Praise for Shards of Light

Under another hand, *Shards of Light* could all too easily have become a murder mystery or a novel of intrigue alone; but there's a larger purpose at work here, and r~~omance enters into an already-complex~~ equation to introduce Shilo   it also her heart. With its different  es and its gentle exploration of a   *f Light* is a beautifully evocative st   hancing a series. It invites reader   y through faith and secrets comes

—D. Donovan, Senior Reviewer, Midwest Book Review

Susan Miura has crafted a tale that is as intriguing as it is complex. It sits on the border of YA fiction, but the characters are interesting enough to keep this adult fully engaged and flipping the pages.

—Cara Putman, award-winning author of
Delayed Justice and *Shadowed by Grace*

The characters are real people, instantly familiar like old friends. Well-written with poignancy and humor, Shards of Light is the perfect curl-up-in-your-favorite-chair novel.

—Gina Detwiler, author, *The Forlorn Series*

Susan Miura's accurate portrayals of the physical, psychological and life-altering affects of a serious injury and the treacherous uphill battle of rehabilitation were on point. The reminder of how God's plans are a part of a bigger picture that we don't always see while focused on our immediate struggles, renewed my faith that He is ever present and working his miracles when the universal timing is right.

—Christine Rojas, licensed occupational therapist

A captivating novel that demonstrates the power of love and courage, while highlighting the brilliance of God's work.

—Yasmeen Bankole,
Congressional Constituent Services Liaison

Other Titles by Susan Miura

Healer

Show Me a Sign

Pawprints in the Snow:
How God Protects Animals from the Cold

Shards of Light

Healer Book 2

Susan Miura

SUSAN MIURA

Vinspire Publishing
www.vinspirepublishing.com

ISBN print book: 978-1-7327112-8-0

Published by Vinspire Publishing, LLC

For my mom in Heaven, whose name inspired
the convent in this book: Le Sorelle di Santa Teresa.
For my husband, children, stepdaughter,
and grandchildren.

And for everyone who uses their own unique,
God-given gifts to love, inspire, encourage,
rescue, and protect others.

"Courage faces fear and thereby masters it."
—Martin Luther King Jr.

Glossary

Bambino	Baby
Buon compleanno	Happy birthday
Ciao ("chow")	hello or goodbye
Cugino	Cousin
Grazie	Thank you
Idiota	Idiot
Le Sorelle	The sisters
Mi cara	My heart (term of endearment)
Molto bella	Very beautiful
Magnifico	Magnificent
Panini	Grilled Italian sandwich
Polizia	Police
Ragazzino	Little boy
Sei guarito	You are healed

Prologue

Riccardo Montella could smell revenge wafting through the night like sweet almond blossoms. The wooded area near the convent provides perfect camouflage for his empty milk truck, which has never seen a drop of milk. His usual cargo is far more valuable. Soon, he will have his little treasures back, and those nuns will find out they messed with the wrong guy. Doesn't it just figure they stopped by his place the same day he was making a pickup from the mainland? By the time he made the round trip from Sicily to Calabria, his place was boarded up, and his two good-for-nothin' associates had vanished…along with his moneymakers.

But Riccardo had ears throughout Sicily. He heard what happened in bits and pieces and finally put it together. Those nuns came by the brothel, stole all nine of his girls, even the little one, then called the *polizia* and vanished.

"Whatever happens next will be their own fault," he mumbles to the darkness, justified in knowing they're simply paying the price for their actions.

Doing wrong has painful consequences. He learned that childhood lesson all too well and all too often. A smug smile spreads across his face as he reminds himself it won't be long before those girls are cowering in the back of his truck, crying and begging. But it won't make a difference. By this time tomorrow, he'll be back in business. No cops, and definitely not a bunch of nuns, are going to keep him down. Customers mean money, and money makes Riccardo a happy man.

But there's been little of that since the Sisters of Saint Teresa decided to interfere.

A twig cracks, jarring Riccardo from his vengeful musings. He freezes, scanning the midnight woods, then pats his holster. Reassured his Glock is still there, he bends to slide his hand over the knife sheath strapped to his ankle. Chances are it's nothing more than some stupid squirrel. But Riccardo doesn't take chances.

∾

"What's he doin' on this middle-of-nowhere mountainside?" The tall one whispers, determined to remain undetected by Riccardo.

"Don't know, don't care. Long as he doesn't make it out alive." A foot shorter than his partner, the second stalker adjusts his night vision goggles.

Weapons in hand, they follow Riccardo's moves, having tracked him for weeks. It is time to get revenge on this traitor who pretended to be their partner then tricked them by using phony nuns. It was no coincidence Ricardo was out of town when they got robbed and narrowly escaped arrest. If they hadn't slipped away just before the cops arrived, they'd both be rotting in jail while that traitor walked free.

Luckily for them, Riccardo is a creature of habit. They knew he'd have Sunday dinner at La Luna Café and stuck a tracker on his car while he dined. Following him to this remote spot was almost too easy.

The tall one pulls a Beretta from his side holster. "I do believe our friend's days are numbered."

His partner snickers. "Yeah, and he just hit zero."

Chapter 1

Shilo

Lemons. Their delicate scent drifts along gentle breezes in the convent courtyard while nuns tend citrus trees and blooming flowers like ethereal garden fairies. *Le Sorelle di Santa Teresa.*

Throughout Sicily, the Sisters of Saint Teresa are famous for the delicious pastries they sell to help support the poor and oppressed. But it is not them I traveled five thousand miles to see. I watch from a marble bench, lost in my own thoughts and expectations, as a woman approaches from across the courtyard. Our blue eyes lock. She continues, slowed by age, with the blazing Sicilian sun glistening on her short silver curls, and I rise without hesitation to approach the great-grandmother whose story set our family tree on fire.

Nonna Marie.

We stop, inches apart, gazing in silence.

I haven't seen her since I was a child, but I'd know that face anywhere. And those eyes, of course. A mirror image of mine, set in a face weathered by the joys and trials of eighty-six years. For all the world, she appears to be an old woman standing on a garden path, harboring nothing

remarkable or noteworthy. But I know better. Because behind my great-grandmother's eyes lies the key to a divine gift
bestowed upon me just weeks before my seventeenth birthday. A gift like no other—so amazing, so unbelievably powerful, that I sometimes wonder if I'm lost in a dream.

"Shilo Marie." The whisper accompanies tears that shimmer in her topaz eyes. No one else calls me by my first and
middle name, yet spoken from her lips, it sounds as natural
as breathing. "Shilo Marie."

Memories swarm my mind, stories of all she'd been
through, and all she left behind. The fall that nearly took her
from this world. The shame that brought her to a mountainside convent, miles away from civilization and an ocean
away from her family. But she stands before me, content-
ment gracing her face, strength blazing in eyes that have witnessed miracles and wonders, and cried a thousand tears. I
close the gap, and we embrace, wrapped in each other's arms
as if we'll stay that way forever. And if that's what she wants,
I will wait.

Because what I came here to learn is worth whatever it
takes.

❧

"So you are the one." Mother Superior's stiff greeting leaves
me wondering if she was less than willing to approve my
summer visit. She sits motionless, wrinkled hands folded on
her desk. "Marie's great-granddaughter from Chicago."

Rain taps the convent windows, weaving tiny pathways
down the panes and onto stone walls that have survived
storms and the harsh Mediterranean sun for nearly five-hun-
dred years.

"Yes, ma'am." Not sure I've ever used that term before,
but it seems appropriate. "Cedarcrest, actually. Next to
Schaumburg." Everyone seems to know Schaumburg, probably because of Woodfield Mall.

Her head tilts. No light of recognition lights her angular face. "As in Schaumburg, Germany?"

"Yes. No. I mean, same name, but it's a suburb of Chicago." My words meet with another quizzical look, reminding me that suburbs are not a thing in some places. "It's a town near the city, ma'am." Another random ma'am, like I have no control over it. Julia would be giggling if she could hear me now, but my little sister's heading back home with our parents...and I am not. Our week-long visit with the Sicilian cousins was crazy fun and ended much too soon.

Now this.

"Please address me as Mother Superior."

Images from "The Sound of Music" dance through my brain. We saw the play at the community theater a few years back. Part of me wants to belt out that song about the hills, just to see if she'll crack a smile, but chances are slim she'll see the humor. I nod.

"You did not join your family when they met with Marie. Why not?"

The unanticipated question tumbles around my brain. It was important for me to meet her alone, to connect one-on-one with no distractions, no outside voices. I planned it that way even before stepping foot on the plane and told my family to visit her first. But how do I explain that possessing The Gift is something no one else can understand, except Nonna Marie? She had it first. She gets it. And we are linked in a supernatural way, incomprehensible to the rest of the world.

"I just wanted to meet her alone. It was...just something I wanted." It is the lamest of answers, but her nod tells me she won't press for more, which is all that matters.

"Marie tells me you are not Catholic."

"No, but I'm Christian. I go to a nondenominational church. We have pastors, not priests." There are other differences of course, but my gut tells me she's well aware of them.

"I see." She gazes at me with eyes that pierce my soul. "You look like her. Not just the eyes. Your mouth, too. Your cheekbones." Her English is nearly flawless. "Is it true you possess The Gift? That you can heal like Marie used to do?"

Another question I didn't anticipate. At least, not so soon, or so directly. I steal a moment by glancing around her stark office. Like my room in the convent, it provides little more than the basic necessities. A crucifix and painting of Jesus are the only wall adornments. I focus on the Savior's face, wondering how to release a truth I guard with my life. But her eyes tell me she already knows why I got exiled to the land of nuns.

"Yes, ma'am. Mother Superior."

She folds her hands and nods, her gesture laden with scepticism. "Tell me, then. When does this happen? How? If you are to stay here for the summer, I need to know more about you."

Clearly, there's no room for small talk. The woman's all business with no apology. She stares at me, unblinking, her ancient countenance intimidating me for reasons I can't explain. My heart reaches for Kenji, but he's a world away, living with relatives on an Indiana farm.

Maybe right this minute he's wondering, like me, how our summer plans got torn to shreds. We were supposed to have jobs, go to soccer camp, and spend lazy days at the beach. Instead, we're living on separate continents, a strategy meant to keep us safe from the gang bangers who want our heads on a silver platter.

I fight the urge to fidget like a fourth-grader in the principal's office and begin with the story of healing an injured dog when I was five years old. The Gift went dormant for twelve years after that until the day I met Tyler.

"I was visiting my Aunt Rita in the hospital and met this little boy who'd been beaten by his father." The vivid image sears my heart. "When I touched his head, I felt warmth in my heart, and the room got hazy. I returned the next day, when Misty, his mom, was there. We became friends after that."

Mother Superior leans forward. "And this is when the healing took place?"

I nod, reliving the scene that is forever imprinted on my life. "I prayed for him. Warmth spread through my body, my arms, then pooled in my palms and fingers. Misty said my hands were moving over Tyler, but I don't remember that part."

My hands clench and unclench as I reveal this highly protected information. No one is supposed to know about The Gift, but spending the summer here comes at a price, and this is it. Mother Superior promised not to divulge my secret to anyone else.

"You could not see?"

I open my mouth to answer then realize there isn't one. At least, not one that will make sense. The warmth filled me with joy...no, something bigger. Love, purity, power, and beauty all combined into light and breathtaking colors. But that will sound crazy. "I couldn't see Tyler, or anything of *this* world, but I could see. Then I passed out."

She studies my face. "Are you saying you saw Heaven?"

Did I? I struggle for words to explain what can't be explained. "It felt that way, but honestly, I don't know. It was just...wonderful."

"Hmm." I sense her trying to decide whether to believe me or write me off as a whacko. "And the little boy...he was healed?"

Images of Tyler's sweet, pallid face fill my head. By the time I left that room, the gash on his cheek was little more than a thin pink line. "That night, the doctor checked his spleen and determined he didn't have to operate. The cut on his face was gone, and his arm wasn't broken anymore."

"I see." She nods. "What happened with your Aunt Rita? Marie's granddaughter. She died of cancer last month. Why couldn't you heal her?"

I gasp, then struggle to take my next breath. Aunt Rita's death hit me like a freight train, and I haven't quite moved past the pain. I miss her laugh, her stories, her hugs that wrapped around me like a blanket of love. I miss her cheering like crazy at my soccer games.

I miss *her*.

"I don't know." I want to say that God decides who gets healed, but the words stick in my throat. Why, how, when? Who to heal, and who not? How does he choose? And what could have possibly qualified me for such a gift? These questions plague me daily. I only hope my great-grandmother can answer them and tell me why Aunt Rita had to die.

Gazing at my hands, I choke back the emotion her name brings to my lips. When I look up, Mother Superior's face has softened. Sadness shadows gray eyes that have probably seen dozens of souls leave this world.

"I'm sorry," she says. "I, too, have lost loved ones. It is difficult. We cannot always know God's reasons, but we can always trust him, yes?"

I nod, knowing her words are true, but taking no comfort in them when Auntie's death makes everything hurt inside.

"We can continue this later if you are upset."

My preference would be no continuation at all, but that's not going to happen. We may as well finish up this polite interrogation now, and be done with it. Anyway, answering more questions will help take my mind off the last one.

"It's fine. What else would you like to know?"

"What is this trouble you are in? Why is someone after you?"

I recap the highlights, explaining how Misty ran away from her foster parents at sixteen, moved in with Jake, and gave birth to Tyler. "It didn't take long for her to figure out Jake was a violent maniac, but she had nowhere else to go. After Jake beat Tyler, Misty discovered he was running drugs for a local gang called The Warriors. That's when my dad asked her to help him with a drug bust."

"Your papa is *polizia*, yes?"

"Yeah, he's a sergeant. He arranged for Misty to deliver the drugs surrounded by undercover cops, but me and my boyfriend kind of got in the middle of it. Now the Warriors want revenge on us."

"That is an interesting story. You have experienced much drama for one so young. You will not find such things here." She points to my phone, which is peeking out of my hoodie pocket. "Nor will you find service for cell phones. They are useless on the mountain. You may call your parents once a week from my phone." She places her hand on the ancient landline sitting on her desk. "We live a simple life, Shilo. Perhaps you will be bored."

I sigh, having wondered that a million times myself. Five weeks is going to feel like a lifetime, but no need to share that with her. "I'll be fine. There's a lot I want to learn about The Gift."

"Well, then." She stands up, indicating our meeting has ended. Finally. "Talk to your nonna. Listen well. Do not make the same mistakes she made. Such mistakes...they can be fatal."

She isn't the first one to utter those words. I've heard them from my parents, and more recently from my Sicilian relatives. I have no intention of healing people to gain fame and fortune, but neither did Nonna Marie. It happened over time, they all say. Slowly building, until one day God took away the power as quickly as he'd given it. Devastated, suicidal, Nonna Marie left society behind and hid away at the convent.

There is so much I want to know about what my relatives refer to as "the fall." What led up to it? What happened after? And most importantly, how do I prevent it from happening to me?

I jerk awake as the numbers 2:07 glimmer at me from the
travel clock on the nightstand. My window shade comes
alive with the menacing silhouettes of lemon, fig, and olive
trees waving in the darkness. By day they were friendly pro-
viders of shade and fruit, but tonight they bend and sway as
though reaching out to grasp something unknown. Was it
the trees that woke me? The wind?

The ivory walls of this room are void of art, except for
the wooden crucifix over my twin bed and the Virgin Mary
oil painting centered above the small wooden dresser. It is a
stark contrast to my own bedroom back in Cedarcrest with
its violet walls covered in photos of friends, Kenji, posters,
the string-art guitar Julia gave me for my birthday, and my
real guitar standing in the corner like a faithful friend.

Footsteps pad softly past my door. I heard them last
night, too, but thought I must be dreaming. Not this time.
Someone around here sleepwalks or performs a mysterious
late night ritual. Maybe it's just hefty Sister Francesca indulg-
ing in the occasional midnight snack. But the footsteps head
in the wrong direction and tread far too lightly. Curiosity
draws me toward the door.

Slow and silent, I turn the knob and ease it open the
width of one eye. Dressed in her flowing white habit, a nun
carries something in front of her with both hands. Not wide
enough for Sister Francesca and definitely not the ancient
Sister Angelina – no limp. She's too tall for petite Sister Celeste. That pretty much covers the ones I know. She heads
toward the room I'd asked Nonna Marie about earlier today
in the barn.

"Shhh, granddaughter," she said. "You will know when
time is right."

It was the same answer she gave when I asked about the
little stone house in the field where several young girls are
living. I've seen them hanging clothes out to dry, playing

catch, reading books. The Meadow House Girls—another mystery on this desolate mountain. Since Nonna wouldn't expound on her cryptic answer, I let it go. At least, on the outside.

Stopping at the door, the nun shifts her burden to one arm, turns the knob with her free hand, then slips into the room. The door clicks behind her, leaving the convent halls silently vacant, as though the lone sister had been nothing more than a transient ghost.

I have to know who or what is in that room. Do they have other visitors with divine powers? Are they sheltering refugees from a war-torn country? Or…is some sort of abomination taking sanctuary within these walls?

Clearly, I've seen way too many movies or desperately seek something to take my mind off missing everyone back home.

My head tells me to stay put, close the door, and return to bed, but my feet don't get the message. They creep down the deserted hallway, finding every squeaky floorboard along the way. Hopefully, the tapping of rain on stone covers my footsteps, as well as my drumming heart. The door looms ahead, staring defiantly at me as if to ask, "Now what?"

Getting caught would render pure humiliation, but that doesn't stop me from pressing one ear to the door while keeping an eye on the hallway.

"This pill will help the pain." The soft, Italian words of the nun inside are muffled, but I hear well enough to understand. "This one will fight the infection in the stab wound. The bullet wounds seems to be healing well. You are blessed to be alive. Thank the Lord we found you in time."

Silence, then the clink of glass on a metal tray.

"You cannot get stronger on pills alone. Here. Try to eat a little. I've brought some lemon bread and minestrone. Come now; eat. Don't worry; they won't find you here."

"Thank you, sister." The voice is raspy. Weak. And definitely male. "You are too kind."

The stranger's simple words are meant to be cordial. Nothing more than a thoughtful expression of gratitude for the care he is apparently receiving from the compassionate sisters. And yet, they ice my skin. Bristle the hairs at the nape of my neck. And I'm not sure which is the biggest mystery; why there's a man in the convent, why he's been shot and stabbed…or why his presence here unsheathes my claws.

Chapter 2

Shilo

"No men in convent. No, no, no." Nonna Marie's words were gentle but firm earlier today when I tried to convince her to let Kenji visit sometime during the summer.

"But you'd like him. I know it. And I promise nothing bad would happen if you let him visit. I miss him so much."

"No men in convent, Shilo Marie. This is strong rule. Only priests."

"But, Nonna…"

"Is Kenji priest?"

"No, of course not."

"Then no."

Safely back in my room, I listen to the melodic rain and wonder what pivotal circumstances could have caused the nuns to override the "strong rule." Obviously, the man was in bad shape and hiding from someone. He could be one of the priests. Scratch that; who shoots a priest? Then again, maybe a nun fell in love with a priest, but he stuck to his vows and rejected her, so she went crazy and…no, this is ridiculous. I've got to get Nonna Marie to fill me in.

Maybe they want me to heal him. My stomach tightens at the thought, which makes no sense because I don't even know the man. The others never disconcerted me, even when I feared my secret could be revealed. Could that be the real purpose for my being here? Were all the circumstances leading up to this moment part of a divine strategy to heal the stranger? But how do I know? If only the questions that pummel my brain could be answered in a Heaven-sent text. Of course, there would be no way to receive it in this technology-free corner of the world. Aside from Mother Superior's ancient rotary phone, this place hasn't changed much since the stone walls were built.

I slip back under the covers, sure my curiosity will keep me tossing until daybreak, but fall into a sleep plagued by dreams of ice: dark, menacing, jagged ice.

ع

"You have thoughts in head, Shilo Marie." Nonna cuts a blood orange into wedges and places them on my breakfast plate, nestled next to a slice of warm date bread. "Tell me."

The fruit is truly deserving of its name. Crimson droplets bead on Nonna's knife, which appears to have just dissected a small animal.

"Nothing, really. Just tired."

"Tired, eh? That is lie. You have troubles." She taps her temple. "In here." She pats her heart. "And maybe here, too. Yes?"

I nod. We've been together only two days, and already she sees right through me. "I was hoping we could talk today." I look at the kitchen table, ringed by the sisters chatting in Italian, though they like practicing their English on me. "In private."

"And so we will." She pours milk from a brightly flowered ceramic pitcher. "Finish your breakfast. We will walk in the garden and talk about life and God and gifts and many things." She hands the cup to me, and I take a swallow, but it is not the two-percent milk I'm used to drinking. And I suspect the fat percentage is not the only difference.

"Drink. Is goat's milk. Fresh this morning. Very good."

"Seriously? Straight from the goat?"

"Si." Nonna laughs. "Where else?"

We finish eating, help clean the kitchen, and head outside, where, if all goes as planned, I will finally get some answers. The green, earthy scent of rain-washed garden mixes with lemonade air. All around us, sunlit droplets hang from flowers, vegetables, and the bright yellow lemons. Nonna gently places her hand under my chin and gazes into my eyes as though searching my mind.

"Come," she says. "It is time to talk."

As we head toward the well-worn dirt path that winds through groves of citrus trees, I see Celeste and Francesca carrying pans of food to the little stone house.

"Are they bringing breakfast to the girls?"

"Si."

"Who are they?" Maybe this time she'll shed some light on the mystery. "Why do they live here at the convent?"

A sad smile graces her face. "It is long story, Shilo Marie. I tell you soon. This is promise. For now, we must talk about other things, yes?"

I nod, still curious, but aching to hear more about The Gift. We walk among the trees, their bright orange and yellow fruits awash in sunlight. Some distance ahead, the ancient olives, grandfathers of the orchard, beckon us with their massive, gnarled branches. Nonna's pace requires us to stop now and then to rest on the marble benches dotting the orchard. Under normal circumstances, this would drive my hyper self insane, but I left normal behind the day I healed Tyler.

She tells me her story, beginning with coming to America when her daughter—my grandmother—was a little girl. Her daughter grew up, got married, and gave birth to my mother.

"After my husband die in car crash, I go live with my daughter and her family."

"Mom told me. She said she was just a kid when you moved in with them." The story's been interesting, though I already knew most of it, but now it's time to move this talk into the present. "Right after that, you got The Gift."

"Yes. Your mama was maybe six or seven when I healed priest at St. Mary's. The Gift, I have it twenty years. And then...well, you know. I dishonor God. I shame my family."

Could it happen to me? The thought has plagued me since the night my parents told me I had The Gift. Nonna Marie did the right thing for decades before losing her way. Will I follow in those misguided footsteps, unable to ward off the pride and arrogance that come with adoration from the healed?

"Every day after that, I wake up and say to myself, 'Marie, how you abuse such amazing Gift?'" A tear slides down her face, breaking my heart for the pain she still endures. "People, they treat me like celebrity, and I loved it. People give me gifts, money, and I accept. Instead of honoring God, I thought only of myself."

She had replaced gratitude with entitlement, and no longer used the gift to glorify God. And God responded by teaching a valuable lesson. He took it back.

"To think, I could still be healing people today." She faces me, those piercing blue eyes shimmering. Odd to think it's what people see when they look at me. "But God, He has forgiven me. Someday, maybe I will forgive myself. But we are close again, He and I. This is all that matters."

I'd heard the stories. Healings failed. People got angry. Her house was vandalized, and she could no longer go out in public without being taunted at every turn. Nonna became a recluse. Her depression began to suffocate her until finally, unable to face another moment of darkness, she tried to take her own life.

"All the terrible things that happen after that, they were consequences. You understand, Shilo Marie? Not consequences from God but from *me*. From the bad choice I make."

The sun is nearly centered in the sky as we reach the welcome shade of the olive grove. A few steps ahead, the sight of a bench brings a sigh of relief to my great-grandmother. There'd been too long a stretch since the last time we sat down. She reaches into her skirt pocket to retrieve her water bottle and takes several gulps before I help her ease onto the cool bench.

"Ah. This is nice, yes?" She recalls the last month of having The Gift, telling me the story of healing a paraplegic soldier. He was her last healing, and she never forgot his face, his joy. He'd been stuck in that wheelchair for years, she said. Dependent on people doing everything for him.

"It break his spirit, Shilo Marie. He had been big, strong soldier. Then he step on bomb in ground and 'boom'. Life changed." But when she met a child with leukemia, then a young mother with a heart condition, and finally a teacher with a brain tumor, nothing happened. She never felt the warmth again. Her story provided the perfect segue to my questions.

"But that happens even now - even with The Gift – and that's what I don't get. How do you know who to heal? Why is it this person but not that one?" My heart cringes at a memory. "Why wasn't it Aunt Rita?"

Frail hands clasp mine. "I know this breaks your heart, granddaughter. So many times, I feel that pain inside. Ask those questions. Get angry."

"So what's the answer?"

She gazes beyond the trees to where the land slopes into a valley. A breeze blows silver strands into her eyes, and she swipes them away, sitting in silence. The question remains unanswered. It's possible she didn't hear it, but something in her expression solicits my patience.

"Faith."

All that waiting for one word. "Faith?"

"That is all. Everything. Trust God. He give you The

Gift, and only He knows how each life touch another life, how it all affects the future in good ways or bad. God, He knows what He is doing. He made all this." Her frail arms sweep the land and sky. "And He made us. Loves us."

"But sometimes it doesn't make sense."

"To you, perhaps. To me. But to God, it makes sense. He sees the whole glorious painting. We see only a brush stroke. *Capisci?* You understand?"

I nod, understanding the concept, but unable to imagine the reality of such vision.

She pats my hand. "Now, I rest my eyes for just a moment. So much walking today."

I'm content to sit and ponder her words while she sleeps. A soft breeze kisses the olive leaves, fluttering the heavy-laden branches. I breathe in the deliciously primal scents of wet earth, ripening olives, grass, and wildflowers.

Faith, she said, is the key. But the problem with faith is that it requires letting go, and letting go dislodges me from my comfort zone. It requires me to relinquish control. Willingly. Confidently. She's saying God gave me The Gift, and as for the rest, He's got it. But...

"Marieee!"

The distant voice reaches me through the trees. I scan the grove but see no one.

"Marieee, where are you?"

The woman's voice sounds closer this time. I gently nudge Nonna and tell her someone is calling her name.

"You answer, please. My voice, it is not so strong."

"We're here!" As the words leave my lips, I catch a glimpse of Sister Celeste riding Carlos the donkey. Behind her, another donkey follows on a lead rope. I help Nonna up from the bench, and we head toward the unexpected visitor.

"What is it, Celeste?" Anxiety tinges Nonna's voice.

The tiny nun slides off Carlos and pats his neck. Worry lines furrow her forehead as she steps closer to us. "Our guest, Riccardo, has taken a turn for the worse. We are very concerned. The infection is bad, and his fever is high."

"I cannot help, Celeste. The power, it is long gone from me."

The sister draws a breath then glances from me to Nonna Marie. "Can we talk, Marie? In private?"

"Please, dear. Speak in front of my grandchild."

Her words don't come quickly, though I'm anxious to hear them. She ties and unties the end of the lead rope then finally nods her agreement. "We thought...all of us agreed...that she should see him now." She looks at me, her meaning unmistakable.

Blood rushes from my face to my heart, pushing it to overdrive. No one is supposed to know. That was the deal. No one. Did Mother Superior betray me?

Nonna takes a step, placing her four-foot-ten self protectively in front of me. "Why?"

"She has your eyes, Marie. And your spirit. We all feel it. We believe she came here for more than safety. We sisters agree God brought her here to heal Riccardo."

"You are just guessing this thing." Nonna's voice harbors a note of anger. And something else. Fear?

"Marie...are we right?"

She's got Nonna in a tough spot, no doubt about it. She lives with these nuns, loves them like family. They took her in when she hit bottom and allowed her to make a home here. No way she's going to lie to them. No way she's going to reveal my secret, either.

Nonna's lips form a thin line as she shakes her head. "I do not trust this man. Something feels wrong when I am near him."

Evasion. Well played, Nonna. But more interesting than her dodging the question is our shared suspicion of this ominous visitor.

"No, Marie, he is fine. Always so nice and polite to us. Always so thankful." The sister's formal way of speaking, laced with a slight English accent, reflects her Oxford education.

Nonna shakes her head. "Then why is here, not in hospital? Why is everything so hush hush?"

"He explained that, remember? He said he witnessed a mafia murder. The criminals caught him and brought him here to kill him, thinking no one would find him for a long time. They left him for dead."

"Yes, yes. But he was alive and crawl toward convent. Sister Sophia, she find him on her walk."

"See? You do remember. Now he fears going to a hospital because they might find him."

"I remember. But we do not know if story is true. There is something —"

"Will you let Shilo pray for him?"

Interesting story, but like my great-grandmother, I'm not buying it. Nonna doesn't answer the sister, who now implores me with her eyes. "Would you, Shilo? Please forgive me for asking a favor of you, especially when you have only recently arrived. I would not ask except for the matter's urgency."

A nun asking me to heal someone seems like a clear sign, despite my unexplainable desire to steer clear of this Riccardo. "Maybe I'm supposed to do this," I whisper to Nonna. "After all, I'm here. He's here. Sister Celeste could be right."

Nonna deflates with a sigh. "I am not saying Shilo Marie has gift or does not. She can pray for this Riccardo. What happens next, God will decide."

Her words set Sister Celeste into motion. She produces a small folding step stool from her donkey's saddlebag and opens it next to the second donkey then motions to me.

"Please help your nonna onto Vincenzo's back." I scrutinize the aging donkey, wondering who's older, Vincenzo or Nonna Marie, and whether there's a remote chance this transportation plan won't end in disaster. "Is there a safer way to get her back to the convent?"

"Shilo Marie." Nonna chimes in before Sister Celeste has a chance to speak. "I may be old, but I can still ride donkey."

Words few people ever hear from their great-grand-mother.

She sidles up to the step stool and holds out her arm, a sign for me to support her. The next few moments require awkward positions and grunts from all parties, including the ancient beast, but in the end, Nonna miraculously sits astride Vincenzo. I walk beside her as our little posse heads back, my arms braced to catch her every step of the way. Nonna says nothing, her disconcerting silence thickening the air around us.

✑

Inside the dimly lit room, so distant from the sunshine that warmed my skin just moments before, Riccardo's pale face shines with sweat. Eyes dulled by fever gaze at me. Through me. I shudder away an emotion that doesn't deserve a label. The man before me is weak, possibly dying, therefore no threat to me or the women in this room. I silently repeat that conviction, willing it to solidify in my head.

Riccardo. Sounds like the guy from the video game Kenji used to play. But no, that was Mario, and there is no shred of resemblance between the man in this bed and the whimsical mustached character who zips around in a go-cart. Riccardo's dark hair matts to his scalp. A faint scar peeks through his face stubble, and another below the tattoo on his left arm, soon to be accompanied by the two new additions. Bruises discolor his face and arms. If there are more, they are hidden by the sheets. I tell myself he's accident prone, but myself refuses to believe it.

There is something about this man. Something unexplainably, yet undeniably sinister. Even in his frail state, he emits an aura that is both vile and frightening.

Sister Francesca whispers to him as they enter the room, to which he simply replies, "Ah, *grazie*," before closing his eyes.

Three nuns and Mother Superior flank the bed in a room identical to mine, though the Virgin Mary above his dresser is bowed in prayer, while mine faces heavenward, bathed in beams of holy sunlight. On some silent cue, the nuns back away from the bedside as though I require a three-foot miracle parameter. Sister Francesca places a pillow on the floor next to the bed then gestures for me to kneel on it.

Creepy.

Like an empty graveyard on a foggy night.

Like an exorcism.

I stay standing as she partially pulls down the sheet, revealing a patch of discolored gauze on his right side. The skin around it is red and puffy, tinged by yellowish ooze.

"This one," she whispers. "The infection is here."

Clearly.

She motions again toward the pillow, but I stay put. If anything is going to happen here, it's going to be on my terms. I turn and face the sisters.

"I can't promise anything." They nod in unison. "And only my nonna stays."

"But child." Sister Celeste walks over to me, takes my hand. "Jesus said that whenever two or more are gathered in His name, He will be in their midst. Imagine the chance of success if we all join in."

"I'm sorry, Sister." I shake my head and refrain from saying more, knowing it would confirm their suspicions about me.

Nonna nods her approval. "Please, dear friends," she says in Italian, "pray for the man in the hallway, while Shilo and I remain here. Surely the Lord will still know the purpose for which we gather. A door between us will not deter Him."

The nuns silently contemplate Nonna's words then turn

toward the door. Habits swishing, they exit like a flock of doves shooed from their favorite branch. The door clicks shut, leaving the three of us cloaked in an oppressive silence.

"Okay, then," I say, more to myself than to Nonna. "Let the prayers begin."

"Yes." Nonna settles into a chair near the bed. "But mine will be for you not him." Her jaw sets just like my mother's when she's tense.

Riccardo lays still, shallow breaths the only indication of life. I kneel next to him, certain his hand will shoot out from beneath the sheets and grab my throat. But his hands, like the rest of him, remain motionless. No point in delaying the inevitable. I gently lay my palm near the wound, silently hoping my skin never touches his puss-bloated infection during whatever happens next. The mere thought of it raises bile in my throat. Choking it down, I close my eyes to begin, wondering if the miraculous warmth will flow through me like it did when I healed Tyler, Rebecca, Kenji and Pat. Or elude me like it did with Aunt Rita. To feel that oneness with God, fully submerged in a love so pure it transports me from this world, would be worth any trepidation I feel about this man.

Heavenly Father, if it's Your will for Riccardo to be healed, please use me as Your vessel. Cure his infection, heal his wounds, and make him well. I trust in You with all my heart. Please make Your will known to me.

Cold. Like sucking in a gulp of February, it ices my heart. But unlike the celestial warmth that floods me during healings, the cold stays contained. It intensifies, transforming blood to ice, freezing the organ essential to my life. Instead of the peace that filled my soul when I healed the others, my mind whirls with fear and anger.

Shadowy images of gray and black form into a skinny little boy, not more than six, tied to a tree trunk. A woman whips his bare back with a belt. The silent image rips through me as each lash contorts his face with pain. The image blurs and reforms. The same boy, now a teenager, enters his home with a stray kitten. Imploring eyes beg the woman for just one act of kindness. She smiles, grasps the tiny creature by the neck, and forces it into a jar filled with water. Torment contorts the boy's face as the tiny animal struggles. He hits his knees, hands clasped as he begs her to free it, but her booted foot shoves him to the floor. By the time he rises, the kitten is still.

Shades of darkness swirl and reform into a familiar-looking man. The boy has grown. He is waving a gun, forcing hazy images into the back of a van. They huddle, emitting painful sounds that hurt everything inside me as the van rumbles down a dirt path and stops at a house with darkened windows. Water leaks from each windowsill, plopping onto the dirt below. The terrified shadows are locked in rooms with nothing but mattresses.

Outside, men line up at the door, money in hand.

I watch it all from someplace outside the convent room, outside this world, where I am invisible to those I watch. As the horrid scenario unfolds, black thorns twist around me, winding around my legs, my torso, reaching for my throat. The putrid fumes of rotting flesh engulf my nostrils. Screams assault my mind, over and over again, thrusting me toward insanity.

And through it all, the ice continues to harden my heart, slowing it nearly to a stop.

Chapter 3

Melody

Gossamer layers of blues and greens flow from the waist of my shimmery leotard. It nearly took my breath away the first time I saw it, but tonight it means nothing. Tonight is *the* night, and *the* man is in the audience. Just because he's here for his little niece and not me doesn't mean I can't make it count. I scan the audience again to make sure he hasn't left, and feel my heart kick it up a notch when I spot him. Blue suit. Middle aged. Nothing extraordinary…just someone who holds the key to changing my life. And all I have to do is dance with the elegance and grace of Misty Copeland: fluid, graceful, yet strong. Otherworldly, like I was born for only this, with moves that take his breath away and command his full attention as he revels in the gentle beauty of ballet.

No pressure at all.

"Five tickets, please." A white-haired woman holds out a ten-dollar bill to purchase raffle tickets that will help pay for renting this college auditorium. I smile a thanks and take her money, while Jenna hands over the tickets.

"I look forward to seeing you young ladies dance tonight."

"Thank you. We'll be in the second act."

She tucks her tickets into her purse and walks away, leaving Jenna and me with our tickets and cash box, but no more customers.

"Wish we were in the first act." Jenna organizes the bills so they're all facing the same direction.

I laugh, wishing the same thing. "But then we wouldn't have had the awesome opportunity to sell raffle tickets."

Her attempt at a smile is betrayed by the sadness shadowing her eyes. "I can't believe you're going." Her voice cracks on the last word. "How will I survive? Who will make me laugh when Miss Bellaire tells me my arabesque is a disaster of Titanic proportions?"

We can't do this now. Not when we need to keep our heads, hearts, and souls focused on the upcoming performance.

"Oh, Jen. Stop." I avoid her eyes, knowing they'll spark emotions I can't afford to express. "If we cry off this stage makeup, Miss B. will have our bunheads."

"I know, but you're the only one in the troupe who doesn't drive me crazy. Now you'll be off dancing with the beautiful people, and I'll still be here."

"Then audition! You can't get in if you don't try."

"Oh, please. I don't have your skills. Your…whatever it is that makes you look like wind and flowers and rippling water. I'm not Joffrey Ballet Academy material."

Love Jenna, hate her defeatist attitude. I wish she could see how beautiful she is. How talented. But in her parents' eyes, she'll never measure up to her Harvard-bound older brother. And to Jenna, those are the only eyes that matter.

"You are. You just don't realize it. Try out, and let them decide."

She shrugs a "maybe," strengthening my resolve to convince her to register for the next audition.

We stand in silence, watching a little girl with a walker slowly make her way up the aisle with her mom. She couldn't be more than six. A shudder runs through me, settling in my heart. My legs can leap and pirouette. Hers can't even walk without assistance. Why did her mom bring her here to watch people doing what she'll never be able to do? It feels cruel. There must be something, even something small, that would make her happy. I make a mental note to visit her after the performance. If I run straight to the lobby after the applause, I might catch her before she leaves. Maybe we could take a picture together, if she wants to. My options for doing anything worthwhile are pretty sparse.

"This place is amazing." Jenna draws my attention away from the little girl. We gaze at the university stage our ballet school rented with a lot of fundraising and ticket sales. We're still over budget though, which is why we're standing here trying to sell more tickets. "This whole campus is amazing. Wouldn't you love to go here?"

I laugh. "I don't think the O'Hara college fund covers places like this. Would be nice, though."

"Know what you mean. My parents couldn't afford this place either. Blake's lucky he got that scholarship."

"It wasn't luck. He got a crazy high SAT score and studied like a maniac to graduate with a 4.0. You should have seen his college admissions essay. Blew me away. They would have been crazy not to give him a scholarship."

Footsteps behind us turn our heads in unison, causing Jenna to lean in and whisper, "Speaking of lover boy…"

Blake grins and takes my hand, but knows better than to kiss off my Petal Pink lipstick this close to show time. His faded jeans bear the tears and paint stains common to the stage crew.

Jenna rolls her eyes. "Guess I better go check on…something."

"Smooth, Jen." Blake never misses an opportunity to harass her. "Someday, people of all nations will be quoting you."

Jenna continues walking and ignores the comment,

knowing it's the best way to annoy him.

"Cool outfit." With thumbs and forefingers, he extends my watercolor wings. "You should wear that tomorrow."

"To the movie? Umm, that would be a 'no.'"

"Well, I wouldn't mind a bit." He winks, then looks out over the audience. "Is he out there?"

I can't suppress a grin. "Left side, aisle seat. Third row."

"Blue suit? Next to the blond lady?"

"That's him."

"Wow. He looks so normal. Who would think he wields all that power?"

I laugh, but truth is, I thought the same thing. There he sits, a nondescript man at a local ballet, blending in with all the parents and ballet enthusiasts. But he is one of the Joffrey's artistic directors, which pretty much makes him royalty to dancers like me. If I wow him tonight, if he notices me at all…well, maybe he'll remember me when the time is right. My stomach constricts at the thought of performing in front of him an hour from now.

"What's it called again? That class you got into?" Blake whispers, continuing to gaze at the people settling into their seats.

"The Pre-Professional Program. The next step up, my next dream, is the Trainee Program, but you have to be invited to audition."

"And that's where Blue Suit comes in."

"Exactly."

The call from Joffrey had come the day after Shilo left for Sicily. Facing a summer without my best friend, I desperately needed something to lift my spirits. Only one "something" was powerful enough to do that, and when it happened, I pirouetted my way across the room to tell my parents, but had to settle for telling Shi over the phone. She was still with her cousins, so I was able to reach her.

"That's so great!" she said. "When I get back, we'll head straight to Schaumburg and hit up Lalo's for guac and celebration enchiladas. It's just sooo great!" But lingering below the enthusiastic greats was a reservation I couldn't deny. And the worst part was, I shared it. The academy acceptance was the highlight of my life, but it would consume me. And we both knew it. With me balancing school and a rigid ballet schedule, and her balancing school and soccer, and both of us with boyfriends, well…our days of sleepovers and long talks on the river path were over. I couldn't even text her about Blue Suit, thanks to her exile to the land of nuns.

"Don't worry. Your solo will blow him away. Just stay focused." Blake leans in close and gently squeezes my hand. "I won't tell you 'go be amazing,' because that's a given. But I *am* going to say be careful, because that platform is garbage." He points to the structure behind us, where I hope to capture the attention of Blue Suit.

I don't know about the construction end of it, but the art students did an awesome job of painting it. The shading actually makes it look like rock instead of wood. In the performance, a girl escapes her captors to reunite with her boyfriend, but has to leap across a dangerous ravine to get away from them. It's my favorite part, and I nearly died when they gave it to *me*.

"That's not the design they should have used." He's back to complaining about the set. "And that dope in charge of stage design is an English major. What does he know about building a set? I would have…"

My hand shoots up to cover his mouth and stop the flow of words I've already heard three times. "Stop being an architect nerd for five minutes. I have no doubt you're going to design award-winning buildings someday, but tonight…just enjoy the performance, okay? I'll be fine. The platform will be fine. Everything's *fine*."

He removes my hand and kisses it. "Fine. Come on, you better go do whatever you ballerina types do when it's ten minutes 'til curtain."

I blow a kiss in his direction, grab the tickets and money,

and head to the designated waiting area backstage. Jen and I check our costumes in front of the dressing room's full-length mirror. I stand a head above her, my mocha skin, high cheekbones and black wavy hair portraying my Nigerian-Russian origins, and contrasting sharply with Jenna's peaches-and-cream complexion. If Mom and Dad were here, with their red hair and ivory skin, everyone would think they were Jenna's parents, not mine. The thought brings Mom's words streaming into my head. *You may not have my eyes or my color, or my blood in your veins, but you have all my heart.*

"You should model." Jen tilts her chin to meet my eyes. "Everyone thinks so."

It isn't the first time I've heard it, and though I appreciate the compliment, I have no interest or time for such a thing. Ballet, and only ballet. It is all that matters.

❧

Stage left, just beyond the curtain, I wait for the cue for my solo. With each beat of the music, my muscles tighten. Will he notice me? Will he pay attention, even if his niece isn't on stage? *Focus, Melody. Become one with the music. Live for the dance. Forget the man who can transform dreams to reality.* Oh, but I can't. I have to be great. Perfect. Nothing less. Years of dancing until my feet bled will mean nothing if I don't impress him. Years of dealing with torn tendons and aching muscles, missing countless parties, movies, bonfires – it all comes down to this moment.

Cued by the music, I *chassé* on stage, acutely aware of each step, each position, the arch of my arms, the stray hair that rebelled against a gallon of hairspray.

The lack of passion.

Miss Bellaire always says passion overflows in me, trans-forming me from dancer to "ballerina extraordinaire." But not tonight. Can he tell from out there, in that sea of heads? I try to concentrate on my next series of steps, which lead me to an angled platform decorated as a rocky cliff. My *pas de couru* takes me up, up, to the six-foot high ledge from which I'll perform my *grand jeté* before landing on a matching ledge, stage right. My moves are stiff, and that hair, that blasted little strand, is dangling right in front of my eye. But it will not be my undoing. I concentrate on every move, every breath, like I've never done before. And it just might be the death of me. Because his trained eyes can discern between concentration and "living the dance." I near the spot from which I vault into my *grand jeté*. When he sees my legs extended in full splits, my back arched like a crescent moon as I ride the air, maybe he'll forget the past few pathetic moments. I push off, legs stretched forward and back, parallel to the floor. Toes point, wings billow.

But something's wrong. Something that never happened during practice.

Those costumed wings, lovely as they are, cannot compensate for the unexpected movement of the cliff beneath my foot. It weakened the push-off, stealing my velocity and distance. Changing my angle. And there is no turning back. No midair do-over. Only desperate pleas to Heaven, begging to be spared from the impending disaster. Gravity weighs on me a second too soon, a heartbeat before my foot would have reached its destination. Instead of landing on the opposite side, it rams the set, inches below the cliff's edge. The sickening crack of bone obscures the music, shooting pain through my ankle, shin and knee, all the way up to my thigh. Gasps drown the orchestra. My head smacks the floor and pain stabs every part of me before darkness closes in like a curtain of death. The music stops.

And the whole world fades to black.

Chapter 4

Shilo

A blinding light silences the screams inside my head. Warm, bony fingers yank my hand away from the man. As the horrific odor dissipates, I breathe in the sweet scent of freshly baked pastries and fresh linens. My eyes open to the panicked face of an old woman, her sparse eyebrows scrunched together forming lines across her forehead. Maintaining a firm grip on my wrist, she tugs me to an upright position, her strength contradicting her age and tiny stature.

"Come. We go." She pulls me toward the door. "*Adesso.* Now."

She's telling me to go, but I don't even know where I am. Or where I've been. Only that this is not my room and doesn't even feel like my planet.

"Who? What?" I resist her long enough to scan the strange surroundings, settling on the wounded man on the bed. He appears to be sleeping, yet his face holds the hint of a sinister smile. Exhaustion threatens to buckle my legs. She persists, tugging me toward the door.

"I don't…" Words elude me. I rub the goosebumps on my arms, trying to elicit a shred of warmth. "I don't understand."

Palming my cheeks, the old woman warms my face with wrinkled hands. Blue eyes gaze fervently into mine, forcing me to look upon a face aged by time and wisdom, dawns and dusks.

"You must listen, Shilo Marie." Her words are laced with love. "You hold Nonna's hand. You come. I will explain, but we must go."

I nod, fully trusting this vaguely familiar woman without knowing why. She opens the door to a flock of nuns whose bowed heads raise in unison. Expectant eyes gaze upon us, but their expectations are a mystery to me. An awkward silence hovers over us, waiting for an utterance to release the tension that formed as we entered the hallway.

"Riccardo remains as he was," she rattles off in Italian. "It is not God's will for him to be healed today." Disappointment shadows five white-rimmed faces. "My great-granddaughter needs to rest now."

"Perhaps tomorrow, Marie?" The heavy one stands, her question entwined with hope. "Is she willing to try again?"

The fog in my brain begins to dissipate, but I'm still not clear about what just happened, or was supposed to happen and didn't. The nun said "Marie"—a name so familiar, yet just out of reach.

"No." Marie's tone leaves no room for dispute. "I never said Shilo Marie had The Gift. That was an assumption."

"She does not look well. Her face is pale as flour. Her eyes...glazed. And look, she is trembling. My goodness, Marie, what happened in there?"

Marie. Marie. I know that name. This woman is someone special to me. There's a connection between us. Something powerful. Extraordinary.

"She is not feeling well, sisters. I'm sorry she could not help our guest. She needs to lie down now."

The old woman sets off with me in tow, like a puppy shadowing its master, assured no harm will come. Nonna Marie. The name comes to me as we traverse the hallways, where marbled saints and angels gaze upon us from alcoves in the walls. The fog clears further, allowing the memories to flood my head. She is my great grandmother, who possessed the healing gift before me. My Yoda, according to Kenji, or my Professor Dumbledore, according to Julia. But unlike me, Luke Skywalker and Harry Potter could control their powers. Choose the when and who. Determine the why or what.

We slip into Nonna's room, collapsing onto stiff wooden chairs where we catch our breath for several minutes, though I'm not sure if our fatigue resulted from the brisk walk or the freak show that took place in Riccardo's room. Nonna stands and lays a small blanket over my quivering shoulders. I wrap it around me, welcoming the warmth.

"You feel cold, yes? Frightened?"

Chilled to the bone—that's what Mom would call it. But this chill penetrates even deeper, icing my soul. The deepest recesses that should never, ever, rise to the surface.

I pull the blanket tighter and nod.

"Bad thoughts in head?"

"The worst. Horrid." My brain is scarred for life. Those images.... those vile, painful, images, will never fade away. "How did you know?"

"Your hand, it did not move. Your breaths, they come fast." She demonstrates with rapid gasps. "I know this thing. This happens when The Gift touch evil." She grabs my hand, which still holds tight to the blanket. "Forgive me, Shilo Marie. I was going to tell you today, but we no finish our talk. I did not trust this Riccardo, but I did not see the evil."

"Why didn't God help me?"

"You are safe, yes? God never leaves you. He protects you."

"*You* protected me, Nonna. I felt like I couldn't move until you pulled my hand away."

"Use your head, Shilo Marie. Who put me in my mama's

womb so I would be here when my great-granddaughter need me? Who made me know to pull your hand? Our God, He protects in many ways."

I nod, still reeling from the horror of that moment. "Every thought, every feeling was…violent, monstrous. Revolting and terrifying."

"And your heart, it feel like ice?" Frail hands rub mine to warm them. She's been through this hell-on-earth ordeal. It's the only explanation for her knowledge.

"I don't ever want to feel that way again."

Compassion infuses Nonna's eyes. "Stay and rest. I get something for you, then we will talk more of this thing. *Capisci?*"

"Yes." A slight haze still hovers around my brain, but I can understand that much. "Can I have some orange spice tea?" I'd brought some from home, along with a few packages of M&Ms, knowing I'd be glad to have my favorites along for this strange journey.

She smiles and kisses the top of my head. "I have something better."

The moment she leaves, I want her back. Talking to her helped dissipate the violent images, but they've crept in again, accompanied by the darkness that nearly sucked me under. "God never leaves you," she said, but I felt light years from Him during the disastrous healing attempt. And now, in the wake of that icy chaos, I'm battling some weird demonic repercussion. Only it isn't much of a battle on my end. Waves of hot and cold course through muscles stiffened by anxiety. Drum beats hammer my head, threatening to shatter my brain. It is hard to think, to breath.

To *be*.

Exhaustion seeks to knock me out before Nonna returns, but I fight to stay awake so I can find out more about this encounter. Why did it happen? If she's right about "The Gift touching evil," then everything I've ever believed tells me the power of The Gift should have triumphed. What can I do to prevent it? This can't happen again. Period. And what if she hadn't pulled away my hand? A shudder zips up my spine, shivering my body, which longs to collapse into a dark, silent coma. But if this was one of my jedi-wizard lessons, and it propels me toward a clearer understanding of using The Gift, then I'll push through.

Please God, I pray, hoping for even a fragment of what I feel during healings. *Please help me.* As prayers go, it isn't much, but my brain refuses to focus on specifics. Anyway, He knows my heart. Knows what I need.

Fatigue closes my heavy eyelids. The crashing waves of hot and cold meld into gentle swells of warmth that quiet the drumbeat and massage stiff muscles. My mind drifts to hugs from my family, my fingers pressed against the supple metal strings of my guitar, the rush of a soccer goal, Kenji's kisses. Sweet, warm, wonderful. The pure elation that envelops me during healings, when the Spirit fills me, and Heaven touches earth. Peace floods my soul...and I know He is with me.

Always.

Nonna returns, vaporizing the lovely images, but not the peace. She is trailed by the enticing scent of chocolate, which rides the wisp of steam rising from a ceramic mug large enough to bathe in.

"You are better." She gazes at me with the shadow of a smile. "The despair, it is gone from your eyes. You see? You knew just what to do. You feel it." She sets the mug on her nightstand, next to a faded photo of herself with my grandparents. How it must have wrecked her when they were killed in that helicopter crash.

"Drink. It is good. It will warm you from inside out. Relax you. Italian chocolate is more rich than American."

I need no encouragement. The aroma alone is enough to ensure me I'll be asking for seconds. My palms wrap around the smooth warmth of the handmade mug, and I inhale the chocolatey deliciousness of its contents before taking the first sip. The velvet liquid is paradise in a cup. I am in love.

"Nonna, this is amazing."

"Is what you need."

What I need is a bigger mug, but that would be called a bucket. "So…what went wrong? How do I make sure it never happens again?"

"Ah, Shilo Marie. This happen too soon. You do not have enough experience. I should have stop you before we enter. My heart, it tells me this is not right. We should always listen to our hearts. Forgive me for letting it happen."

"Not your fault, Nonna. You rescued me. But why did I need rescuing? God trumps evil, right? So this never should have happened."

"When a person touch fire, it burns, yes? So we know not to touch fire."

I wait for more. And wait. Take a sip of chocolate ecstasy, and wait.

And then I get it. Riccardo's the fire. "It was a warning." Her nod affirms my insight. "Powerful, terrible, so there'd be no mistaking the message. He's a danger, Nonna. To all of us."

"Yes."

The warm mug in my hands is no match for the chills that surface from her simple acknowledgment.

"We have to do something. We have to get him out of here. Call the police."

"The sisters believe his story, believe he is good person." She shakes her head. "What would you tell *polizia*, Shilo Marie? You tell them you feel his evil?"

She's right. The cops will think I'm crazy. My mind whirls around ways to justify our suspicions. "Couldn't we just tell them there's a guy here who's been shot and stabbed? That should interest them."

"Only Mother Superior has phone, and she promise him she will not call *polizia*. You see? Is problem."

Is problem all right. I savor the last gulp of hot chocolate and set the mug down. "What do you think he's done?"

She shakes her head. "This I do not know. But if the Spirit warns us, then it is very, very bad."

A foggy image fills my head, making the chills return. "There's a truck. He forced people into a truck or van or something."

"You see this when you pray? You see faces? License?"

The image offered up no clarity. I shake my head, wishing I knew more. "I'm sorry."

Endless possibilities ramble around inside my head, each more horrid than the last, but all I have is that hazy image, and gratitude for Nonna's intervention. "This happened to you before, didn't it? That's how you knew to pull me away. How you knew what I felt before I even told you."

"*Si.* Two times this happen."

"Who pulled you away?"

"First time was in America. Your mama was a little girl. She pull me away. Our relatives in the room say 'What you doing, Annie! Do not touch Nonna during a healing!' But your mama, she knows something is not right. I tell the people to leave her alone. She sees with the faith of child. Best kind of faith. She rescue me."

"Did you ever find out what he did?"

She nods. "He kill the neighbor family." Her eyes gaze beyond me, surely looking past time and space, into a memory that seared her soul. "Next time was in Sicily. I knew the sign, so I force my hand away. That time was a woman. Two times she had a baby, and two times they disappear. She tells us someone take them. We all feel sorry, but after that day, I knew. Those poor babies." She glances away from me, but it doesn't hide the shimmer of pain in her eyes, even after many decades. "I sneak around her house while she is away and find the dirt, you know, like someone dig, so I tell *polizia*. They think I am crazy, but they look and find both babies."

Nonna yawns. It's been a long day for both of us, so I

suggest we go our separate ways until dinner, knowing she'll take a much-needed nap. She readily agrees, and I retreat to my room, happy to be alone. Happier still to see Sister Celeste's guitar leaning against my bed. She hasn't touched it in years and wanted me to have it during my stay. A quick tuning and it's ready to rock-n-roll, though I go with a ballad instead, losing myself in the music. Loving the feel of the smooth wood against my body, the frets against my fingertips. I close my eyes and strum, and for just a moment…I am home.

Six-thirty, and still the sun bathes the mountainside, lighting the bronze adornments on the convent door like golden treasure. I wander out to the garden, lacking anything else to do now that dinner is over and Nonna got called into a meeting. Something about money and refugees. Over by the sunflowers, Sister Celeste is focusing on a butterfly with a camera that may be the most modern technology I've seen since my arrival. A black case at her feet holds two more lenses and other equipment I can't identify.

"*Ciao!*" I walk closer, treading carefully to avoid the array of vegetables and flowers at my feet. "Nice camera."

She grins. "This is my, what is the proper word? Interest? No, hobby. But it is also a way for us to make money for the poor. We sell my photos in the piazza when we sell the pastries. For this reason, I am allowed to possess the camera equipment and a laptop." The butterfly glides away, lighting on a delicate lavender blossom. Celeste takes a stealthy step toward it and bends her knees to get the angle she desires. Five rapid shots later, she shows me the gorgeous photos. The butterfly in the foreground nearly comes alive with clarity and detail, while the flowery background is blurred like a beautiful dreamscape.

I shake my head. "That's amazing. Gorgeous. How did

you do that?"

She hands me the camera, looping the strap over my neck. "I'll show you. If you can remember a small amount of math, and some simple concepts about lighting, you will find it is not difficult."

The next hour flies by as she explains aperture and shutter speed, depth of field and ambient light. She demonstrates the dials and buttons, telling me to shoot the same subjects with different settings to see how the photos change. I'm fascinated over and over at how adjusting the settings lighten, darken, or completely alter the image. We head toward the small pasture adjacent to the barn, where a kid goat and his mom are enjoying the summer evening with the mama pig, her six pink piglets and our resident donkeys, Carlos and the ancient Vincenzo. All of the barnyard creatures are peacefully munching or nursing, except the ever-energetic kid, who is frolicking playfully around his grazing mama. With guidance from Celeste, I switch to a fast shutter speed, increase the ISO and take a few shots as the young goat runs and leaps like a joyful toddler.

"Now stop and check before continuing. Is the lighting good? Is the photo blurry, or no?"

We scroll through the pictures, laughing at the baby goat's pure adorableness.

Celeste grins. "Very nice. I believe you are a natural. Good composition. Good lighting. Good enough to sell at the photo table next week when we go to the piazza."

Her words elicit an unexpected excitement in me. I've always enjoyed taking pictures, mostly with my phone, but this...this is a whole different perspective of the world. And I love having control over the way a moment is captured. Control is a rare and precious commodity in my life these days.

"So you sell your nature photos? Do you shoot anything else?"

"Oh, yes. With photography I can share our world with

others. Photos of the nuns baking, laughing, praying, tending to the garden and animals makes us less mysterious to the villagers." She scrolls through the photos in her camera until she finds some taken earlier in the week. My favorite is the closeup of Sister Angelica rolling dough for her special croissants. The camera captures her weathered skin, her nose dusted with flour, and the determination in her eyes as she takes on a task worthy of a much younger woman. "These pictures, they make us more…human. That helps us build relationships with them. Photography is like an international language. Everyone understands photos."

Vincenzo saunters over, nudging me for a scratch between the ears. I'm happy to comply, especially after hearing the story of this sweet, smelly beast getting rescued by the nuns when he was starving and neglected. The old donkey presses his face against me, loving the attention.

"Even better, my photos show them the world of the refugees we support. How they live, the school we built. We did that with donations and also with profits from pastries and my photos. Photos can be powerful tools in helping people understand a situation, or identify with people who are different from them. You see?"

"I do. I get it." Her words open a door to a world I'd never considered. My excitement grows, blooming into something more. Something bigger. Possibilities of using photography to…to what? Details are hazy, but there's something new forming in my head, and I can't wait to see what develops.

I look toward the mysterious stone house in the meadow, where the youngest girl is sitting on a large rock, gazing at the sky. Another two are tossing a frisbee to each other. They motion for her to join, but she shakes her head. "What about them? Are they refugees?"

Celeste sighs. "They are refugees, yes. But different. Special."

"I don't understand."

"Your nonna asked us not to speak of them to you. She said she would explain. But I will tell you this: they were in a very bad situation, and now they are better. Not fine, but definitely better. Safer. Please do not ask me any more questions. I made a promise."

Her request halts a thousand questions. Who are they? Where are they from? Why are they here? I want to know about their families, their histories, and their 'bad situation.' Instead, I nod and look toward the barn.

"Let's go inside and shoot the chickens." It only takes a heartbeat for the spoken words to reach my brain. "Oh, man, that sounded bad."

Celeste laughs. "Come. We will shoot, but only with the camera."

We turn to go, my mind switching from thoughts of the girls to camera settings I'll need inside the barn, where only a small amount of sunlight streams in through a couple of windows. Church bells chime, freezing our steps and beckoning my companion to her evening prayers.

"Oh, I will be late. I must hurry, but you may keep practicing. Keep the camera while you are here. I have another." She runs off as I shout a 'thank you' that doesn't begin to reflect the gratitude swelling inside me. Maybe I can find a nice gift for her when I spend the day out with my cousins. I take another step toward the barn. Those weird chickens, with their crazy feathers and layers of colors, will make great subjects. But the girls…

I glance again toward the meadow house, where the three have been joined by another. That leaves five remaining inside. Nonna didn't want the sisters telling me about them, but no one said I couldn't visit.

Bad situation. So cryptic. I turn away from the barn and head toward the meadow. They don't notice me at first, but as I draw closer, one sees me and calls out to the others. Each turns and freezes. I wave. The three frisbee players draw close to each other, then walk to the rock where the little one is sitting. Her gaze is no longer on the sky. Like the others, she's focused on me until they form a miniature human wall in front of her. They are right around my age or younger, except for the child on the rock. She's more like Julia's age, and even skinnier than my little sister. Moments ago, there'd been laughter as they tossed the frisbee, often missing their target. But there is no trace of laughter in those faces now. Only suspicion…and fear.

"Hi." I smile, speaking Italian and hoping a friendly tone will thaw the ice, but they neither speak nor move. "I'm Shilo." Nothing. I search for words, wishing I'd headed for the barn. Chickens never make you feel awkward. "Do you speak Italian? Or English?"

The girl with the ponytail steps forward. "I speak Italian. Little bit." She points to the girl next to her, somber eyes peering into mine beneath a forest of black lashes. "And she."

"Nice to meet you. I'm staying in the convent." I point to the building, not sure how much they're understanding. "I'm Marie's granddaughter."

"Marie?" A hint of a smile graces a face that modeling agents would battle to represent. Full lips, tawny skin, charcoal eyes. But there's no denying the pain in those eyes. "Marie." She says something to the other girls, but the language is like nothing I've ever heard.

"Marie help us. Marie good woman."

"Yes. She's my grandmother." I omit the word 'great,' figuring it would be too confusing.

Eyebrows scrunch. "Grandmother?"

"Oh!" Miss Eyelashes speaks up. "Grandmother. I know word." She says something to her friends that sounds like "jadah," followed by "Marie."

"I am Shilo." I try the introduction again, this time pointing to myself. "What is your name?" Ponytail understands and says her name is Myriam. Lashes is Nada, and the one who doesn't speak Italian is Cyrine. They say nothing more, and we face each other again in awkward silence. No one tells me the name of the youngest, so I look at her and they get the hint.

"She name Farah," Myriam says. "No speak."

At least I'm not the enemy anymore. It's not much, but I'll take it. If only I could communicate more with them. And then it hits me.

"Would you like to see photos?" I pick up my camera and step closer, showing them the photos of the little goat frolicking in the pasture. The three older girls smile, and one even giggles.

"Awww." Cyrine holds the camera and continues staring at the photo. "Goat baby very pretty." She turns to show Farah, who glances, then looks back at the ground. I scroll to show them more photos of the flowers, piglets, and Vincenzo, which solicits "oohs" and "ahhs," along with a few smiles. But not from skinny little Farah, who draws her knees to her chest, wrapping her arms around her legs. Whatever happened to that girl, it wasn't good, and having me around is just making things worse. I tell the girls I have to go, and point from me to the convent. We part with waves and goodbyes, and I turn to head back.

"Bye." The now familiar accent is attached to a voice I've not yet heard. A small voice, barely there, listless and heavy with sadness. One simple word, yet the emotion it elicits in me could fill volumes. Because despite the sorrow permeating that word, something about my visit inspired her to speak. I turn to see three shocked faces, and Farah's eyes meeting mine.

"Bye, Farah. Is it okay if I come back again to visit?"

Myriam translates for her, and she nods. My heart smiles as I finish the short trek to the convent, walking beneath an orange-streaked sunset sky.

Chapter 5

Melody

Ammonia races through my nostrils and slams into my brain. My eyelids fly open to bright lights, strange faces. Calm voices. I scrunch my nose.

"You got hurt, but we're going to help you. Just relax. You passed out, so we had to use smelling salts."

Pain stabs my knee, which is fixed in a bent position. Beyond the pain, something feels wrong. Out of place. But I can't move to see or touch it, because my back hurts as bad as my knee. Through clenched teeth, I hold back screams that would shatter this auditorium.

"Try to relax. Do you know your name?"

What did he say? Drugs. I need drugs. *Oh, God, please. Do something.* "Pain." The word squeezes out between my teeth. "Pain. Help."

"We're going to help, I promise. Can you tell me your name?"

"Melody. O'Hara." Now the drugs. Please. Use a needle, I don't even care.

"I'm Brian. I know you're hurting, but I have to ask you a couple more questions. Do you know where you are?"

"Auditorium. Ballet show."

"Have you ever had a concussion?"

"No." Each word is a struggle that sends more pain raging through my body.

"We're right here, honey!" Mom calls from a few feet away.

Brian glances toward Mom. "Ma'am, please. Time matters right now." He turns back to me. "Are you allergic to any medications?"

"No."

"Where does it hurt?"

"Everywhere."

"The most?"

Pain shoots through every cell in my body. I try to concentrate on origin points in a desperate effort to move this along. "Knee. Back. Foot."

"Okay, Melody. We're going to put a neck brace on you, then place you on a backboard. Please remain still. We'll do something about the pain once you're in the ambulance. Again, try to relax. Deep breaths. You're going to be fine."

Brian and another guy slide their arms under me. I am terrified that the unbearable pain will reach new heights, but they keep me immobile from the floor to the backboard to the gurney. The next few minutes are a whirlwind as they take me through the stage door with my parents and Blake trailing behind. Deep breaths prove useless. Nothing can break through this pain. Everyone's moving so fast. A needle slides into the vein on my hand and is taped into place. Brian scoots down so he's eye level with me.

"You're doing great, Melody." The ambulance heads out, siren wailing. "Right now we're getting some Fentanyl into you. Just a tiny bit. It's a powerful painkiller and works fast. You'll feel better any minute now."

Even as he speaks, the pain begins to dissipate. Thank God. One more minute of that pain would have killed me. "Okay. Feeling it."

"Good." He smiles and stands up. "It's just temporary,

'til the docs can see what's wrong."

"Why can't I straighten my knee?"

"Don't try. You need to leave it alone. Doc will take care of it." He steps out of the way so Mom can see me.

She's a train wreck. Silent tears rain down her cheeks. One hand is clenched, the other wraps around it. She must be hating it that Dad's not here, but they only had room for one. She reaches over and holds my hand; the one without the miracle drug needle. My muscles relax as the drug completes its job.

"I love you, Mellie Bear."

"Love you, too, Mom. I'll be okay. Promise."

Her tears pour faster.

"It doesn't hurt now. Really."

"What?"

So hard to hear each other over the siren. "Doesn't hurt. Good drugs."

She nods, leaning forward so I'll hear her next words. "The first time that adoption lady put you in my arms, I swore I'd never let anything hurt you. I was supposed to protect you."

My heart breaks for her. "You can't, Mom. Life happens." I push myself to raise my voice over the constant wailing and obnoxious air horn that cuts a path as we race through traffic. "You said it's how we respond that matters." It takes everything to get the words out, because in truth, the timing was the worst, and it's ripping me apart. Will the Joffrey drop me? Will I ever have a chance of getting into the Pre-Professional Program? Did everything I've worked for, sacrificed for, dreamed of, hit the floor and shatter with me? To think, I wanted that man to remember me, and now, well… he definitely will. And on top of everything else, it could be weeks before I can start my Joffrey classes.

Mom tries to smile through her tears. "Using my own words on me, young lady?"

My eyes open to an unfamiliar room, where Mom sleeps on a bed next to mine and Dad is slumped in a chair. A plastic tube connects the needle in my hand to a bag filled with clear liquid. A machine tracks my heartbeat, another hums softly, its purpose unknown. My right leg is in a cast from my toes past my knee, while my left knee is snugly secured to a padded board. Last night's unwanted memories flood my brain. A doctor carefully pushing my dislocated knee back in place, more doctors and nurses examining my back, my head, asking questions, taking me for X-rays upon X-rays. But the hardest memory to endure, the one I try in vain to obliterate, is the discussion about a spinal injury and multiple ligament tears. A discussion that ended with the word "surgery."

"No!" I shouted. "I don't have time for surgery. I just got accepted!" I told them I'd do anything—stretches every day, physical therapy, whatever, but I have to be in that Joffrey class when it starts next week. Mom told the doctor that I'd been through too much to have this discussion right now. They injected something into the bottle flowing into my vein, and that's where the memories end.

The pitcher of water on my bedside table makes me realize I'm insatiably thirsty. I reach for it, unprepared for how difficult that simple task will be. The small move serves as a painful reminder that my body smashed into a hard floor from six feet up. Stiff, achy limbs attempt again to reach for the water, but I can't suppress a groan when pain shoots up my spine. Mom's eyes open at the sound. In a heartbeat she's at my side, pouring the water and asking how I feel. Her words wake Dad, who asks the same question.

"Kind of achy, but not too bad." I downplay the pain, hoping to convince them to take me home. "Probably just needs some intense stretching and physical therapy. Pretty sure I'll be okay for class."

They avoid my eyes, glancing at each other with a silent

message that annihilates any hope within me.

"What?" I ask the question, not wanting the answer.

"You're hurt pretty bad there, Muffin." Dad hasn't called me that in ages. It always warmed my heart, but not today. Chills crawl up my arm. My mind screams, *"Don't say another word! Don't say all those bad things that are coming next!"* Maybe if he doesn't say them, they won't be true.

"For starters, you've got that broken shin bone. Tibia, Doc called it. That'll take a few months to heal, lass. Maybe more. And your spine got jarred pretty hard. Doc says you sprained your back, but here's the great news: there's no fracture or dislocation. That's a very big deal, Mellie. Huge." He forces a grin, knowing, like me, that calling it 'a big deal' doesn't stop it from sucking. "And the even better news? It's treatable. Should be okay in six weeks or so with physical therapy and such."

"I don't have six months or even six weeks. And if that's the good news, what's the bad?"

He looks at Mom. "You want to tell her, darlin'?"

Mom shakes her head and puts her hand to her mouth. Her eyes squeeze shut. A tear escapes down a face riddled in pain. Not like mine from yesterday. Worse. The kind you can't cure with meds.

Dad gets up from his chair and plops down on the side of my bed. "The knee's the bigger problem, Mels. I guess there's four main ligaments in there, and you tore at least two of 'em, maybe more."

"My ACL?" I remember my knee swollen like a softball and the ER doctor draining blood out of it with a needle. I nearly fainted…again.

"Yeah, and another one, too. Hold on." He pulls a folded piece of paper out of his pocket and peers over his glasses to read the scribbles. "Oh, here it is. Your MCL. It's the, umm, medial—"

"Collateral ligament. I know." Over the years, some of my ballet friends have suffered MCL tears…among other things.

"They're thinkin' there could possibly be nerve damage, too. I've always been straight with you, and today's no different. You need surgery, lass. No gettin' away from it. They fixed the break last night, but Doc's gotta go in and reconstruct your knee tomorrow. Of course, with all that going on, it might be hard to do the stretches you need to heal your back. Long and short of it is...could be awhile before you're functional again."

Not 'back to normal'. Functional. It's not a Dad term, so he heard it from the doctor. My head tries to wrap around the implications of that word, knowing I should ask. But the question won't form on my lips. Instead, I turn to Mom. "We'll have to contact Joffrey. Ask if I can register for the next session."

"Mellie," she sighs, then kisses the top of my head. "This is going to take a long time. Do you understand? Your knee will be functional eventually, but..."

There's that word again.

"But as for dancing, I don't know. That's a lot of strain, even on a strong, healthy knee. I'm sorry."

I try to sit up, but the back pain keeps me down. Frustration tangles with pain until my insides just scream.

And scream.

And scream.

But no one hears.

"What are you saying, Mom?"

"The doctors don't believe you'll be able to perform again. They wanted you to know, so you don't have false hope. Truth is, it's just not...it's not..."

"Not likely." I finish for her, preferring to say it myself than to hear it. I close my eyes. A heat wave sweeps through me, borne of anger, frustration, an aching loss that comes from watching a dream crushed beneath a thousand 'if onlys.' If only I hadn't obsessed over Blue Suit in the audience. If only that strand of hair hadn't distracted me. If only my *grand jeté* had sailed one inch further. If all those things hadn't come into play, Blue Suit would have seen the dancer everyone else sees, and I wouldn't be lying here like a tattered rag doll.

Mom strokes my hair, compassion flooding her eyes. "We're going to do everything possible, you know that, right?"

I nod, because the words 'I know' are stuck in my throat.

"Doc's coming back this afternoon to talk about everything," Dad says. "We're not leaving your side, so if you want to sleep, talk, eat, anything, you just let us know."

"I want to be alone." I didn't mean for it to sound angry, but anger is all that's pulsating through me right now. Like a toxic wave, it crashes through my thoughts, my heart, my words. And the only ones here to get hit with it are the people who love me most.

"But sweetheart…"

"I want to be alone. Just alone. Please."

"Blake's planning to come at ten."

"No!" The last thing I want is to paste a smile on my face for Blake. "Tell him not to. Not today."

They leave, saying they'll be back before the doctor comes. A dusting of guilt spreads across my anger, but I brush it away. Tears slip onto my pillow, and I brush those away as well, but the supply is endless. How is it possible that one wrong move, one flash in time, could ruin my life? But wait. This is me, Melody O'Hara, who's been resilient since I entered this world and got dumped on a doorstep at three days old. If I can come this far from a start like that, I can overcome a few dents and dings. Functional. I'll give them functional. By this time next year, I'll be dancing like this never happened, and people will say, "Can you believe it?" And yeah, it's going to be hard and painful, but to dance again…for that, I'll do anything.

❦

"I'm sorry it's not better news, Melody." The doctor is handsome, for an older guy, with a fatherly bedside manner that would be sweet, if his words didn't make him the person I hate most in this world. "I've gone over and over your X-rays with Dr. Lopez, one of our best orthopedic surgeons. He'll meet with you later. Your knee will be in good shape with surgery and therapy, but for a performing ballerina, "good" is not good enough. Dance takes a toll on knees, Melody. What you need would take a miracle."

"Medical miracles happen, right?"

"They do, but don't expect that. Not with these kind of injuries. Take comfort in knowing your spine will soon be back to normal. Things could have gone much worse."

If that's supposed to be comforting, it falls short. I get it. I could have died. Could have ended up in a wheelchair permanently. But in this moment, this dark, miserable, desperate moment, nothing could be worse. I want to leap out of this bed and pound on his kind, compassionate face. His doctor's oath states, "First, do no harm," and he just did the worst possible kind of harm.

He destroyed my hope.

Chapter 6

Shilo

"Wake up, Shilo Marie," the soft voice whispers in my sleep. "Wake up. Today you are seventeen!"

My eyes open to the morning sun and Nonna standing at my bedside.

"*Buon compleanno*! Happy birthday to you. Big day. Your cousins, they come to take you out for all the day." She bends down to kiss my cheek. "Time to get dressed and eat. They arrive soon."

Her words wipe the sleep from my brain. Finally seventeen. And finally spending a day away from the convent. By the time they arrive, I'm waiting outside, though admittedly not expecting an entourage of two cars and a motorcycle. I don't even remember meeting some of these people, especially the cute guy on the bike. The next ten minutes are swamped by passionate embraces and kisses and "Happy birthdays" in both languages.

My last birthday hug comes from my cousin Angelo, just a year older than me. "This is my friend, Domenico." Angelo gestures to motorcycle guy, who gets off his bike and takes both my hands in his.

"Ah, Shilo, you are beautiful as they say." And before I

take my next breath, he kisses both my cheeks. "*Buon compleanno.*"

"*Grazie,*" I say, fighting the blush I can't control. "Nice to meet you."

"Much nicer for me." His eyes linger on mine until Angelo punches him in the arm and calls him an "*idiota,*" thus proving that guys are guys in any country.

Domenico laughs. "It is worth the pain to stare into those *magnifico* eyes. Such eyes, like drops of the Mediterranean."

I'm no stranger to comments about the color of my eyes, or people asking if I wear colored contacts, but the way he says it, well…that's a whole different story. Not that I'm interested. The best guy on the planet is waiting for me in Indiana, and he's my one and only. Still…it's nice to get a little attention from someone besides Nonna Marie. Someone with sexy brown eyes and a smile that, at the moment, renders me speechless.

My cousins tell me we are spending the day in Taormina, a mountainside resort town overlooking the Ionian Sea. Jules told me about it before I left. It's one of those places that draws artists and writers like bees to honey, and it's got a medieval village with stores and restaurants.

Angelo's five-year-old sister, Bianca, takes my hand. Like most Italian kids, she's already learned some English, but just barely. "Gelato!" She tries to fill in the rest of her sentence with the cutest grin I've ever seen. "You eat?"

I scoot down so we're eye to eye. "I *love* gelato," I answer in Italian. "It's my favorite dessert in the whole world. We'll get some together, okay?"

Her grin widens to Grand Canyon proportions, and she nods hard enough to set her ponytails swinging. "Yes, *cugino* Shilo. Oops. *Cousin* Shilo." Her attempt at English takes her adorable level to new heights. "Bianca and cousin Shilo. Gelato."

"And after gelato, we will visit Teatro Greco, the ancient Greek Theater." Angelo lobs an arm over my shoulders, like the brother I never had. "It is thousands of years old."

My aunt says we should be on our way, since it's a forty-minute drive from the convent. She opens the car door for me, but I'm stuck in place by Domenico's arm, which is securely wrapped around mine, while Angelo's is still looped over my shoulder. I'm beginning to feel like the middle of a *panini*.

"You like motorcycle?" Domenico's bike gleams in the morning sun.

"Um...yes?"

"Would you like to ride with me?"

More than life itself. The only thing better would be driving it, but since I've never ridden one, that might be a bad idea. My mind is torn between not wanting to give him the wrong impression, and wanting to ride on that bike so badly I can almost feel the rush of wind in my face. Who knows when I'll get this chance again? Kenji doesn't have one, and my parents wouldn't even let me blink in the direction of a motorcycle. A person really shouldn't let an opportunity like this pass by. I can always make it clear that I have a boyfriend...after the ride.

"Okay. Thanks."

Angelo rolls his eyes. "You be careful with my American cousin," he tells Domenico. "This whole family will beat you if anything happens to her."

Domenico hops on and revs the engine in reply. In minutes, we're flying down the convent's dirt road, my arms wrapped around this hot stranger as I embrace the speed and freedom of my first motorcycle ride. He could drive me across Sicily and back and I'd never ask him to stop.

Forty *fantastico* minutes later we park in one of Taormina's narrow stone streets, lined with picturesque shops, cafés, and no shortage of gelato stands. My bare leg brushes the tail pipe, which results in a tiny burn on my calf. Small, but irritating. I place my hand over it, but the only warmth I feel is the heat emanating from my sizzled skin. Domenico pours his bottled water on it and says we can probably get a band aid from one of my aunts, who all carry purses the size of small suitcases.

Views of the sun-sparkled sea that separates Sicily from mainland Italy take my breath away. Sweet and savory aromas drift our way as we walk past pubs and bakeries selling everything from wine and coffee, to paninis and cannolis. I'm particularly enticed by the *salumi*, a deli where a variety of salamis and sausages hang from the ceiling. But it is the ancient Greek Theater that draws me in, transporting me back in time with its crumbling walls that have stood tall through countless storms and more than two thousand years of humanity.

Who moved the tons of rock to create this huge outdoor theater? Who filled these seats through the centuries, watching plays and concerts under the stars, or beneath the blazing Mediterranean sun? Were there girls like me, glancing past the stone walls to the azure sea, wondering what the future had in store? Was there anyone, in all that time, who harbored The Gift? So many years, so many people. There *had* to be someone.

Beyond the theater walls, cliffs drop to the Ionian Sea, forming coves with sandy beaches. My cousins tell me that, after lunch, we'll take the cable car down to the beach. But first, we will wander through town, exploring the shops that hold colorful, handmade ceramics, leather goods, souvenirs, and so much more. Our first stop is a gelato stand, where my cousins insist I have at least three flavors, then argue over which three are the best. In the end, I let little Bianca choose for me. Lunch is at an open air café overlooking the sea, where we watch artists painting on easels as tourists stroll by or stand at the cliff wall, mesmerized by the view. After lunch, we join them, and I click away using Sister Celeste's camera. It is impossible to capture the true essence of this place...but I try. My favorite is a closeup of an artist painting a seascape, with the real life seascape in front of him.

"Look." Domenico slips his arm around my waist and points out to the shimmering water. "You see that hazy line at the water's edge? That is the coast of Calabria. Very beautiful there. Big national parks, waterfalls, lakes. You should visit."

I nod, wondering if the arm thing is just normal Italian friendliness or a hint of something more.

My cousins ask if I would like time alone to contact my friends and family, and bring me to a café where I can plug in my charger. What better birthday gift than a chance to connect with everyone I miss? They leave me by a window overlooking the sea, probably knowing I can't get enough of it, and promise to return in an hour. I grab my phone and touch Kenji's name first. Love my family, but if I don't talk to Kenji, I'm going to implode. With every ring, I silently beg him to answer.

"Blue?"

Finally! How I've missed hearing him call me that.

"Hey, you. How's farm life?"

"Not great. Not terrible." Voices fill the background. And one, distinctly female, asks, "Where you goin'?"

To which Kenji replies, "Gotta take this. Be right back."

The fact that he didn't say the word 'girlfriend' is not lost on me.

"Who was that?"

"Just hanging with neighbors from down the road. Met them when me and my uncle helped their dad mend a fence. They're our age, so it's cool. And they introduced me to their friends."

"Wow, you made friends already. That's...great."

"Hey, happy birthday! Can't believe I'm not celebrating with you. I was gonna take you on that Ferris wheel on Navy Pier. I had a whole day planned. Man, that sure blew up. How are you doing? How's your great grandma and the nuns? What's it like in Sicily? I miss you so much, Blue."

That's more like it. I tell him about the convent, meeting Nonna Marie, drinking goat's milk, the breathtaking views of the mountains and sea. I tell him I'm spending my birthday in this cool medieval town. I leave out the part about my creepy encounter with the convent's sinister mystery man, so he won't worry, and the motorcycle ride with Domenico, ignoring the wisp of guilt that rides on that omission.

"Hey, Chicago, come on." It's the same girl's voice from before, calling him from somewhere in the background. "We're heading into town."

"Chicago?"

"Yeah, she calls me that. Told her I'm from a suburb, but...she's a little crazy."

Is there a hint of affection in those last four words? My heart stops beating as I read volumes between the lines. It's only been a week, and some Daisy Duke has a cutesy nickname for him.

"Oh." I laugh, for lack of anything to say.

"Anyway, it's good your cousins took you out today. At least you have them to hang out with."

"Yeah, they're great. Domenico, too. I blame him for this burn on my leg, though." I laugh. "He didn't warn me about the tailpipe."

"Tailpipe?"

"Yeah, on his motorcycle. When I slid off the seat, my calf touched the tailpipe. Man, that thing was flaming hot after the ride to Taormina. Don't worry, though. Not that bad. I'll be more careful on the ride back."

"What? Who is this guy?"

And the passive-aggressive shot hits its mark. "My cousin's friend. He's studying to be a geography teacher."

"He's in college?"

"Yeah, just finished his first year, but they only go to high school for three."

"Chicago, you comin' or what?" Farm girl's voice sounds way too close to the phone, which means she's way too close to Kenji. *My* Kenji.

"You should probably go. You've got that big trip to town."

"Yeah, well…call me again when you can, okay? I miss you. And Blue? You should ride in the car with your cousins on the way back. They'd probably like to hang with you, ya know?"

And you should not *go into town with whoever's calling you 'Chicago.'* But I leave that comment inside my head.

"Maybe. I'll see. Bye, Kenji. Miss you, too." I hang up, harboring a heaviness I had not anticipated.

Next up are my parents and Jules, who all get on the phone and sing "Happy Birthday." Mom tells me she's teaching a new cooking class next month, Terrific Tarts, and says Misty's doing great in North Carolina and calls every few days. Jules is all excited about leaving for science camp. Dad gets on and says there are some interesting twists in the saga of the Warriors, whose desire for revenge is partially the reason I'm here.

"We've got two in jail for that drug bust you almost ruined, two more for breaking into Misty's apartment. Another one's in critical condition—got high and wrapped his car around a tree. If he survives, he's going to jail. And you won't believe this, Shi-girl—one of 'em married his pregnant girlfriend at City Hall. Saw it with my own two eyes. He came up to me after and said, 'You won't be gettin' no more trouble from me, Sarge.' Said they were heading to Wisconsin for a fresh start. At this rate, that gang will be nothin' by the end of summer, and that suits me just fine."

His words send my spirits soaring. If the gang's not a problem, then this whole Sicily thing can come to an end. "Me, too. Does that mean I can come home?"

"No, sweetheart. Not yet. Give it time. We need you and Kenji out of the mix for awhile. Should be safe enough by the end of summer, though."

My hopes crash to the café floor. Experience tells me

there's no use in pursuing that discussion, so I might as well accept my fate and move on. "Did you guys see Melody's ballet?"

There's a pause before he answers. "I had to work."

"What about Mom and Jules? They saw it, right?"

Another pause, followed by muffled words. He's blocked the phone with his hand. "Mom says it was good. She'll tell you more when you get home."

Two calls, two traces of something suspicious. I can't pinpoint why his words unsettle me, but my intuition whispers that all is not right with the world. At least, not the small part to which I'm connected. But my time is running out, and I'll have to revisit this conversation next time around.

"Okay. Well, guess I'll go. I just have a few minutes to text my friends before everyone comes back."

"Love you, sweetheart. Be careful out there. We'll talk to you soon."

I take some cell phone shots of the sea and artists painting in the palazzo, and send them to Melody, Brittany and Lauren with a text. Brittany and Lauren respond right away and we do a few rounds of catch ups and miss yous, but nothing from Mel. She's probably tied up with ballet, but I'd really hoped we could connect. There will probably be a card from her at the convent when I get back, and maybe even a package. She'd never forget my birthday. I smile, remembering the crazy soccer ball cake she made last year and her gift of our photo in a pretty 'friends forever' frame. My cousins return and I tuck away my phone, knowing it will be little more than a useless hunk of metal once we return to the land that time forgot.

By the time we pull up in front of the convent, I'm ready to plop down in my stark little room and pass out. My cousins repeat the lengthy hugging, kissing scenario that started my day, and Domenico asks if I'd like to go with him to a place called Gole dell'Alcantara. Since *gole* means throat, I can't imagine what he's talking about.

"The Throat of Alcantara is a gorge, with high canyon walls and the Alcantara river running through it. People come from all over to see it."

That sounds way too amazing to pass up. But…Kenji. On the other hand, I'm in Sicily, and it would be crazy not to see something more than the convent. And it's not like a date, it's just hiking and hanging out by a river. But…Kenji. I decide to take a risk and do the right thing, knowing the tempting offer may disintigrate on impact.

"Here's the thing. It sounds great, but I have a boy-friend."

A mischievous smile forms on his lips. "I do not see this boyfriend."

"Funny."

"I joke. We are just friends, you and I. That is all. I thought you would like to get away from convent for a day. If no, I understand. But this place, it is *molto bella, magnifico*, so beautiful. You would like it much. But…is your choice."

Dark eyes smile at me and they are *molto bella, magnifico*, so beautiful. Oh, man, my heart should not be beating at this rate. I'll just say no and help the sisters bake pastries tomor-row. That's the right thing to do. It's just a river. We have those back home. That's it, then. The answer is definitely no.

"Okay. Yes. I'd like to go." Somewhere between my brain and my mouth, the words got lost in translation.

"Good. I will pick you up at ten in the morning. Day after tomorrow. Yes?"

"See you then."

I am wiped out from a day walking miles through the stone-cobbled streets of Taormina and wandering the gor-geous beach, and stuffed from gelato, lunch, and a cannoli I shared with little Bianca. So when Nonna Marie asks me to accompany her to the kitchen, I pray there's some tiny chance it doesn't involve food.

The birthday cake nearly covers the table and bursts with yellow marzipan bejeweled with the bright reds and oranges of sugared fruits. Set in the center of an inlaid marble platter, it towers above neat rows of almond cookies and cream puffs that encircle it like feather-topped showgirls. It's worthy of a Food Network cake competition and could feed everyone on this side of Mt. Etna. Next to the platter sits a stack of three gifts wrapped in white paper, hand-painted with colorful birds and flowers, thanks to Sister Francesca's artistic hand.

The sisters light candles and belt out "Happy Birthday" in a mixture of English and Italian that is hands down the most hilarious thing I've ever heard. A video of this would get a million hits easy on YouTube, but I wouldn't make this precious moment public for anything. Sister Celeste laughs hard enough to send tears streaming down her cheeks. I blow out the candles and the sisters erupt in applause.

"Make wish, Shilo Marie," Nonna says. "Wish good. You seventeen now – all grown up." She presses her palms against my cheeks and kisses my forehead. "And so beautiful, yes? Not just outside, Shilo Marie. Inside, too, where most important."

The infectious laughter of the sisters dissipates my earlier bout of homesickness and concerns about Riccardo. Even though I thought my birthday would be spent celebrating with Kenji and my friends, this is a pretty good alternative. A huge slice of the gorgeous birthday cake is placed in front of me, and despite the day of decadent consumption, I dig in. What else is there to do? Sister Francesca watches, waiting for accolades, and I don't disappoint.

"This is amazing! You made this? It's incredible. I love it."

"Oh, it is nothing. Just a cake. Anyone can do."

Here we go, round two. "No, seriously. This is the best cake I've ever eaten. So delicious."

"Good. You eat up, and I cut you another piece."

I'm going to die. There is nothing but pure sugar running through my veins and saturating my body. I decline the second piece with all the grace I can muster, but she still looks disappointed.

My empty plate is replaced with the gifts. From the nuns, an ivory lace shirt, handmade by Sister Mary, who sells them in town. It will look awesome over a tank. Mother Superior gives me a painting of the convent, surrounded by the flowery gardens and surrounding hills and valleys. I will love having it as a keepsake. Last is Nonna's. I carefully untie the ribbons, careful not to tear the artistic wrapping, and unveil a miniature, hand-painted guitar with a stand. It's unique and extraordinary and I love it more than words can say. I thank everyone with a hug, and Sister Celeste whispers that this night has been the most fun she's had in ages.

As we're cleaning up, one of Riccardo's regular caretakers walks in and heads straight to Mother Superior. A whispered conversation ensues, followed by the first smile I've seen on Mother Superior's face. She turns to face us.

"Riccardo's fever is down! His infection is clearing up, and he is hungry. This is good news, sisters. Very good news."

Many "Praise the Lords" and "Thanks be to Gods" fill the room as the nuns revel in the news. Nonna glances at me, her eyes no longer smiling. We were safe as long as Riccardo was incapacitated. But whoever he is, whatever evil lies within him, is sure to surface once he's better. And from the sound of it, 'better' is blazing toward us like a meteor.

Chapter 7

Melody

I scoot over so Blake can sit on the side of my bed, wondering what I'll say when he asks why I haven't let him visit. Truth is, I don't even want him here now, cute as he is with that huge bouquet of flowers in one hand and a smiley balloon in the other. The flowers are fine, I guess, but that stupid balloon... I just want to jab it with scissors. How dare it smile when my life is over?

"Hi, Mels." He sets the vase down on the nightstand and ties the balloon to my hospital bed. It bobs its yellow head, mocking me with its big black grin. "I thought this stuff might cheer you up a little."

"Thanks. The flowers are gorgeous."

He bends down to kiss me, then sits on the edge of the bed. "I wanted to come sooner, but your mom said you didn't want company." I can't help resenting the hint of hurt infusing his words. This is not about him. This is *my* time to suffer. *My* world that just crashed and burned. I don't have compassion to spare at the moment. For the past three days, all I've heard from my parents and the medical types is, "At least your back will be normal again." Well, yeah, that's great, but it won't get me into that Joffrey Academy class, and my toes may never touch another stage.

"I was here for the surgery, though. Did they tell you?"

"Yeah. Thanks."

"Sorry to hear they found some nerve damage in your knee. I was hoping…you know. Anyway, you feeling okay? Need anything?"

He's trying. Really trying. But how do I answer that? Part of me wants to tell him I wouldn't be here if I was okay, and what I need, he can't provide. But even in my current state of self-pity, I know that's not fair.

"No, thanks. The surgery's done, I've got physical therapy scheduled. All I have to do now is heal."

He smiles, clearly happy to hear my positive words. "You'll be dancing again in no time, Mel. You're not one to let a little setback get you down."

He doesn't know. I want to tell him, but he seems so happy in his delusion that I'm going to bounce back and hit the stage. There's more than that keeping the words inside, though. There's the tears that will spill out with the words. The tears I don't want him to see.

"Yeah. That's me."

His smile fades. Apprehension shadows his eyes. "What's going on, Mels? You're a better dancer than actor." He places his hand on the huge thigh-to-foot brace protecting my knee. "Is it this? Don't let it get to you. It's temporary. Just remember that. It's not forev…"

"Stop it!" I didn't mean for it to come out that loud, but I'm also not done. "Don't sit there and tell me everything's going to be okay. It's not. It never will be again. Don't you get it?"

"But the operation went well. I heard the surgeon. And you're coming home in a couple of days."

"Just go, Blake. I'm tired. Please, just go."

"Talk to me, Melody. What did I say? This isn't you at all."

He's right, it's not. At least, not the old me. Not the

version that fought dyslexia and came out with straight As. Not the girl who started dancing at the ripe old age of eleven and beat out seasoned dancers for the solo. This is a new Melody—full of self-loathing for making a rookie mistake. Rotting in self-pity. And New Melody just wants to be alone, even if it's unfair to Blake, who waited three days and waltzed in with that smiley balloon and a truckload of optimism.

I lie on my back and stare at the ceiling, hating the drops that slide down from the outer corners of my eyes.

"Mel." He plucks a tissue from the box on my tray table and dabs my eyes. "I'll go if you want me to, but …"

"I do. Want you to. Sorry I yelled. Sorry I don't want company. It's just…I'm tired. Probably from the meds."

"Okay, then. You take care. I'll call you tonight." He lifts my hand to his lips and kisses it, then disappears into the hallway.

I wait a moment to be sure he's gone, then grab a pen from the tray table and jab that smiley face right in its black eye.

❧

"Oh, my. What happened here?" Adanna, my favorite nurse, picks up the crumpled remains of the balloon. An awkward silence fills the space where I should have replied. She tosses it into the garbage. "Well, I am sure your nice boyfriend will bring another."

And I'll kill that one, too.

Adanna checks my pulse and examines all the wires and dressings. "How are you feeling today, Melody? Is your pain manageable? Do you need anything?"

"I'm fine." I want her to go…and I don't. I love her subtle accent, and the way she smiles at me. Something about Adanna just feels comfortable, even now, when I don't want to be around anyone.

She takes my hand, her ebony skin a shade darker than mine, and sits on the edge of the bed. "I will not pretend to know what you are enduring, or tell you everything will be all right. I do believe it will, but I have been in a dark place where it did not seem possible for me, either." She rubs her thumb across the top of my hand. "When our dreams and plans are destroyed, we have to force our hearts open so new dreams have a way to enter."

Her velvet voice takes the edge off my anger, but I have no interest in new dreams.

"Melody, you are more than a ballerina. Much more. Reach inside and find a new passion. A new calling. I have seen people leave this hospital without the function of their bodies or brains. Many others on a gurney headed for the morgue." She gives my hand a squeeze. "You are alive, you can walk, your brain is perfect. What will you do with such a blessing?"

All of my despair settles in my throat, which painfully constricts as I stare at the ceiling. For the second time today, streams trail down the outer corners of my eyes and seep into my pillow. A blessing. As if there's a shred of anything good about this nightmare. I don't want to talk about me or my future, but I want her to stay, just for awhile.

"What happened to you? Your dark place."

"Ah, that is a long and painful story, before I became a nurse and a happy mama. Now I must check on other patients. But if there is time when I am finished, we will talk."

"Okay." For the first time since entering this building, my thoughts are on something besides me. I hope she has time to come back and talk.

"The magazine lady will be here soon. Take one. Reading is a good distraction." She pats my arm and heads out, leaving me alone with my misery.

As promised, the magazine lady stops by, followed by a guy with a juice tray, and another guy who changes my sheets. Transitioning back into my bed is no easy feat, with pain pervading every move, but it finally happens and I'm more than ready to close my eyes and drift off to a place where, at least for awhile, I won't hurt…or think…or dwell on what might have been.

"Hey, you, wake up!" Jenna's voice breaks through my peaceful journey from the land of despair. Like Blake, she totes a balloon, and I am eternally grateful that its brilliant colors simply spell out, "Get well soon," even while knowing that's so not going to happen. Three other members of my troupe traipse in behind her. A hug fest follows, with everyone acting like I'm made of papier mâché. It's just as well, though. Our normal way of hugging, like we do after performances, would probably kill me.

"We've been so worried about you. Everyone's asking about you, Mel. You're all over the chat room, Twitter, Instagram. Dancers from other troupes are even talking about it."

"I don't get it. How do so many people know about this?"

"You know, the video."

My stomach churns. Everything inside me says don't ask the next question, but I have to know. "What video?"

Four dancers exchange glances, and say nothing.

"*What* video, you guys?"

"Guess I shouldn't have said anything. I just wanted you to know how much everyone cares about you after seeing the fall."

This can't be happening. Can. Not. Be. Happening. My worst, most humiliating moment is traversing the world via social media. There are probably people from Africa to Iceland laughing hysterically as the ballerina butterfly leaps to her doom. But maybe, just maybe, there's a remote chance that I misinterpreted her comment.

"And they saw the video where, exactly?"

More glances, more silence. Lucie steps out from behind Jenna and hands me a bouquet of flowers. "Pretty much everywhere, Mel. Sorry. We figured you knew."

"Let's see it." Why I want the torture to continue is beyond logic, but something in me needs to see what the world is seeing. I can't be the subject of a "trending now" without ever having seen it.

"You sure?" Lucy sets the flowers on my windowsill, where they can bathe in the afternoon sunlight.

I nod, and she pulls out her cell and finds it way too fast. I stare at the screen before me, watching myself approach my demise. Arms extended, chin up, back arched, wings shimmering. My mind screams, "Don't do it, Mel!" But the video me continues on with her *grand jeté,* and for the first time, I see it all the way everyone else did. The way the whole world is seeing it now. My foot rams the fake cliff and I drop like a bowling ball, smacking my back and head on the stage while groans and gasps erupt from the audience. Video me lays motionless, wings flattened like one of those butterflies somebody kills to put behind glass.

Never to fly again.

Chapter 8

Shilo

Last night's news plagued me with restless sleep. Riccardo is on the mend, which means we need to do something fast. If the sisters won't believe us, we've got to tell the police, but getting to them or even contacting them presents a problem I struggle to resolve. My eyes sweep the amazing mountain-side view of the valley and distant peaks. Gorgeous, but desolate as well. Other than the stone house where the mystery girls live, there are no human life forms within walking distance, and Vincenzo, the donkey, isn't going to get me anywhere. Pretty sure I could outrun him. There's the van they take to sell pastries in town, but Mother Superior will never let me take it, or even call the cops from her land line.

Domenico! He's coming tomorrow. He'll take me to the police. But there's still the question of what to say. They're not going to listen to some crazy American teenager who believes a man is evil, but I could tell them he's been shot and stabbed. That should count for something. I ponder ways to convince them this guy is pure venom as I head toward the pasture with Celeste's camera dangling from my neck.

"Shilo Marie!" Nonna stands in the barn's rustic

doorway. "Come fast." She waves me over and I fly, noting the urgency in her voice. She ducks back into the barn, and I follow, immediately immersed in the scents of hay, wood, grain, manure and feathers. It is at once sweet, musty, earthy and natural, and while I don't love it, I find it weirdly inviting. My eyes strain to adjust from the blaring sun outside to the barn's muted lighting. Nonna stands at the sheep enclosure on the far side, holding a pair of latex gloves that match the ones on her hands.

"Put on. You help me today. Baby coming now. Hurry."

"Baby?" This can't be good. I don't do babies. They're so breakable, and they've got that scary soft spot on their heads. Who could possibly be having a —

A sheep bleats as it stands atop a clean bed of hay. Thick slime hangs from her butt, where something black protrudes—something that strongly resembles a lamb nose. The mama sheep heaves, pushes, and flops down on her side.

"Our poor Carina," Nonna says. "She have hard time. We must pull to help, but my strength, it is not so good these days."

She has got to be kidding. I add 'animal midwife' to the growing list of weird data I never knew, or imagined, about Nonna Marie. Didn't see this coming. Nor did I foresee my role in it. Part of me selfishly wishes Domenico had picked me up *today*, but one look at Carina's wooly face assures me my presence here is needed. I gather up my guts and send up a prayer for guidance, because whatever comes next is going to require some help from above.

"You watch, then you do. See? Like this."

A miniature white hoof hangs out next to the baby's nose. Nonna slides one hand under it, as the other disappears partway into the mama sheep's opening. Meanwhile, the dangling mucus has gotten longer and is now blotched with blood. My stomach flips over, liquidating my breakfast and threatening to send it sailing.

"I don't know anything about this, Nonna. Let me run and get someone. You don't want me killing that little thing."

"No time, Shilo Marie. Baby comes *now*. Is good experience for you."

Carina bleats and grunts, but her lamb stays put. Kenji is the one living on a farm, yet he's hanging out with friends while I'm playing sheep doc. The irony of this situation is not lost on me. Carina stands, pushes, and lays again, still making no progress. My heart breaks for her, and now I'm worried that baby is going to die before entering this world.

"Not on my watch, Lambie," I whisper. "Here goes." I take a breath and mimick Nonna's move, gently tugging the leg and neck simultaneously, trying to ignore the slimy birth sack. It doesn't budge much, until Carina pushes.

"Now, Shilo Marie. But gentle, gentle."

I pull, Carina bleats, and suddenly a goo-enveloped newborn is laying half on the hay, half on me. And I am so completely enraptured by this new creation, so beautiful, so fragile, that I forget to feel nauseated by the birth sack sliming my bare leg. The proud mama sheep turns to lick the black velvet face of her baby. It is, by far, the most beautiful sight I've ever seen.

"You see, Shilo Marie. Mama sheep, she knows what to do. No one tell her. She does not have to think. Is this way with The Gift. You will know. God will put it in your head." She pulls a clean rag from a box in the corner and carefully wipes the newborn.

"So you don't think I need to hang out in hospitals or war zones—places like that?"

She smiles and sets down the rag to take my hand. "No. Live your life like always. When you feel the warm in your heart, then you know. You do not go looking. He will send you."

Lambie struggles to stand on skinny legs covered in damp fuzz. Her dark eyes and black nose contrast adorably with her curly white wool. On her third try, her legs do their job. Carina continues her tongue bath until Lambie reaches beneath her for her first meal of warm milk.

"But when? How will I know?" I can't tear my eyes away from this new creation, even as I ask Nonna the questions that have burned inside me for months. "How do I prepare?"

"Same way you know the other times you heal. You no need to prepare. You no need to wonder how or when. You just do, Shilo Marie." She holds a bowl of water in front of the exhausted Carina, who eagerly drinks while her baby nurses. "No bragging, no accept money or gifts. Just do in secret, as best you can. Remember, you are not the one with the power. You are…how do you say? Vessel. You understand this word?"

I nod. He's the potter, I'm the clay forming into a pot. Got it. I sigh, realizing there's been a small warehouse of anxiety inside me since The Gift was revealed. It's been packed full of fears about whether I'm meeting God's expectations for being a healer, but according to Nonna, the only thing I need to do is be willing when the moments arise. Willingness has never been a challenge. The temptation to want or expect payment? Not even on the radar. But keeping it secret…now there's a task.

"What if there's people around? How do I hide what I'm doing?"

"Oh, Shilo Marie. You worry about things you should no worry. If God lead you to someone, God will make a way. You have to trust, yes?"

Nonna's expert hand tenderly wipes away most of the sack with a warm, damp towel. She lets Carina take care of the rest. When she's satisfied that mother and child are fine, we rinse off in the little creek behind the barn and head toward the convent, where a man is waving to us. He holds a leash attached to something in the convent's van.

"*Ciao*, Ezra, *ciao!*" Nonna's voice trills with more

excitement than usual as she greets the man who works as a driver, handyman, landscaper – pretty much whatever the nuns need at the moment. "Where is my girl?"

Ezra gives the leash a tug, and out steps a massive gray beast that might, or might not be, a dog.

I freeze in mid step, grabbing Nonna's arm so the creature doesn't crunch her like a doggy treat. What looks like the spawn of a lion hooking up with a grizzly stares at us with eyes set deep in its charcoal face. A dense mane encircles the muscular neck and shoulders, which easily reach my waist. Padded bear paws appear capable of trekking across Siberia and back. I don't even want to think about the fangs inside that muzzle. Dark eyes remain locked on us, probably contemplating which one to snack on first.

"Ah, my *bambina* is back! Come, Liona, *mi cara*." Nonna claps her hands, and the thing responds with a joyful woof. "Finally, you return from doctor. No more chocolate for you, young lady." She shakes her finger at the furry beast, which raises one paw as though swearing off chocolate for good.

Nonna attempts to step toward it, but I hold her back. "What is it?"

"Liona is Caucasian Shepherd. No fear, Shilo Marie. She is good girl." She pats my hand. "Now you let go."

Nonna is smiling, Ezra is smiling, and even the giant beast seems to be smiling. Against all my instincts, I let go, and Nonna steps toward Liona and extends her hand. Gentle as a bunny, Liona sniffs her from elbow to fingertips. I suspect it will be the last I'll ever see of Nonna's arm. A big pink tongue emerges, slobbering her hand in a loving, saliva infused greeting. She laughs like a child.

"Ah, my sweet girl is back. And soon, Liona, you will have a friend to help you guard."

"Just a few more weeks, Marie. Then you'll have your new pup." Ezra scratches the shepherd between her ears. "I should take her now. She could use a good run after riding in the van."

"Yes, yes, you go, Ezra. Thank you so much."

He walks off with Liona, who trots with her tail curved like a fluffy crescent moon over her brawny hindquarters.

Nonna watches until they're out of sight, still grinning like a little girl. "Very strong. She will do a good job."

"Of what? Eating the nuns?"

Nonna laughs. "No, no. Protecting girls." She points to the meadow house. "There."

The mystery intensifies. Now my curiosity fixates more on their need for a guard monster than who they are. "Protection from?"

"Very bad men. How you say in English? Ah, pimps. Sounds funny, like a cookie, but not funny at all."

Since arriving at this convent, there are times I've felt like I've been thrust into the middle of a made-for-TV movie; the kind with plots so crazy, they aren't even remotely believable. This is one of them.

"They're prostitutes?!"

Nonna nods.

"You're telling me that the peace-loving, pastry-baking Sisters of St. Teresa own a house of prostitution?"

She sighs, shaking her head. "Of course no, Shilo Marie."

I release a breath, glad to know something got seriously lost in translation.

"The *church* owns the house," she continues. "We just run it. Take care of girls."

"The prostitutes?"

"They are no more prostitutes. Now they can be young women. Now they can live. You see, Shilo Marie, the evil men, they capture the young girls, force them to sell their bodies. The girls are locked up. Beaten. Starved. They have no choice. No life."

Human trafficking. Modern day slavery. I remember being horrified when I first learned of it a couple of years ago. How could such a thing exist in this day and age? And now the victims have become more than statistics. They have names and faces, and experiences too horrible to fathom. I picture Myriam, Cyrine, Emily and little Farah, so young, so sweet, ripped from their families, forced to…no, I can't go there. Bile churns in my stomach. A blast of fiery anger rages through me. What kind of messed-up excuse for a human does this to other humans?

"How did they escape?"

"Ah, that is the good part. We rescue."

"We? You and the sisters?"

She nods, beaming. "Oh, yes! We plan it very good. We have help from two men. Strong, with big muscles. Perhaps they have guns, too," she whispers, "but we do not ask this, and they do not tell." She hooks her arm into mine and we start walking toward the convent door. "We pay them with the pastry monies."

I force my mind to move past the image of nuns selling pastries to hire thugs, so I can hear the rest of the story. "What about Ezra? Was he there?"

"Oh, no. He has wife and children. They have been through so much, Shilo Marie. They flee from Tunisia ten years ago with two sons. Then, they have baby girl with bad heart. She die two years ago, poor child. So, you see, this is why we no tell him. Too dangerous."

Too dangerous for a middle-aged man, but not a little flock of sisters.

"And the police? You called them, right?"

"Well, you see, it is like this. We no call *polizia* until we leave."

There was a time when I would have been appalled at this statement. I have moved beyond that time.

"But listen, this is good part. The two men, they spy for us. They tell us of hidden place outside Palermo where girls are kept. We drive two hours on Sunday, when brothel is closed. One spy, he dress as priest. Other spy, he hides van behind hill."

I wait for her to start laughing, to admit this part of the story is just a really inappropriate joke, but she just goes on like she's giving a book report.

"We come to door, ask if we can pray for girls. The pimps, they do not like this idea, but we convince. The girls come out. So young, Shilo Marie, it break my heart, but I must stay strong."

We reach the convent's stone door, intricately carved with flowers, leaves, and cherubs, and retreat to the coolness of the vestibule.

"We soon find out some are from Italy, some are refugees from Tunisia. The little one, she is one of the Tunisians." Nonna shakes her head. "I worry most for her."

Lambie's birth and the walk back to the convent have taken a toll on my great-grandmother. Weariness graces her face, even as the nuns vs. pimps story unfolds. I guide her toward a worn, but well padded bench beneath a painting of three crosses on a hill. The gifted artist captured the anguish of Good Friday with incredible realism, infusing it with the bittersweet beauty and sadness of the crucifixion.

"We meet with each one, pretend to pray, and whisper the plan. Is good Mary speak little Tunisian. This help."

I mentally record every word, imagining the expressions when I relay this to Kenji and my family, wondering if anyone will even believe it.

Nonna Marie smiles, and I know the crazy story is about to take another leap. "Meanwhile, Sisters Francesca and Celeste go behind brothel with firecrackers. Then boom, boom, boom! Firecrackers, they explode, and bad men grab guns and run behind house. You see? They think someone is shooting guns. Our man drives van to us very fast, girls get in, and off we go like wind."

"Didn't they chase after you?"

"Oh, I forget. The man dressed like priest, maybe he do something to bad men's tires. I do not know. We pray for this to be forgiven, just in case."

"Nonna, for goodness sake, you're eighty-six years old!"

"Yes. That is what make it work. The bad men think old women like me and Sister Angelina cannot cause problem for them."

Emotions ricochet inside my head. That was stupid, dangerous, and undeniably the bravest, most selfless act I've ever heard of in my life. Nothing I've done comes close to what Nonna and the sisters pulled off. But I could have lost her before I even got to know her. "You guys could have gotten shot, or killed, or who knows what. I can't believe you got away with it. That was amazing…and flat-out crazy."

She puts a hand to my cheek and smiles, her eyes glistening. "That, Shilo Marie, is God at work."

Chapter 9

Shilo

Morning dawns with sunlight streaming through the arched stone windows, illuminating my room with a dreamy glow. As sleep fades from my brain, I remember today is my outing with Domenico, and my heart simultaneously leaps with excitement and twinges with guilt. But, really, it's just a day out with a friend, no different than what Kenji's doing in Indiana.

Nonna and the sisters are done with breakfast and cleaning up by the time I get to the kitchen, but, as always, there's a plate of pastries and blood orange segments waiting for me. And as always, it's enough for three people. As I reach for a piece of orange, another piece topples off the plate and onto my white shorts. With a normal orange, this would not have been a disaster, but—

"Ugh. This will never come out." I dab at the small red blotch on the hem of my shorts.

"You no worry, Shilo Marie. We have something. Go down hall, look in the closet near your room. You will find blue bottle. This is very, very good for take away stain."

I head down the hall toward Riccardo's room, where I remembered seeing a utility closet. The blue bottle is there, just as she described, but the skull and crossbones logo on the bottle next to it surprises me. I see Francesca coming around the corner and figure she'll have an explanation.

"Good morning, sister." I speak loud enough for her to hear me from the other end of the hall.

"Good morning! Can I help you find something?"

"No thanks, I found what I need. But why is there a bottle of poison in here?"

She walks toward me with finger to lips.

"We should be quiet so we don't wake Riccardo. We had a rat problem a while back. Just a few in the basement. We hated to use poison, but it was necessary."

Must have been a difficult choice, given the way they love animals, but I can see why they did it. A few rats could destroy their pastry business.

The homemade stain remover worked miracles on the red blotch. With my shorts back to being white, Nonna and the kitchen crew send me off with a picnic lunch to share with Domenico, who shows up right on time. In a car. I try to mask my disappointment, but oh, how I'd been looking forward to another motorcycle ride. He gets out and hugs me a little longer…and tighter…than expected. Solid abs press against me through a navy blue T-shirt that suddenly feels ridiculously sexy. I should pull away, but he said we're just friends, and Italians are affectionate by nature, so I'm just reading too much into it. Probably.

"Today we drive so we can talk, yes?"

Since there's really no choice, I assure him that's a great idea and get in, mentally pushing Kenji out of my head. There's nothing wrong with this. He's doing things that obviously involve female company, so why should I think twice? Anyway, I'm just sightseeing, that's all.

"Ah, beautiful Shilo. The sun, she shines for us. We have a perfect day, yes?"

I nod and open the basket. "Nonna Marie packed some food for us."

"Very kind. And you have your swimming suit?"

I partially lift my shirt to reveal a black and aqua patterned suit. He nods, but his smile disappears. "You do not have bikini?"

I laugh. "No, I left it at home."

"Maybe I buy you bikini."

Maybe you no buy me bikini. "This is fine. Really."

"Hmm. I do not agree, but is your choice."

Once we get off the topic of my swimsuit, the conversation flows surprisingly well. Domenico thrives on playing tour guide, describing sights along the way and even throwing in some interesting stuff about temple ruins we see here and there. When we stop to let a shepherd and his flock cross the road, I jump out and take pictures like crazy, with a fast shutter speed to freeze the motion. I remember Celeste's instructions and vary the aperture to get some completely in focus, and others with the sheep contrasted against a blurry background. Next, I zoom in on the shepherd, who scoots down to push a large rock out of the path of his wooly troop. My closeup shows the shepherd's face, his hand clutched around his staff, and the velvet faces of his curious flock as they investigate his action. Can't wait to show Celeste.

"May I see?" Domenico points to the camera, and I show off my work. "Very nice. You will have much opportunity to take beautiful photos at Gole dell'Alcantara. In English, *gole* means throat." He wraps his fingers around his own throat to illustrate. "We go to Messina, to the Alcantara River. Mt. Etna, she formed the land by the river with lava. She is very active volcano for millions of years. Still erupts, you know?" Domenico takes both hands off the wheel, gesturing wildly while making sound effects.

The car veers toward a grassy bank and I grab the wheel. "Watch out!"

But Domenico laughs, placing one hand on the wheel and patting my leg with the other. "You are so funny, Shilo.

American girls are no different than Italian girls."

I'm about to remove his hand, which still rests firmly on my leg, when he begins gesturing again, this time leaving his left hand on the wheel.

"So, the lava, it forms the ground. Then the river cuts through for many years to make a path, you know? But some of the water goes around the lava to make islands." His passion for geography shines through his words as he talks passionately about the place we're about to visit. It will make him a great teacher someday."Also, there are waterfalls and high rocks in some places. Very high, like walls. You will like it, this I promise. Many boys take girls there. It is a nice place to be with a girl."

Warning bells gong inside my head, but they don't drown out his words, or the way he said them. I start to say, "Remember, I have a boyfriend," but he laughs like he knows it's coming, and I give him an eye roll instead. He pats my leg again, and I want to hate it. Really, I do. But his tank flaunts arms chiseled from marble, and he's fun and interesting, and we're flying down a dirt road surrounded by nothing but vineyards and valleys. And he smells so good.

Kenji. I force the name into my head. Close my eyes and picture his face smiling at me, his lips on mine. Walking hand in hand at the carnival where he won that goofy stuffed rhino. He'd held it up to my face and made smoochy sounds as if the rhino were kissing me, but when we stopped laughing, the carnival lights and sounds disappeared as we kissed for the first time. The sweet memory strengthens my resolve. I open my eyes to the sunlight reflecting off the blue topaz ring Kenji gave me the night before I left.

With each passing mile, the landscape becomes more amazing. Domenico's descriptions didn't begin to portray the otherworldly beauty of the geometric shapes, some rising up like mammoth pipe organs, others grouped at angles as though a celestial hand tossed them down to build a campfire. Mount Etna's convulsions had lifted and twisted them, while Alcantara's rushing waters polished them to a smooth pewter gray as it swept through the land to expose two sheer cliffs of basalt. It reminds me of the Devil's Tower in Wyoming, where we went on vacation a few years ago.

As we continue driving, Alcantara's "throat" opens to a wide valley floor, where small pebbly islands beckon, and children laugh and splash in the surrounding waters. Domenico parks, and I grab the basket.

"You see? Beautiful, yes?"

"Amazing."

He grabs my hand, like it's no big deal, and heads toward the last deserted mini island. His hand feels warm and strong, and stirs something inside me that was better left unstirred. I'm about to let go when we hit the cold water and I instantly slip on a flat rock. He laughs and holds me up. Maybe holding his hand is a good idea, purely for practical reasons. The water deepens and he grabs the basket, holding it over his head as we frog-kick over to our little piece of earth, perfectly situated right near the gorge's entrance.

Domenico takes the towel covering the basket and lays it on the ground. "Your nonna was very kind to provide this food. Good time to eat, yes?"

He doesn't have to ask twice. I'm ready for whatever culinary treasures the basket holds. The aroma of fresh baked bread rises from the basket as he unwraps two sandwiches, nestled next to plump purple grapes. At the bottom of the basket lies something wrapped in white paper and tied with string.

"Perhaps it is amaretti. Your great-grandmother, she makes the best."

I reach in for the package, hoping he's right. Those chewy almond cookies rank side-by-side with gelato for best eats in Sicily. Or the world. Pulling open the paper reveals a stack of amarettis. We each go for the cookies before the sandwiches.

"Now, we go into El Gole." But instead of moving

toward the water, Domenico takes both my hands and gazes into my eyes. "I like you very much, Shilo Giannelli. You are a fun girl. Smart. Very pretty. I want this to be a good day for us. Are you enjoying?"

"Yes." I search for something more to say. Something about Kenji—a reminder that I'm off limits, but each thought feels too awkward to verbalize.

He brushes my windblown hair from my face, cupping his hand under my chin. "I like you very much," he repeats, but this time the words are a whisper as his face nears mine. I pull back, catching movement from the corner of my eye.

"Ciao, Ciao!" A soggy little boy appears from nowhere, as though the river just spit him up onto our island. Bright orange swim trunks sag around his skinny little waist. He pushes the dripping hair from his face to reveal pink cheeks and sweet chocolate eyes.

"My name is Stefano," he rattles in Italian. "Do you want to see my guy?" He holds up a small plastic action figure with a dark green cape. "He has special powers. He has laser eyes and he can fly! Were you going to kiss?"

"Umm." It's the only response I can muster on such short notice.

"My mamma and daddy used to kiss. But then my daddy died. A bad thing happened to his heart. It broked and the doctors couldn't fix it. Me and Mamma came here today cuz we need a happy day. That's what mamma said."

Tears glaze my eyes, and it only took half a heartbeat.

"Stefano!" The firm but gentle voice comes from an adjacent island. "What are you doing bothering people? Come back here. They want to be alone. Come on now." She turns to face us with an eye roll and a laugh. "Please accept my apology. I just looked away to get a towel, and he disappeared. That boy doesn't stay still for a moment."

"No problema, *signora*," Domenico answers. "He's a good boy, and he's welcome to visit us for a few moments before we go swimming in El Gole."

"Can I go with you?" His hope-filled eyes stare as though a blink might ruin the possibility of a "yes."

"No." Domenico smiles, letting him know it's a friendly rejection. "First you have to grow a bit more. El Gole is very deep in some places, and you are still a little one."

"But I'm a great swimmer! *Really* great."

I stifle a laugh at his conviction.

Stefano faces his mother. "Aren't I a great swimmer, Mamma?" He megaphones his hands as he shouts across the water. "Can't I swim in the deep part with my new friends?"

"No, no, no, Stefano. You just visit for a minute, then you come right back here."

"Yes, Mamma." Domenico and I glance at each other and smile, as Stefano lets loose a long, dramatic sigh. "My mamma worries too much."

"Your mamma loves you." I answer in Italian, glad to be nearly fluent. "She just wants to keep you safe."

"My daddy loves me, too. Mamma said he even loves me from Heaven."

"Absolutely." I swallow hard, not wanting him to see that his innocent words are tearing me up inside. "He will keep loving you forever, and he'll wait for you there in Heaven."

"You talk funny," Stefano says.

"She is from America," Domenico says. "You know, the United States of America?"

"Oh, I know about it. People must all talk funny there. I'm going to school this year. I'm a big boy now. Mamma got me a backpack and crayons and everything." He provides a detailed description of his school, teacher and friends.

"Stefano, time to come back now." The now familiar voice interrupts from our neighboring island. "Come, I will watch." He says goodbye and jumps off the island, hands held high and dark hair flying straight up as he hits the water. Three sets of eyes watch as he half walks, half swims to his mother, his bright orange swimsuit practically glowing beneath the water.

"Thank you for letting him visit," she calls to us.

"Our pleasure," I reply.

Domenico shakes his head. "Poor child." He switches back to English. "It is very sad his father died."

"No kidding. Tough for his mom, too."

We sit in silence until he asks if I'm ready to go in, then removes his T-shirt and shorts to reveal a form of swimsuit I've only seen in photos from the 1970s. I've heard they were commonly worn in Europe, but didn't think about it. Until now. At this point, about ninety percent of Domenico's gorgeously sculpted body is naked, with the rest packed into a very small, very tight, Speedo. Guilt envelopes me again at the thought of Kenji witnessing this scenario. But it's not my fault. Domenico's choice of swimsuit cannot be blamed on me, and there's nothing I can do about it.

We wade toward the gorge's entrance, then swim as the chilly water deepens. Black geometric forms stretch toward the sun, simultaneously graceful and monstrous. I look around in disbelief at the eerily beautiful surroundings. Further up the gorge, our world becomes little more than rock, water and sky. Miniscule water droplets on the sheer rock face refract the light into a thousand tiny mirrors.

Domenico reaches a rock and holds on, gesturing for me to do the same. "Are you a good swimmer? Strong?"

I nod. "Why?"

"In some places, the water reaches over twenty-one meters deep."

I do the math and come up with seventy feet, more or less. Not a problem, but he might have asked a little sooner. We travel about a quarter of a mile as the light and darkness dance together through narrow passages and twisted, gleaming prisms of rock. Julia would adore this place. She just has to see it someday. It would be a geology dream come true.

Few others share the gorge on this remarkable journey. We reach a shadowy area that, in any sci-fi movie, would clearly serve as a portal to another realm. Domenico's hand on my arm interrupts my thoughts. He points ahead, where a series of waterfall rapids warn us to turn back. I nod, having already experienced the deadly dangers of rapids, and swim in the opposite direction toward the shallows for a much-needed rest before heading back. Domenico does the same. The handful of other swimmers must have retreated earlier, because only the towering rocks witness his face coming closer to mine as he slips his hand around my waist.

"Shilo."

He whispers my name in a way that makes me feel naked, then adds "*mi cara*" and I turn to butter. Warm lips touch mine, gently at first, then more passionate. I place my hand on his arm to push it away, and feel the solid bulge of his muscles. Everything about this moment feels delicious and irresistible and electrifying. He's the devil in a Speedo, and I've failed in resisting temptation.

Completely. Totally. Failed.

If Kenji knew, he'd be crushed. And leave me forever. Trust has never been an issue for us. His face fills my mind – those dark eyes, that shaggy black hair and adorable grin. Those lips, soft and firm and wonderful. And his incredible heart, that entwines with mine in ways I can't describe. He is one of the few who shares my secret, and has witnessed the miracle first hand. The thought of him finding out I kissed another guy slaps me back to reality. My hand flies to Domenico's chest and pushes.

"I have a boyfriend."

He smiles, gazing into my eyes from an inch away. "But you are not married, Shilo. You are only seventeen, yes? Perhaps it is time for a new boyfriend, at least while you're in Sicily."

He doesn't get it. It doesn't work that way. Not with me and Kenji. "No, I'm sorry. He's got my heart. My whole heart."

"I understand." I feel his warm breath on my face. "Just

one more kiss. That is all. Just one."

I push again, this time scooting backward to increase the distance. "No. No more kissing. Let's go back. I'm freezing."

I turn and kick without waiting for his response. We swim back in silence, an awkward tension hovering over us. But it's not the tension that weights me down. It's the shame. This never should have happened. I could have stopped it, but didn't. Guilt continues to admonish me. I try to drown it with thoughts of Kenji and my renewed, impenetrable commitment to him, but guilt is not easily muffled. The late afternoon sun nearly blinds me as we approach the opening and our little island beyond. I catch a glimpse of something orange bobbing next to the rocks. My pet peeve: people marring nature with plastic bags. I head over to grab it, with Domenico following, but as we go behind the rocks, I realize the orange thing is swim trunks.

And they are attached to Stefano's limp body.

Chapter 10

Melody

I'm as fragile as a newborn lamb, and I hate it. Asking people to hand me my iPad, refill my water pitcher, walk me to the bathroom. I just want to go home and never see anyone from this hospital again. Except for Adanna. She's pretty cool, but she'll be out of my life soon, so really, what's the point in even talking to her? Everyone else here just makes me crazy. Each one telling me I'm so "fortunate it wasn't worse," as if the complete annihilation of my ballet career was just a blip on the radar. I don't even know who I am anymore.

"Good morning, Miss Melody!" Ginessa, my physical therapist, is way too perky for nine a.m. "Ready to start building up your muscles? Get back some flexibility and strength?"

"Nope."

The smile takes a little dip, but she recovers. "I know this is hard. Really, I do. But once you start getting some movement back, you'll feel better. Promise."

Promise. She has no clue how one fall, one moment, destroyed all my hard work. My hopes and dreams. My future. Physical therapy isn't going to bring back any of that. *Don't*

*tell me you can promise me anything worth promising, you bouncy PT
with your perfectly healthy limbs.*

"Not today. I don't feel good."

This time her smile fades and doesn't return. "Just try a
few stretches. You'll see, it will help you feel…"

"I. Don't. Feel. Good. Just leave. Please."

"You know you can't be discharged until we see some
progress. And you don't feel good because you are in pain
because you're not stretching."

Ginessa has a point, but I can't deal with her today. Or
anything. I close my eyes, hoping when they open, she'll be
gone.

"How about this: we'll do a short session today. If you
want to be done after twenty minutes, we'll be done. Sound
good?"

My eyes remain closed. I refuse to acknowledge her perky
existence.

She sighs her defeat. "I'll have a nurse come check on
you." Footsteps head out the door. Finally.

I have ten minutes of peace before Mom calls to ask how
I am and whether I've talked to Blake today, which I haven't…and don't intend to.

"He called here, you know. Asked if he could visit today.
He said he tried to call your cell and the hospital room, but
you didn't answer. Your relationship is your business, Mellie,
but please don't leave that boy hangin' if you don't want him
in your life. That's not fair."

A lot of things aren't fair. And she knows I didn't answer
on purpose. There's no room for romance in my life right
now, or trying to have conversations like the old me, or kissing, or anything to do with Blake. When he sees what a disaster I am…it's just not going to work, that's all. Might as
well cut ties now, instead of dragging this out.

"Yeah, okay, I'll talk to him."

"Good. We're leaving in a few minutes. See you soon."

"You don't need to come. I'm tired."

"From the physical therapy?"

"Yeah." It just slips out, followed by a tinge of guilt. But I'm in no mood for justifying why I don't feel like dealing with the PT today.

"Don't lie to me, Melody Yasmeen O'Hara. Ginessa just called." She continues with all the reasons therapy is important, regurgitating words like muscle atrophy, mobility, and agility. It is the first time since the crash that her words are anything less than sympathetic. "Don't you want to leave the hospital? Don't you want your independence back?"

"Yes." I speak truth, but wanting and believing are two very different things. Right now I can't even see that light at the end of the tunnel. The combination of pain, weakness, and casts has blinded my vision of the day when independence is a reality.

"Therapy is your pathway out. You know that. You *can't* let this beat you, Mellie Bear. Where's that fiery spirit I love so much?" She chokes on the last words. It must be painful on her end, too, but nothing compared to what I'm going through. Still, her pain surprisingly takes the edge off my anger. I didn't think there was room left in my heart to feel sympathy for anyone but me.

"I'm sorry, Mom. I'll try next time. Just not today. I can't." Unexpected tears stream down my cheeks. "I just can't." I turn toward the door at the sound of footsteps and see Adanna waiting for me to end the call. "I have to go now. Nurse is here. I'll see you and Dad later, okay?"

And now I face yet another conversation, when all I want to do is crawl under a rock and die. What I'd give to just lie here for the rest of today, with no one talking to me or checking my blood pressure. No one looking at me with their sympathetic eyes or telling me I have to take a pill or stretch my muscles.

Dear World, go away.

I hang up and Adanna immediately launches in with, "What is this I hear about your therapy?" Her firm tone and knit brow punctuate her words.

"I know, I know."

She hands me a tissue and I swipe the tears from my cheeks. "Can we just talk about something else? Please?"

"No." The faint scent of vanilla and coconut drifts my way, just like every time she enters the room. I breathe in, hoping she doesn't know why, and let it seep into my senses, tranquilizing the horned monster inside me.

"Melody." Her lovely accent makes my name sound like the first note of a song. She places her hand under my chin. "Look at me."

Adanna's box braids are neatly wrapped together at the base of her neck, accentuating her high cheekbones. Fatigue dulls her mocha eyes today, but there's something else. A familiarity I can't explain, yet I'm sure I've gazed into those eyes before.

But that's impossible.

"You look tired."

A soft smile graces her face. "I am a working mama of two, so being tired is normal for me. But that is not what I want to talk about. *You* need therapy, young lady. Every hour you lie here without moving, your muscles atrophy and lose flexibility. Your back becomes stiffer, more painful. You prevent healing. Maybe you will never be the ballerina you wanted to be, but do you want to be stuck in a wheelchair?"

"No."

"So you need to…"

Why can't I shut her out like the therapist? "Do my physical therapy."

"Ginessa will be back after lunch, and you will be nice and cooperative. Not for me, not for your parents. For *you*."

"Yes, ma'am."

She grabs the folding chair by the wall and drags it to my bedside, checks her watch, and sits down. "You are having a rough day?"

My vision blurs. *Rough day.* Is that what you call the end

of the world?

"I have a few minutes. Are you up for a story?"

Her 'dark place' has haunted me since she visited yesterday. Imagining the possibilities has been my only respite from wallowing in self pity. I nod.

"It is not a story I often share. Can I trust you to keep it to yourself?"

I place my hand on my heart. "You have my word."

"Well, then." She nods, as if encouraging herself to begin. "Here we go. When I was fourteen, a white couple came to my village in northern Nigeria, just outside Sokoto."

My ears perk. "Nigeria? I'm half Nigerian."

"I suspected as much, but we are discouraged from asking a person's nationality. So these people, they did not have American accents like the missionaries that sometimes brought food and medicine. We did not know from where they come. With friendly smiles and sweet tones, they introduced themselves as Vera and Peter."

"They spoke your language?"

"English is the national language in Nigeria. Most people speak Hausa and English. So these people, Vera and Peter, told the mothers there were good jobs in America for girls my age."

She's got every fragment of my attention. I heard about this in World Cultures class. Something about people going to really poor villages, where the locals are barely surviving, and offering jobs to young girls. But it's all a horrific scam, and the girls are usually never seen again.

"You have to understand, Melody, that we lived outside Sokoto, which is very poor. My parents struggled to feed me and my sister and brothers. When they said American parents will hire us to take care of their children, our mothers got very excited."

I reach for the pitcher and squeeze my eyes as pain radiates through my back. She jumps up to pour me a cup, then sits back down.

"They showed us photos of beautiful houses and said we can live in such houses and get paid. We could even send money back to our families. I cried because I did not want to leave my family. My mother cried too, but wanted me to go. Our family was desperate. It would only be for two years, the couple said. Then we would come back to Nigeria with lots of money for food and school. The next day, I left with Vera and Peter and six other girls from my village."

"It must have been hard to leave your home."

"My family." Her voice cracks, and she pauses. "We were very close. We all hugged each other so tightly that last day." She turns toward the window and blinks those deep brown eyes. Even the sadness in them feels hauntingly familiar. She glances at her lap, then back toward me. "I never saw them again."

"What happened?"

"Too much to tell it all. After many days of travel, first in a small plane, then in the belly of a boat, then the back of a truck, we arrived in Chicago. We were exhausted, dirty, hungry, and frightened of being in a foreign place. We arrived late at night, but not at a house; at a massage parlor, though I didn't know it back then. Two scowling men inside unlocked the door and gave money to Vera and Peter, who left without goodbye. We did not understand what was happening. The scowling men glared at us and hurried us down a long staircase into a dim basement. One had cold gray eyes and a small scar on his cheek. 'We own you now,' he said. It was our first night as slaves. In less than twenty-four hours, my friends, all virgins like me, would become prostitutes."

"Not you?"

She shakes her head. "The man with the scar, Vlad, said he wanted 'a piece of chocolate' for himself. When he grabbed me and dragged me upstairs, away from my friends, I was terrified beyond words. He brought me to his apartment above the massage parlor. My time as his slave was horrible, but my friends…"

Again, her voice cracks. She takes a breath. My heart is torn between wanting her to stop reliving the pain, and craving the rest of the story. "You don't have to finish. It's fine. I understand."

She nods, and gives my hand a squeeze. "The men came every day but Monday. Those poor girls. My job was to cook, clean and do laundry when Vlad was not using me. He was an angry man. A rough man. I never stopped shaking, even when he was not around. Four months later, I knew I was pregnant. When he figured it out, he beat me, but my baby was strong. She did not leave me."

She has closed the door on the room where my self-pity has been thriving. In this moment, my heart bleeds only for her, and those unfortunate girls whose lives became a living nightmare.

"When the time came for delivery, he brought a couple of the girls up from the basement. They did not know what to do. While I was in labor, he showed us a birthing video online, then gave them water and towels. 'Clean up the mess when it's done,' he said, and left the room. So there we were, three terrified kids, trying to deliver a baby. You can only imagine."

No. I can imagine a lot of things, but not any of what she just described. It is lightyears from my life with my mom and dad. I've had my challenges being half black with snow-white parents, like hearing people's rude comments and feeling the assault of their blatant stares. Growing up in mostly white suburbia, I've had strangers touch my hair, as if that were perfectly okay, and store clerks follow me around to make sure I wasn't stealing. And there was that obnoxious, disgusting man who came up to me after one of my best performances last year and said he "always wanted to do it with a black girl." Yeah, I've had my challenges. But this...

I take a breath after forgetting to for the last few seconds. "Was the baby okay?"

Adanna smiles. Not the sunburst grin that often graces

her face, but the smile that emerges when you're graced with a bittersweet memory.

"My little girl, she was beautiful. So beautiful. And healthy, despite everything. Vlad said we would take her somewhere the next day. I begged him to let me keep her. I said I'd do anything. I begged God all night to protect her. And then, a miracle. Vlad was stomach sick, probably from something he ate. God gave me two extra days with my sweet daughter. I nursed her and hugged her and kissed her nonstop. I did not even want to sleep. Did not want to miss one second with her."

"What happened to her?"

"We brought her to a big house across from a church. I think it may have been a convent. It was late at night. Very dark. Someplace in the country, I believe, because we were away from the city lights. He took her from my arms, and in that moment, my heart ripped apart. Those scars have never healed. But at least I knew she would be away from Vlad."

My whole heart aches for that young Nigerian girl who experienced a lifetime of trauma by the time she was sixteen. Anxious to hear the rest, I keep silent, hoping she'll continue. But Adanna checks her watch and stands.

"Now I must—"

"No!" It comes out a little louder than I'd intended. "I mean, please, don't leave without finishing the story."

"I must. There is still much of the story to go, and the hospital is not paying me to be a storyteller. If there is time after I tend to my other patients, I will tell you the rest."

"Okay." I nod. There's no way to justify her staying here instead of doing her job. "And Adanna? I'm sorry that happened to you. When you said you went through a dark time, you weren't kidding."

"Oh, Melody." She shakes her head and I catch the glint of a tear. "That was not the dark time. That was only the beginning."

Chapter 11

Shilo

Oh, God, please. Not this.

We simultaneously grab Stefano and flip him over. Domenico starts mouth-to-mouth resuscitation.

"Stefano!" The boy's mother calls from a few feet away, blocked from us by the rocks. "Where are you?"

"He's here!" I wave her over. She heads toward us, unaware of our horrific discovery. But as she nears, her eyes widen. Her mouth opens in a silent scream, contorting her face with a terror I never want to witness again. She grabs my hand, stares at Domenico trying in vain to clear Stefano's lungs.

"Stefano," she whispers. "My baby. My baby. No, no, no." Never have I heard so much pain in a person's voice.

Domenico shows no intention of giving up, even as little Stefano turns a pale shade of blue. Despite the witnesses, there is only one thing left to do. Nonna said if God leads me to someone, He'll provide a way for me to do it. I step out in faith.

Please, God, make this happen.

I place my free hand on the boy's arm, fearing I'll feel nothing. Fearing that, for reasons unknown to me, God will choose to let this child die. But the moment I touch his chest, The Gift envelopes my heart.

Thank You.

"Stop." My command surprises Domenico, who takes his eyes off the boy for the first time since pulling him out of the water.

"No, I must keep going. I will not let him die."

"Listen to me." It's not a request. Every second counts, and there's no time for explaining everything to him or risking it being overheard by anyone else. "You know about Nonna Marie. I'm like her. Understand?"

"I cannot trust in a legend right now. There is no time to lose, Shilo. This boy is dy…" He stops himself as he looks at Stefano's frantic mother. "We cannot take the chance."

"There's no time to argue. I can't do anything once it's over. This will work. He's given me the sign. Now move. I'm not asking."

"You better be right." Domenico's face softens from defiance to compliance. There is no time to contemplate the reason. I jump in.

"What?" his mother shrieks. "What is happening?"

I take her hands, gaze into her eyes. "I can help him, I promise. But I need a towel. Go quickly."

She splashes through the water, urgency driving her legs like an Olympian. I turn to Domenico. "I had to get her out. Just stay here. Don't say a word."

I place my hands on the boy's chest, knowing just below the surface his small lungs are filled with the water he happily played in just a short while ago. Water that blocks his life-giving oxygen. I close my eyes.

Heavenly Father, you are the only one who can save Stefano. Please heal him. Remove the water from his lungs and let him live to touch other lives and renew his mother's crushed spirit. Breathe your life into him.

Warmth. Wonderous, mystical, lifegiving warmth. It permeates my heart, gently spreading through my chest as it fills me with peace beyond understanding. Waves of tranquility wash over me, lifting me to the place where the colors of love swirl around me in a sky-blue haze. I submit mind, body and soul to the Creator's power – power that flows into my shoulders and down my arms as I continue to pray. Silence replaces the lapping of water against rock, the distant voices of swimmers and the gulls calling to each other overhead. Soft, sweet silence. I am one with the Spirit.

Like soft beams of sunlight, the warmth glides past my wrists and into my palms. Swirling colors become more vibrant as the power intensifies in my fingers. And then…the miracle. The healing power radiates from my fingertips, draining my energy as it infuses Stefano's limp body. His chest heaves, pressing against my hands as a dribble of water spills from his mouth onto the rocky ground. I open my eyes to see Domenico turning Stefano's head so the water flows out. Stefano sucks in the lifegiving air with ragged gasps.

His mama returns, drops the towel, and covers his face in kisses. She scoops him up with both arms, holding him to her chest as she rocks back and forth, crying, kissing, thanking God. Thanking me.

Domenico stares as if I were an apparition. Somewhere in my foggy mind, I find the same words I said to Kenji just a month ago on that bloody Kentucky riverbank, where he and little Rebecca nearly lost their lives.

"Please don't tell." My words are weak now, so different than a few moments ago when I found Stefano floating in the water, but it's the best I can do. "Get me back to the convent. I'm tired. So tired." The words steal my last bit of energy. I want to get to the car before I collapse, but there's nothing left. As Domenico stares, still speechless, I lay down on the smooth gray rock and fall asleep.

Thin wrinkled fingers envelop my hand as I open my eyes

to see Nonna Marie sitting at my side. Her mouth turns up slightly at the corners, eyes glistening.

"Ah, Shilo Marie, you finally wake. You did good. Domenico, he did good, too. He carry you from car to your room and tell me everything."

I blow past the image of Domenico carrying me—an event that would normally drag me down to new levels of humiliation—and search my mind for the 'everything' she's talking about. Images flicker in the haze. Wind in my hair. Towering prisms of rock. Cold water. Sunlight and shadows and a stolen kiss. But there was something worse, just out of reach, and finally my mind catches the painful memory.

"Stefano! Is he okay? Tell me he's okay."

"Si, *mi cara.*" She brushes the hair from my forehead. "The little one, he is fine."

I can still hear his mother's sobs, feel her terror and the relief that followed. If God allowed me to heal Stefano, maybe he will act on my prayer to carry the widowed mom through her grief. Thoughts of her spawn a new concern.

"Does she know? Did she see?"

"Do not worry, Shilo." Domenico's voice startles me. I turn my head to see him standing by the window. "The boy, he left with his mother as if nothing happened. She did not see the miracle." He walks over and sits next to me on the bed. "She believes we helped him. Breathed into him. I do not know the word in English."

"Resuscitation."

"*Si.* That is all she saw. You were smart to send her for the towel."

As comforting as that is, it doesn't change the fact that Domenico witnessed the whole thing and now another person knows. This secret is spreading like an oil slick. It won't be long before someone lets it slip, or sees it as an opportunity to grab a chunk of fame. Or money. And all it will take is one.

"Domenico, you can't tell. Not a soul. One word to

anyone could ruin my life."

He takes my hand. Not in a flirty way, like in the car, but with a steady gaze that ensures his confidentiality. "I understand. I will not betray you. On my life, I swear it." His intensity is both comforting and humorous.

"So what do you think of the legend now?"

Domenico's brow knits into a "V" as he collects his thoughts. "I am not the same person I was this morning. That is the only way I can say it. To see a miracle of God, it changes a person. Please forgive me for not believing. It is one thing to read or to hear. But to see…" He shakes his head. "There are no words."

"Ah, Domenico, you see miracles every day." Nonna Marie reaches across me and pats his hand. "The sun, she rises. The stars, they know when to shine. Prayers are answered; hearts, they mend. Babies come. People give their time and money to help strangers in need. Our God's miracles…they are all around."

Domenico nods, but says nothing. Poor guy. This must be overwhelming, even from a bystander's perspective. I've had some time to wrap my brain around it, and it's still too huge to comprehend. To be consumed by the Spirit is indescribable. But to watch it, well, that's got to be mind-blowing as well. At a lesser level maybe, but still mind-blowing.

"How long did I sleep?"

"Three hours. You slept in the car. Then I carry…"

"Yes, I got that. Thanks."

A gentle rap on the door prompts Domenico to rise and open it. Sister Celeste peers sheepishly past him, holding a blue envelope.

"You have received a letter, Shilo."

"Thank you."

"I am happy to see you feeling better. We were worried when we saw the young man carrying you from the car. We have all been praying."

Seriously, this needs to stop. I'm momentarily grateful for

the lack of cell phones and access to social media. "I'm fine. Thanks, Sister."

"I am sorry to say your gentleman must leave now." Her face pinks beneath her winged hood. "Mother Superior's orders." She turns to Domenico. "I'm sorry, sir. There are rules. Please do not think me rude."

"No, no, Sister. It is fine. I am grateful to have stayed this long. *Grazie.*" He holds out his hand for the envelope. "I will take it for Shilo."

Sister Celeste leaves and Domenico hands me the envelope I'm sure is from Melody. She probably just forgot to mail it on time for my birthday, or didn't realize how long it takes to reach Sicily. Especially up here on Mt. Etna. Pretty sure it came by donkey express. Domenico holds it out to me, but as I reach out, he snaps it back.

"Let me see." He grins and stares at the return address. "Who wrote a letter to our Miss America?"

"Give it to me. It's from my friend."

"Boyfriend?"

"No. Now let me see it."

He laughs and doesn't notice Nonna's hand reaching for the envelope. In a blink, it's out of his hand and safely in mine. Nonna winks at me.

"We girls join together, yes?"

Close enough. "Absolutely."

"Come." She hooks her arm through Domenico's. "Shilo Marie will be fine now. We will let her rest." Nonna kisses the top of my head, and they leave me alone with my card from Melody.

Only it's not. The return address is from Tarboro, North Carolina. It's great to get a card from Misty, and I can't wait to hear all about her new life with the Howells, but...why isn't Melody writing to me? I don't have to ponder the reason for long. The answer is short, simple, and obvious. Ballet. Always ballet. It will forevermore take priority over our friendship. And I get it. Really. But can't she take five minutes to send me a letter?

I open the card and out falls a photo of Misty and Tyler, holding a "Happy Birthday, Shilo" banner. Behind them, the Atlantic tide reaches for their sandy feet. Laughter radiates from happy faces, and I long to jump into the picture and join the fun. The Misty before me is nothing like the one I first met in the hospital. Those red-rimmed eyes, that greasy ponytail. Her skinny body draped with one of Jake's big T-shirts. Her face shadowed with pain as she gazed at Tyler, wondering if he'd survive the beating from Jake. But Misty's living in a different world now. Free from Jake's grasp, enveloped in love, and finally part of a real family.

Her handwriting fills the left side of the card.

Dear Shilo,

You'll probably get this late. Sorry. Life's been crazy, but really good. North Carolina is beautiful. Never thought I'd be living in a place like this. I'm taking two classes at the community college – English Comp and Intro to Sociology. Maybe I'll be a social worker someday. Then I can help some kids so they don't turn out like me. That would kinda make all the bad years worth it.

Tyler's doing great. He adores the Howells and has a couple of friends down the block. Cousins, too! The Howell's sons (they're my brothers, now that I'm officially adopted) and their wives have been really nice to us. It's just weird being part of this whole big family now. So glad Jake's out of our lives and can't hurt us anymore. Don't know where I'd be right now if it wasn't for you and your family.

Anyway, I hope it's okay for you over there in Sicily with the nuns and all that. Send me a letter or something, if you can. I miss you a lot. Feels weird to say that to someone.

Misty

I miss you, too, Misty.

That girl, she was definitely unexpected. Out of the blue, she and her little son crashed into my world and sent it spinning. Toughened my skin a little, too. Meeting someone who grew up in foster homes and had a baby at sixteen—someone who tolerated abuse just to stay off the streets—well, that changes a person. I reread her letter, haunted by the line, "Maybe I can help some kids so they don't turn out like me." Considering everything, Misty turned out pretty great. With the love and nurturing she's getting from the Howells, she'll probably figure out she can reach for the stars and grab a whole armful.

Chapter 12

Melody

A new day, a new stuffed animal. My parents arrive with a giant lion sporting a shimmery turquoise bow, pink mums, a novel, and candy bars – my favorites from years ago.

"There's no room for candy in a dancer's diet," my coach says. *Used to* say. I guess it doesn't matter now. Just when I think Mom is done pulling things out of her tote bag, she reaches back in and produces three magazines – none of which are ballet related. I'd forgotten there were other kinds. The cover of the top mag gleams with the violet and orange streaks of a sunset sky over ocean waves.

I lay it on my lap. "A travel magazine?"

"We have a surprise for you, Mellie." Mom's got that Christmas morning grin. The woman really loves giving more than anyone I've ever met. "We're going to take a family trip. A big one! And *you* get to decide where. Mountains, oceans, cities, wherever you want."

"Soon as you're better, lass," Dad chimes in. "We're long overdue for a trip."

What he doesn't say is that trips took a backseat when all of their time and money was spent on ballet. Classes, costumes, shoes, private lessons so I could catch up to those who started years before I did. We made it to Disney World when I was twelve, which was great, but that was our one-and-only.

Mom nudges me over and sits at the edge of the bed, then picks up the magazine.

"This might be fun to look through for ideas. There's a whole big beautiful world out there, honey." She flips through pages, stopping at an aerial view of a lush island. "Ohh, would you look at this. Isla Mujeres! It's in Mexico. I've heard it's wonderful."

My throat thickens from an onslaught of opposing emotions. Self-pity, love, anger, gratitude, fear. I don't want to travel. I just want to dance. That's it. One thing. Strolling the beaches of Isla Mujeres or wherever isn't going to magically fix everything. I want to scream those words at her, but they won't come out. Nothing about me is functioning right. Not even my stupid voice. And look at her, with those hopeful eyes, aching to hear even a hint of excitement from me. I squeeze my eyes shut, trying desperately to hold in the tears, but they stubbornly squeeze through my lashes.

"Oh, Melody." Mom kisses my head and asks Dad to leave us alone for a few minutes. When I open my eyes, he's gone.

She takes a breath, stares at the sheets. Whatever she's about to say requires a moment of summoning strength. "You'll dance again, sweetheart. Not professionally, but you'll dance." Her eyes rise from the sheets to lock with mine. "Just for the joy of it, and is that so bad? You think I don't know a trip can't make up for what's happened? 'Course I do. Just like I know you're too smart to fool. You know the trip's a distraction, but it's more than that. It's a way of remembering there's so many good things in the world."

If she thinks I've forgotten, she's right. My mind can't produce a single image of a good thing in the world, like I just don't subscribe to that channel. Logic tells me they're out there, buried deep in my pre-accident memories, but no 'good things in the world' are revealing themselves these days.

"Beautiful and miraculous people, places and things," she continues. "Random acts of kindness and selflessness. Opportunities to make a difference. To let your light shine. Life is never about one thing or one person or one dream. You can't do that, Mellie. It's the old saying about putting all your eggs in one basket. Sometimes baskets break. At some point or another, we all need a spare basket. A Plan B. I wish this didn't happen to you, more than you can imagine. But it did, and you need to accept that, do everything you can to get yourself better, and move on."

She's acting like all I did was scrape my knee and everything will be fine in a few days. "Move on? Like it's—"

"Easy? No. It's not easy. There will be a lot of things in life that aren't easy. And each time one comes along, you handle it, even if it's hard, and then you move on."

"What about you? Did you ever have to *move on*?" My words are saturated in an attitude I can't seem to control. What does she know about life kicking you in the gut?

She glances out the window. When she turns back toward me, there's a sheen to her eyes. "Melody Yasmeen O'Hara." Her words emerge just above a whisper. "You know you're adopted. What does that tell you?"

"That you couldn't get pregnant." Which is nothing like what happened to me, but I know it broke her heart, so I take the attitude down a notch.

"Dad and I, we wanted a house full of children. Four, at least. That was the plan. That was *my* dream. And it nearly killed me when, month after month, it didn't come true. Finally, the miracle - I got pregnant. We were so excited, we went out and bought little booties and a great big teddy bear, and started looking at cribs and rocking chairs."

She'd told me she couldn't get pregnant, but never in this much detail, or with so much emotion. I hang on her words, waiting to hear what comes next, knowing that child never made it into the world. And what came after that? Me. I was the resolution to the problem.

"Then, the miscarriage. Followed by another. And another. Each time, it ripped my heart to pieces. His, too. It was Dad's idea to adopt."

"That's different than this. I understand it was painful. Really, Mom, I do. But it's different."

"Is it? I had a dream. A plan for my life that meant the world to me. It never crossed my mind, not once, that my dream wouldn't become a reality. Does that sound familiar? Then you came along. A new reality. Better than anything I ever dreamed of. God's plans for us don't always match ours, but they're always better."

And there it is. The God factor. It was only a matter of time. The problem is, He let me down. Maybe it's not right to feel that way, but feelings are feelings. I know He didn't make the accident happen, but He didn't prevent it, either. And here I am. Broken.

"Well, I sure hope that new plan comes along soon, cause I can't imagine what's better than attaining the goals I worked so hard for. Struggled for. Even *bled* for. Gave up a social life, lived in a constant state of stress trying to keep up with stupid homework and ballet."

"I know, honey. I know. That's why I talked with your nurse, Adanna. She said she has someone she'd like you to meet. Someone you can relate to better than me."

Perfect. Mom and Adanna teaming up to enlighten me. "No thanks."

"Melody, you are never going to move on if you don't start making an effort. Give this woman five minutes of your time. What can it hurt? But first, for goodness sake, do your exercises, take a shower, come back to life. You can't discover what it has to offer if you don't come back."

Dad walks in with yet another stuffed animal. My room is starting to look like the hospital gift shop.

"Couldn't resist getting this koala." He sets it on top of the travel magazine, which still rests on my lap. When I get back home, if that *ever* happens, there's going to be little room for me amidst the furry menagerie.

"Remember how much you loved them when we went to the zoo? We should go back there when you're a little more mobile. Whaddya think, lass? Wouldn't that be fun?"

I want to throw the koala against the wall and scream like a toddler that I don't ever, ever, ever want to to back to the zoo, but oh, the love in that man's eyes. And the pain. He doesn't have a clue how to help me, but he's trying. God knows, he's trying.

"Yeah, that'll be fun. Maybe in a month or so."

He clears his throat and tosses a quick glance to Mom before focusing back on me. "You know, that boy is sitting in the waiting room. He said the nurses told him to wait 'til we left, but he's holdin' some flowers and seems pretty anxious to see you."

I sigh. "I'm really tired." I've overused that lame excuse, but my brain can't think of anything else right now. "Can you tell him not today?"

"He drove over here to see you and paid good money for those overpriced flowers from the gift shop. I'll tell him to only stay five minutes. How about that?"

I nod, when everything inside me is saying 'no,' and they leave to give me and Blake 'some space.' When he enters, I can't see his face behind the bouquet of brightly colored mums and roses, and I wish it would stay that way. It would be easier to do this break-up without seeing the disappointment shadowing those captivating eyes. His cologne reaches me before the flowers – woodsy, earthy, clean as rain. At once, a million Blake memories flood my mind. Kissing backstage, sneaking onto the studio roof and watching the sun set, riding those silly paddleboats on Volkening Lake. I shove them away.

"Hi, beautiful. Been missin' you. Tried to call a few times, but there's never an answer."

"Sorry. Thanks for the flowers." The obligatory words emerge in a monotone, my attempt at preventing him from glimpsing my heart.

He places the vase next to the last one he brought, then kisses me, quick and dispassionately, like anything more might break me. The chair is occupied by Mom's magazines and the giant koala, so he sits on the edge of my bed. "How you doin'? Your dad said I can't stay long. Everything okay?"

I cringe at the question, wishing no one would ever ask it again, then respond with the answer he, and everyone else, wants to hear. "Yeah, fine."

We make small talk about the weather, school starting soon, his job working backstage at the college, and the type of exercises I have to do. Our words are forced. Stilted. Nothing like the long, easy talks we used to have, sharing opinions, dreams, frustrations, and triumphs. He glances at his cell to check the time, probably thinking Dad is waiting to make sure he leaves.

"Whoa, it's been ten minutes. Guess I have to go...unless you want me to stay."

"Honestly, I could use a break. The meds make me tired."

"Okay, I'll get going, but I'll be back tomorrow and I'll call you tonight."

He stands, gazing at me and probably weighted down by the guilt of wanting to move on with his life. Might as well make it easy for him.

"That's okay, you don't have to."

"I *want* to, Mel."

Liar. "I just want to focus on healing right now, and fig-uring out what comes next. I'm not in a good place, and can't seem to get there."

"We can do this together. I'm here for you. You know that, right?" He reaches for my hand, but I move it away, not wanting to feel the warmth of his skin on mine.

Why is he making this harder? I gave him the perfect out. "It's something I need to do on my own, Blake. I really need some space, but I'll call you when I'm ready, okay?"

He opens his mouth to speak, but Ginessa struts in pushing a cart with resistance bands, exercise balls, and the thing that stimulates my muscles.

Blake looks from me to Ginessa and back again. "We'll talk," he whispers, and walks out, leaving my heart in shards on the hospital floor. I tell myself the breakup was my choice, but that reminder does nothing to repair my broken pieces.

"Sorry, did I interrupt something?" She positions the cart in a corner.

I shake my head, wanting her to leave, but hoping the stupid exercises will take my mind off the new variety of pain that's sucking me under.

"Ready to try this? It will help strengthen your back." She holds up the resistance bands and demonstrates where to place them and how to pull. I reach for the bands because I promised my parents, because somewhere deep inside, I really do want to get better, and because maybe, if the universe doesn't hate me entirely, everyone will leave me alone when it's over. I comply like a marionette through each command, hating every painful move and hating Ginessa even more, but it finally comes to an end and she leaves.

In the wonderous silence that follows, Mom's words echo through my head. *Life is never about one thing or one person or one dream.* Did I let my focus on one solitary goal ruin my life? Is there even a way to move on from here? It's the kind of thing I'd talk to Shilo about, but she's not here. If she knew, she'd be on the next plane home and would talk to me all night if I wanted. But Shilo can't know about this. If she comes home and those gang guys got hold of her...I don't even want to think about what might happen. Even in this totally messed-up state, I still want my best friend safe more than I want her with me.

"I see all your visitors have left." Adanna's melodic voice breaks through my thoughts. It's her first appearance today, and my emotions can't decide if they're happy to see her or disappointed the moment of solitude has already ended. "Are you enjoying your time alone?"

"Yeah, it's nice."

"I won't stay long, but wanted you to know my friend Chen is coming tomorrow. Your mother told you about her?"

"The woman who's going to inspire me to move on? Yes. She told me."

"Would you like to know something about her?"

I so don't. In fact, I could live happily without ever meeting her, but for my mom and Adanna, I'll go through the motions. I shake my head. "Can we just talk about the rest of your story instead? I really want to hear it."

"Promise me you will meet with my friend and be nice. Otherwise, the rest of my story will remain my secret."

"No one said anything about being nice, but okay, I will. Promise."

"Then I will continue. Where was I?"

"You left your baby at a house. Possibly a convent."

"Oh, yes. On the way back, while grief was tearing me apart, Vlad said he didn't want me anymore for himself. I had three days to heal, then he was going to move me to the basement with the other girls."

"You mean…"

"Yes."

I'm no expert on babies, but I know it takes a lot longer than three days to heal before your parts are in working order again. Poor thing must have been terrified.

"What happened?"

"My mind was racing. I had to escape. Had to find my daughter. Then Vlad told me to start doing laundry in the morning. He said all the sheets from the basement needed to be washed. Even though I still hurt badly from giving birth, I was glad for the opportunity to go outside. You see, we did not have a dryer, so the sheets were hung in the yard. A huge wooden fence encircled the yard. Very high, with points on top."

"A picket fence?"

"Yes, picket. But way high. In that moment, a plan began to form. In the basement was a large, metal bucket, which I wrapped in the freshly washed sheets. I placed it in the laundry basket, with more sheets piled on top. You could not tell a bucket was inside. Vlad was drinking beer and watching football in the house. He must have assumed there was no way for me to escape over the tall fence, especially in my condition. But he was wrong."

In my head, I picture the young Adanna, just two days after giving birth, formulating a strategy to escape. I see her heading into the yard with her basket of sheets, hiding the bucket inside, and fear for her.

"I went to the fence, turned the basket upside down, set the bucket on top, and stood on it. It was wobbly, but now I could reach the top. I tied a sheet around one of the pointed tops, climbed over, and eased myself down on the other side using the sheet like a rope. It was very difficult, and I was in much pain, but it worked. Now I was free, but I was weak and bleeding, and I had no idea how to find my baby."

I can hardly wrap my head around that level of courage and strength. "How did you do all that after just having a baby?"

"Because I would do anything to find her. Anything. And the first step to getting her back was to escape. You must understand, Melody, the pain in my body was nothing compared to the pain in my heart."

That's easy enough to understand. My situation is nothing compared to hers, but it's the loss of my dream that hurts far more intensely than all the physical stuff.

"I began to run and just kept running, so afraid Vlad had

seen my escape. Everything about Chicago was foreign and frightening, but I just kept putting distance between me and that horrible place. Finally, I could run no more. Blood streamed down my legs and I was exhausted. There was a church ahead, so much bigger than any I had ever seen. I barely made it up the stairs and through the doors. The last thing I remembered was seeing the sunlight pouring in through a beautiful stained glass window."

"What happened next?"

"I woke in a bright room, with a kindly faced woman. Not Nigerian, but black like me, which made me feel safer. She placed a cool cloth on my forehead and told me not to be afraid, that everything would be all right. She said a doctor was on the way. That lovely room would be my bedroom for the next five years. And that doctor? He became my father-in-law."

My muscles relax as the story concludes with Adanna finding a safe refuge, but there's still something I don't understand. "I thought you said things got *worse* after you left the baby at the convent."

"Oh, Melody, my baby girl was gone. Nothing could make up for that. The pastor and his wife were very kind to me. They are my family now. But I did not even know where we left her. It was dark, the ride was long, and I spent it staring at my baby, knowing she would soon be gone. My grief was nearly unbearable, but Pastor James and Tiana helped me through it. And Owen, of course. My Owen."

"Owen's your husband?"

She answers with a nod.

"What about the other girls?"

"The police came that day. I was so afraid of them, but they were nice, too. I gave them the name of the massage parlor and they found three of the girls. But the others were gone, and so were Vlad and his partner. When he saw that I had escaped, he must have fit as many girls as he could into his car and fled. The three were eventually sent back to our village in Nigeria."

"Why not you?"

"I could not leave. My child was somewhere in the Chicago area, and I was determined to find her. Even though I wanted to see my parents and siblings, I could not leave without my baby."

The machine connected to my IV starts beeping and she stands to stop the noise by pressing a button, then repositions my arm so it lays flat.

"So much happened in the years to follow. Many good things. But for years, I was plagued by an overwhelming darkness that tossed me back and forth from sadness to anger. Thank God for my new family, the church congregation, and my wonderful Owen, who helped me realize that not only does life go on, it is still worth living. I went to school, improved my English, became a U.S. citizen, and married Owen. We had two beautiful children. But I never found my baby girl, and never stopped praying for her."

"I'm sorry that happened to you."

She checks her watch, a sign that she'll be leaving me soon.

"Thank you. My anger and sadness are gone now. I try to make the most of life by helping others heal. It was not a goal I had as a young woman, but after everything that happened, it emerged as my goal and became my passion. I am grateful to be doing it."

Neither of us say a word. I can't help but wonder what happened to that girl, if she got adopted, like me. How sad that she missed out on having Adanna for a mom. I look at her, so beautiful and smart. Proud. Brave. What if she hadn't climbed that fence? What if Vlad had caught her? The image of what could have been makes me shudder, and my heart breaks for the girls in that massage parlor basement.

"Adanna!" My other nurse walks in, a note of surprise in her voice. "I thought you were off today."

"Yes, I just stopped in to make sure this stubborn girl

was doing her physical therapy."

Her words catch me off guard, until I realize she's not in uniform. How did I not notice? "You're not working?"

"No. I am visiting. And now I must go, because I promised my family egusi soup and jollof rice tonight, and I still need to buy tomatoes."

A wave of gratitude washes through me as I realize she visited me on her own time. Why would she do that? Adanna stands to go, looking at me with those penetrating eyes, and there's no denying I've seen them before. Maybe in a dream. I don't know. And I sure don't know why I want to hug her like I hugged my parents when they left. She'd probably think I was ridiculous, so I just thank her for visiting and promise to do my exercises and "be nice to that handsome boy."

Chapter 13

Shilo

It's time for the dead zone – that exasperating stretch of night when I'm not tired, don't feel like walking around the deserted grounds, and can't play my guitar because of the 'silence after eight' rule. Without a cell or computer, that leaves me with books, but I've read everything I brought, and some of the convent's books, too. The pretty box of stationery from Melody perches on my dresser, reminding me I owe Jules a letter. Her last one to me hinted of loneliness. She was excited about heading off to science camp, though, so I can ask her about that and hope she responds by telling me she had fun and made friends. That girl seriously needs a few fellow nerds in her life. I pull out the little wooden chair and plop down, always amazed at how incredibly uncomfortable it is, wondering why I don't have lower expectations by now.

Dear Rockhound,

Hey kiddo, it was great to get your letter. I can't wait to hear about science camp and all the cool stuff you did there.

I stop to grab a bag of M&Ms from the desk drawer, noting there's only two bags remaining from the stash I brought from home. *Please let there be a store in town that sells them.*

> *Hopefully, you didn't blow anything up. Last week I went to a place called Gole dell'Alcantara. Google it – you'd love it. There were huge rock pillars that looked like…*

Rap, rap, rap.

The knocking breaks the silence, causing my hand to jerk and nearly topple the little hand-painted guitar perched on the desk. Nonna Marie doesn't stop by this late, and the nuns are in the chapel for evening prayers. *Rap, rap, rap*, harder now. My head fills with the creepy image of Edgar Allen's poem. *Rap, rap, rap.*

Quoth the raven, "nevermore."

A small gray cloud of uneasiness hovers overhead as I step toward the door. Dad always says, "Listen to your instincts. People get victimized because they don't listen to the warning signals in their head." But not here. What could be safer than a convent? The thought does little to comfort me as prickles rise up my spine. I open the door and freeze, unable to remove my hand from the doorknob.

Riccardo.

"*Buongiorno, signorina.*" His eyes remind me of the coyotes I've sometimes seen in the forest preserve back home. When they're hunting.

Another Dad saying: "Don't look down. It's a sign of weakness." I gaze straight into eyes so dark I can hardly tell the pupil from the iris.

"*Buongiorno, signor.*" I make no attempt to smile or open the door further. I know what he is, and though my heart breaks for the abused little boy he was, I cannot risk letting that compassion guide my actions.

His smile ices my spine. "So you are the American girl. I

heard whispers about you when I was half dead with fever. They say you have The Gift; that you can heal. I am still fighting the remnants of my infection, but I am nearly well. I came to thank you."

If I healed him, there would be no remnants, especially after this many days. Hard eyes continue to peer into mine, as though searching. For what, I don't know, but I desperately wish Liona was with me, with her giant teeth and bear paws.

"I just prayed for you. I didn't heal you. You should thank the nuns, they took good care of you."

"Oh, but look at me, young lady. I am walking and talking. When they found me, I thought the end was near."

A flash of something shiny and silver in his pants pocket catches my eye, but I don't want to draw his attention by changing my gaze.

"How did you know where to find me?"

"Not so difficult, really. The hallway is dark and empty, the sisters are in prayer, and your doorway had a crack of light beneath it."

"Oh. Well...thanks for stopping by. You should probably get more rest. Goodnight."

"Let me leave you with a thought, *signorina*. This wonderful ability you have, it could be very profitable. We would make good partners, you and I. Many people would pay a fortune for what you can do."

An aura of evil emanates from him, stiffening every part of me. I shake my head, forcing myself to maintain eye contact.

"No. I'm not interested in profit, or partnering. I have nothing to offer you." I start to close the door, but he blocks it with his hand.

"Oh, but you do. Just consider it, and we'll talk more when I am stronger. Very soon, I think." Emerging through his Dracula grin, the words are clearly meant as a threat. "Yes. There is much potential for wealth from this Gift. One way or another. Goodnight, young healer."

He turns to go and I close the door, reminding myself to breathe, while listening to his footsteps grow fainter. The click of his door closing at the far end of the hall provides a modicum of comfort, though I can't help but wonder which side of the door he's really on.

One way or another.

Prickles rise on the nape of my neck and creep down my spine. I slowly turn the doorknob, like I did that first night, and crack it just enough to peek out. Only St. Francis, patron saint of animals, inhabits the deserted hallway, his marble features staring out from an arched alcove. Sweet woodland creatures, so expertly carved they seem to breathe, gather at his feet.

Drumbeats replace heartbeats in my head as I silently close my door, lock it, and push the wooden chair in front of it. The chair isn't even capable of keeping out Sister Celeste, but at least it would alert me if he tried to break in. And maybe, just maybe, I'd have a chance.

Heart pounding, thoughts swirling, I lay awake until after midnight, wondering how I could prevent having another conversation with him. "Profitable," he'd said. That is not a word that will ever be associated with The Gift. *Ever.*

❦

Hurried footsteps in the hall awaken me to an unfamiliar brightness emanating from beneath my bedroom door. The hallway light is on…at three a.m. Something's wrong. It is way too early for anyone to be up, even the sisters. More rushed steps follow, as though they long to run but know it's not allowed. Knocks on doors, strained voices, the rustle of robes as nuns pass my door. There's more drama in this little convent than I've had in three years of high school. I toss back the white cotton bedspread and reach the door in two steps, thankfully remembering the chair before I trip over it. Ear pressed against the wood, I fail to catch the whispered words as they head further down the hallway. Except for one.

Volpe. Fox.

It's not a word I knew in Italian until Sister Celeste told me that sometimes a fox makes it past the dogs and into the barn. Not surprising, considering the convent dogs are nothing like Liona. They lay in the shade all day, occasionally flicking away a fly, then sigh from the exertion. Pretty sure a fox, even a really old, crippled fox, could sneak past them without ever breaking into a run.

I slip on jeans and a T-shirt and head into the utter blackness of a night without lights, except for the bobbing flashlights over by the barn. The same barn where little Lambie lives with her mama, along with the baby goat in my photos, and the litter of piglets. *Please don't let it be Lambie.* My feet break into a run as my eyes follow the beams ahead. The chances of tripping over something in this utter darkness are nearly a hundred percent, but I push forth, begging my eyes to adjust. The voices of Celeste, Francesca and the red-headed nun whose name I never remember rise and fall from within the barn. The beams are no longer visible, but a faint glow emits from the barn door. I pick up the pace. Nearly there, my foot hits something lumpy and soft, a high-pitched yelp splits the night, and I sail through the air in slow motion. My scream shatters the night just before my head smacks the earth.

A warm, damp nose sniffs my face, nudging me for signs of life.

"Move away, Bruno." The voice comes from Red. "It is the girl," she calls out. "Marie's granddaughter."

More voices come to me before my eyelids can function.

"Oh, no!"

"Is she okay? Can she move?"

My eyes finally open, only to be blinded by beams of light bobbing in my direction.

"Shilo, speak to me." Celeste is on her knees, brushing the hair from my face. "Are you all right?"

Am I? I take a breath, and the momentary fog begins to clear. "Yes. Is Lambie okay? And the baby goat?"

"*Sí, Sí.* They are fine, but the fox got into the barn."

"Oh, no. The piglets?"

She shakes her head. "He took some of our baby chicks. The hens are very upset. Now, what about you?"

Relief washes over me, then a tinge of guilt for being glad it was baby chicks and not Lambie. I slowly rise to a sitting position.

"I'm okay. Tripped over the dog." Dirt clings to my knees and palms, both of which sting from the fall, but it's my ego that sustained the worst damage.

Celeste sweeps her flashlight until it lands on my canine stumbling block, Bruno, who is totally beyond the incident and once again flopped comfortably on the ground. From the henhouse, a clamor of screeches and clucks rise from the frightened chickens. That mama hen will likely spend every night in fear of the fox's return. I know the feeling, but my fear is centered on a far more dangerous *volpe.*

❧

As I cross the meadow, guitar and camera in tow, I see Myriam, Cyrine, and a girl I don't recognize tossing a ball to Liona, who happily runs to retrieve it and waits for the next toss. She doesn't have to wait long. The girls are enjoying the game as much as the giant dog. Little Farah sits on the same rock where I saw her last, knees tucked against her body, head down. She is safe here, but that doesn't erase the horrors that were done to her. Or the others. The images sicken me, ripping through my heart. But I came to lift their spirits, if that's possible, so there's no room right now for anger and sadness. Myriam spots me and waves, then alerts the others, who do the same. I wave back, hoping we can communicate more on this visit. Since Nonna said some of the girls are Italian, I'm hopeful that will make it easier. And a little music couldn't hurt.

"Hello, Shilo." Myriam speaks first. She points to the girl I don't recognize, who must have been inside when I visited the other day. "This Emily. Is Italian." Emily is lighter skinned than the others, with waist-length brown hair a little wavier than mine. She looks at me, but does not return my smile. I get it. These girls have little reason to smile. At least she'll understand me if I speak in Italian.

"Hi, Emily. I'm Shilo, Marie's great-granddaughter from the United States. I'm staying with the nuns for the summer."

"Hi." Still no smile, and no other words forthcoming.

I reach into the camera bag and pull out a container. "We made these cookies for you this morning. I hope you like them." I hold out the container and she takes it with a polite "*grazie*." I glance over at Farah, then back to Myriam and Emily. "How is she doing?"

"Not well. She barely eats."

Myriam looks at me and shakes her head. She doesn't know the words to tell me about Farah's broken spirit. Her depression. Her pain. But no words are needed. My throat thickens as heartache threatens to close it completely. I want to cry. I want to yell at the heavens and sob until my brain dissolves, taking with it all the horrific thoughts of what happened to them. I want to shake my fist at God and scream, "How? How could you let it happen?" But I know He is not the author of evil, and that His heart breaks for these girls even more than mine. I know He gave Nonna Marie and the others the courage to rescue them. Still, my heart wishes He'd sent a thunderbolt down to obliterate every man that touched them.

I set down the camera bag, loop my guitar strap over my neck, and walk toward the rock.

"Hey, Farah."

Her face remains pressed against her arms.

"Do you like music?" I strum a few chords. The other girls join me, and two more emerge from the house. "Can I play a song for you?"

Still nothing. The girls gather around me, staring. The two new additions whisper to each other. I can't imagine a way for this to feel more uncomfortable, and regret coming, but that doesn't change the fact that I'm standing here with my guitar and need to do something. Anything. I strum a few more chords and Farah raises her head. It isn't much…but it's enough. Almost without thinking, I launch into an Italian song I learned years ago from Aunt Rita. Maybe she's guiding me from Heaven. I'd like to think so. Halfway through, some of the girls are swaying to the music, and two have the trace of a smile. Farah just stares, but her head remains up, a little higher than when I began. The music won't fix their messed-up lives and stolen innocence, but in this moment it feels right, and I no longer regret my decision to visit.

When the song ends, Myriam steps closer to me. "Is good."

"She's right." Emily joins her. "Please play another."

I do. And following that, at their request, I play another, and another. During the fourth song, Emily opens the cookies and passes them around. One of the girls brings a chair from the house, and sets it next to me. I sit, and the others plop onto the ground and encircle me. Halfway through song number five, they clap to the beat, and grace me with more smiles. Even from quiet Emily. Farah comes down from her rock and sits behind the circle, ignoring the space they make for her, but she isn't alone. Ever the protector, Liona saunters over and sits next to her. Farah wraps a frail arm around the dog's neck, and with her other hand reaches into the cookie container. Yes! She's going to put some food into that scrawny little body. My joy is short-lived, however, when she offers it to Liona, who gently retrieves it before annihilating it with those monstrous teeth.

I pause to pull out my water bottle and ponder ways to get through to Farah. The music was a good start. Maybe there's a way to bring it into her world – a place too dark for me to comprehend. I call her name, motioning for her to come to me, with little expectation that will happen. And yet...she does. With Liona at her heels, she stops in front of me and I stand, looping the guitar strap around her neck. I reach for her hand, slowly, gently, as if touching a newborn. She stiffens, but allows my hand to hold hers, guiding it toward the strings. Before we get that far, the sunny day melds into a misty blue haze, while the faint sound of Farah's heartbeat echos in my head.

And warmth floods my heart.

Chapter 14

Melody

Chen Song is not what I expected, but I don't know what I expected. She strolled in with a "Hey, Melody" like we'd known each other for years, and stretched out her prosthetic arm for a handshake. Now she's waiting for me to answer her question – a question that has no answer. At least, not one I'm willing to give. And I don't even know why she asked, or why I should respond. What's the point? But she's sitting there with those expectant eyes and that whole life-is-awesome thing going on, which should annoy the crap out of me, but it doesn't. She's actually likable. *That's* the annoying part.

"So? Did you come up with anything?" She had offered up three minutes of small talk about losing her arm two weeks after qualifying for the Olympics. Basketball had been her life since fourth grade. That's all the background I got before she dove right in. I don't even know what she's doing with her life, or why she's here. Scratch that. Adanna. That's why she's here.

"It's complicated."

"Nope." She grins. Something she does *a lot*. "It's the easiest thing in the world. Just say the first thing that comes to mind. What do you want that is possible to attain?"

Repeating the question doesn't help extract an answer from my brain. I knew exactly what I wanted and did everything humanly possible to attain it. Less than a week ago I could have answered without stopping to think. But now…now everything's different.

"I want to be a professional ballerina."

"Nope. Not possible to attain. I know it's hard to hear, but that's your new reality." Compassion shadows her eyes, despite her tough-love words. "Try again. Search deeper. What really matters in the grand scheme of things? Say you're dying, what do you want to look back on and think, 'Yes! I did that. I had that.'"

She's not going to cease and desist until I offer up something she considers acceptable. Her question begins to infiltrate my mind, moving past the I-don't-want-to-answer barrier and into the contemplative zone. It weaves past the standard ballet answer I've been giving for the past decade and into a secret corner where I hide certain thoughts, questions, and desires, many of them connected with my adoption. If I reveal one, maybe we can move on and be done with it.

"I want to find my parents."

Chen's brow crinkles. "Adanna says your mom and dad think you're the sun, moon, stars, and a few rainbows thrown in for good measure. So…"

"Slight exaggeration, but yeah, kinda. I want to find my bio parents, though. I'm adopted."

"Ohhh, didn't know. Okay, that's a good answer. Really good. What else? Remember, think big picture."

Clearly, we're not done with it, though someone in my crushed-beyond-hope circumstances should be able to rest without constant challenges from everyone.

"I don't know. Just being out of all this pain and doing stuff for myself would be good. I *hate* this!"

A grin spreads across her face. "Perfect. You *should* hate

it. So how are you going to find your parents and get your body back in shape?"

She's forcing me to think when I'd rather just ask for more painkillers, drift off to sleep and forget this ever happened.

"Come on, Mel, it's not rocket science."

"Don't you have someplace to be?"

"Nope."

If she says, "Nope" again, I'm going to fly out of this bed and pummel her, even if she's got six inches on me. Even if my entire body is broken.

"I took the morning off just to hang with you."

I roll my eyes. So rude, but I just can't help it. Her annoying traits are starting to outweigh the likeable part.

"Didn't ask you to."

"I'm aware. But somebody did it for me, and today, you're the lucky recipient of my pay-it-forwardness. So, what's your plan? Start with the bios."

A laugh escapes me. The bios. She's so weird.

"Look at you, laughing! I mean, it was kind of small and pathetic, but still, laughing is good. You reminded me of someone just then. Oh, yeah, Adanna. You look like her when you laugh, but her laugh is big. You know, the kind that makes everyone else laugh, too. Anyway, back to the plan. Still waiting."

I don't have a plan. The whole concept of the future has been too painful to consider. Since the day I heard my leg would be little more than 'functional,' I've been taking life one miserable hour at a time. Maybe if I answer a few more of her questions, we can finish the interrogation and she'll tell me more about what happened to *her*.

I push my weary brain to focus. What steps would I need to take to find my biological parents? The Internet seems useless if I don't know their names, so Step One has to precede any kind of online search.

"I could hire a private investigator, but that's expensive."

I mumble the statement, surprised my thoughts were audible at all. Chen nods her affirmation. "I could see if the adoption agency will release any info. Guess that would be the best starting point." Saying the words out loud makes me wonder why I've never done it.

"Great! Start today."

"What? Do you see where I am?"

"So what? You've got a laptop and a phone. That's all you need to start. Look up the agency, see who to contact. Ask your folks if it was a closed adoption or what. Ask them to bring the adoption papers. Who knows what info you'll find by the end of the day."

Her energy level is simultaneously infuriating and contagious.

She grabs my cell from the tray table and holds it out to me. "Start now."

This girl is crazy. Certifiably insane. Intolerable. I grab the phone and call Mom. Her tone reflects her surprise, but she agrees to bring the papers and go through them with me.

"Look at that. You got started. How does it feel?"

"It feels like you're way too perky and optimistic. I don't even know if this will lead to anything." My words conceal the unforeseen emotion stirring inside me. What might be revealed about my adoption before this day is over? I push away the flicker of excitement, but it just keeps on flickering.

"It will lead to a whole lot more than you laying there doing nothing. Now, for your body. It's a mess, and that's your fault."

Wow. After all I've been through. The pain. The heartbreak. Surgery. Crushed dreams.

"Seriously? You just said that? Let's give that a big nope." Maybe using her favorite word will make it clear.

"Yep, it is. Rumor has it that it took you days to start the PT, and you do the bare minimum. So, what do you need to do?"

I roll my eyes. "Cooperate during PT sessions."

"Nope. Give it one hundred and fifty percent. Dive in like it matters. Like your life depends on it, because it does. What else?"

I fantasize about her disappearing in a puff of smoke, but that's not going to happen, so I'll just keep answering. At least it will help pass the time.

"Do the exercises when I'm not in a session."

"Yes, until you can hardly stand it. And do everything you can for yourself, even if it hurts. If someone reaches for the water pitcher, politely tell them you want to get it yourself. You will hate the process, but guaranteed, you will *love* the results."

"You think you know everything."

The light in her eyes dims to normal human level as her grin recedes to a thin line.

"No, Melody, I don't. But unfortunately, I know *this*. I know what it's like when one stupid thing that literally takes a fraction of a second steals all your hopes and dreams. I know the pain. It rips your heart out. It attacks you physically, mentally, emotionally, and for me, even spiritually. I know how it feels when the black weight of depression blinds you to all that is good or possible. And I know how much you hate it when some stranger tries to intervene."

I nod. She lost her arm, and I haven't given a thought to what she went through. Until now. Words stick in my throat as it thickens with pain. For her. For me. For everyone that is fine one moment and broken the next. I avoid her eyes, staring straight ahead while knowing she sees the tears flowing down my cheeks. This weak, sad, pathetic shell of me has got to go.

"I'm sorry. I didn't come here to make you cry. I'm not good at this like Adanna." She reaches for my hand, but I jerk it away. "I'll go."

Chen picks up her purse and stands, until I grab her arm. The surprise on her face matches my own. I didn't want her to come, and now, for reasons I can't quite explain, I don't want her to leave. She's the first person I've met who lost the function of a limb, thereby losing the career she'd worked at for years. Adanna's story was painful and inspirational, but so different than mine. Maybe Chen can offer up something, some little diamond in this dark cavern, that will help me figure out how to survive.

"No. Please. I want you to stay. But don't comfort me. Everyone else does that and I'm tired of it. I'm drowning in compassion. It's very sweet, and I know I'm lucky to have people who love me, but what I really need is, well, someone like you."

"Hey, I know someone like me." She laughs and grabs the physical therapy handout left earlier by Giselle. "Let's start with this."

And she's back.

"Nope."

"Are you mocking me?"

"Yep. I'll do the PT stuff, but first tell me about you. What happened? How long did it take to recover? What are you doing now?"

A sigh escapes her lips, the kind that reflects the agony of what's about to be said.

"When my family heard I qualified, they planned a celebration party. My aunt has the biggest house, so everyone was heading there, about thirty relatives. We're on the expressway - me, Mom, Dad, my twin brothers - and we're driving under a bridge when the world explodes. At least, that's what it felt like. Glass flying, bodies flinging against seatbelts, crashing again and again as cars hit us and we hit them."

"Why? What happened?"

"Somebody dropped a brick off the bridge."

"*What?*" No way I heard that correctly.

"Yeah, it happens. They got the guy, though. He was drunk and thought it would be funny to drop a brick onto the expressway. That pretty much sums up his motive. It crashed through our windshield. We were all in bad shape. Like, *really* bad. They had to cut us out with one of those jaws-of-life machines. My arm got crushed from the elbow down. Everyone had broken bones and gashes." She stares out the window and takes a breath, the way I do when I'm trying to stifle a sob. "Dad's head wound took a long time to heal. He still has memory problems, but he's pretty good now."

"I'm sorry that happened. That's messed up." My words feel insufficient for expressing how incredibly messed up that really is.

"Yeah." She turns toward the window again, probably wondering for the millionth time how different her life might have been if that stupid, horrific, random act of violence never happened. After a moment, she reaches down and unzips her backpack to pull out something wrapped in tissue paper, and sets it in her lap.

"Yeah, so I came home from the hospital and went into my room, where I had shelves full of basketball trophies. I grabbed the one that was different than all the rest cuz it was glass and very colorful, with hues of red and gold. It was also my favorite. I looked at it one last time and ran my thumb over the 'most valuable player' inscription." She glances down at the wrapped package before her eyes meet mine. "Then I hurled it against the wall. Just whipped it with everything I had."

Didn't expect those words, but I get it. Right now, right here, stabbing the smiley balloon was the best I could do. Smashing something against a wall would have been far more satisfying.

"My mom ran over and tried to comfort me, but I wasn't interested. She picked up most of the shards and tossed them in a bag, then vacuumed the rest. But she forgot to take the bag, so that beautiful trophy, all shattered like me, just sat there in the corner of my room."

Ballet trophies line the shelves of my room back home.

Plastic, metal, ceramic – each topped with miniature ballet shoes or a graceful ballerina performing an arabesque or pirouette. Will rage send one of them sailing into the wall?

"Fast-forward a year. It's my twenty-first birthday and this woman starts talking to me during my prosthesis appointment here. She's been through some crap, too. Way different than mine, but just as painful. And we started meeting for coffee once a week, even though she had a job and kids. She did that for me, a total stranger, and helped pull me out of the dark muck I'd been wallowing in. Helped me reconnect with God, too."

Mom's words from the other day echo in my head. *God didn't make this happen – don't you forget that, Mellie. But He's the one that will carry you through it…if you let Him.* My response was to close my eyes and pretend I fell asleep. Just not sure how I feel about God right now.

"As my perspective began to change, so did my life. It was a slow process, I'm not gonna lie, but I was finally moving forward. Long story short, I went back to school, became a psychologist and love it, and on days off I volunteer at the horse rescue farm. Love that, too. And when I get a call from the person who helped pull me up, I drop everything and come running."

"I thought Adanna called you."

"Yep."

"She was the one who pulled you up?"

"She was amazing. Still is. And now she's set her sights on you, so look out, Melody O'Hara, because between the two of us, you haven't got a chance." She laughs and I do the same until she stops and stares at me, shaking her head. "It's uncanny. Even your eyes resemble hers."

"I'll consider that a compliment." Adanna is one of those beautiful people, like you can almost see the love glowing inside her. If Chen thinks I have anything that remotely resembles her, I'll take it.

"Definitely. Okay, now you've got a couple of good

goals, but you still need to work on the big one. You know, the if-you-were-dying thing I said earlier. But I don't expect you to come up with that on the spot. Wrap your brain around it while you're doing PT and searching for the bios. Combine what you care about with what you're good at and mold those things into a new goal." Chen pours herself some water from my bedside pitcher and takes a gulp. "And if your brain starts reverting back to your old dream, just stop. That's the devil gettin' into your head. You're vulnerable right now. To him, that translates into 'easy prey.' Do not let that happen. Got it?"

"Yes ma'am."

"Yikes. You just aged me thirty years."

I smile for the third time in an hour, after not smiling for a week, and point to her still-unwrapped package. "What's that?"

"Oh! Geez, almost forgot. I made three of these after I emerged from the trenches of self-pity. One for me, and two for others who might need a little encouragement. After Adanna told me your story, I grabbed this one for you." She unwraps the tissue to unveil a brilliant sun, pieced together from the red and gold trophy shards. It dangles from a thin chain as she holds it by the window.

"It's a suncatcher."

I gasp, blown away that she created something so beautiful from the broken mess, and that she's giving it to *me*. Sunlight streams in through the hospital window, lighting the shards like shimmering gems.

"I don't know what to say. It's gorgeous!"

"Thanks. I gotta admit, I like it better than the trophy." Chen stands. "Well, I better get goin'. I have appointments this afternoon. I know you're leaving in the next day or so, but would it be cool if I stopped by your house next week?"

"Yeah. Definitely."

"I'm going to expect to see a huge improvement, you know. Maybe we'll even shoot a few hoops."

"Umm. Can we take your expectations down a notch...or three?"

Chen laughs. "Okay, but you'll be surprised at how fast you recover once you start putting some effort into it. Take care, Melody. See you soon."

She leaves and I feel like a meteor just swooshed through the room, because even in her absence, a wave of cosmic energy remains. I shake my head, still staring at the open doorway.

"What just happened?" Only my gang of stuffed animals hears the question, but I couldn't help but say it out loud. I'm still a mess in every way possible, but there's a new element to my mess now that wasn't there an hour ago. It is tiny - small as a match spark - but hints at the possibility of fanning into a raging fire.

It is hope.

And it is everything.

Chapter 15

Shilo

Sweet scents envelop the kitchen as Nonna and I help the nuns pack pastries in boxes to sell in the *piazza*. Flaky crusts stuffed with honey-almond and hazelnut fillings. Crispy cannoli shells waiting to be filled with sweet ricotta, with their ends dipped in crushed pistachios. Biscotti, amaretti cookies, and fresh strawberry cassata cake. For a sugar junkie like me, it would be Heaven on Earth … if it wasn't zero dark thirty. If I wasn't exhausted from spending half the night trying to figure out a plan to heal Farah. If only I could have one cup of coffee, or even one precious, glorious sip.

I am going to die.

At least my late night musings resulted in an idea that could potentially work. Nonna said whenever God leads me to someone, He'll makes a way for me to accomplish my task. So far that's happened, so I'll have to trust that it will happen again. When we're away from the sisters, I'll tell Nonna my strategy and see what she thinks. Farah needs a miracle, and that's exactly what she's going to get. If my idea works out, none of the girls will ever know what happened.

"Where is the chicken?" The red-headed sister pushes food around in the refrigerator, then turns toward those of us working at the counter. "The chicken. It's gone."

"I didn't eat it." Sister Francesca is the first to respond. "Everyone always thinks it's me."

"I was asking everyone, Francesca. I wasn't accusing you."

"It was in there last night." Celeste carefully tops cassata cakes with a pretty pattern of fresh strawberries. "It must be there. A cooked chicken doesn't just fly away." She laughs at her little joke.

"Well, it's definitely not here, and it was supposed to be our dinner tonight." Red closes the refrigerator in defeat. "I like to have something ready so we don't have to cook after selling in the *piazza*. This is quite odd."

"It wasn't me, that's all I know."

Something about Francesca's words hurts my heart. She has probably had a lifetime of comments about her weight. Celeste puts the final touches on the last cake and holds open a cardboard box so I can place it inside. I grab Francesca's boxes too, and add them to my cart.

"*Grazie, Shilo. Grazie mille.*" She is one of the few who prefers to communicate with me in Italian. I offer up a "you're welcome" to her "thank you very much" and push my pastry-packed cart outside, where the ever-loyal Ezra loads everything into the back of the mini van. Emphasis on mini. The sisters follow, lead by Nonna Marie, and we squeeze in like sorority girls in a Bug. My little group is quieter than usual, but like me, all are suffering from caffeine and sleep deprivation. All except Nonna, who is already playing tour guide as we begin the hour and a half cruise down Etna's slope toward Acireale.

"You will much enjoy Acireale, Shilo Marie. Such lovely views. Pretty fountains. Good shops, too. And, oh, the *duomo*! This you will love. So beautiful, it will make you cry."

In the days before I left for Sicily, Jules had told me about the 400-year old *duomo*; a Catholic cathedral with huge gothic towers that looms over the *piazza*. Asking "What's a *piazza*?"

resulted in an eye roll, before she explained that it's like a town square with no streets running through it and usually has a fancy fountain with statues and carvings. It was one of a billion 'fun facts' she enthusiastically shared about the area near the convent. She was particularly excited about the geology of Mt. Etna, which apparently has superstar volcanic soil that grows amazing grapes and olives. When she started to toss out phrases like "organic acids, high porosity, and nutrient rich," my eyes glazed over and my brain excused itself from the conversation.

In front of me, sunrise begins to illuminate the breathtaking vista of Etna's slopes, artfully dotted with vineyards and olive groves. We pass a grove of trees bursting with lemons the size of grapefruits. That girl sure knows her stuff.

Nonna points to a shop in the distance. "You see? You see store there? They sell olive oil and honey and the *best* torrone. Always fresh. We come back after sell pastries and buy for your mama and papa."

That's actually a great idea, and I tell her so. Everyone in my family loves torrone, with its chewy nougat and almonds. Fortunately I brought money, thanks to Jules telling me that *piazzas* are surrounded by cafés, bakeries and shops, and there's usually artists selling paintings and ceramics. Maybe I'll find something for Celeste, to thank her for letting me use her camera and opening my eyes to a whole new world. And I definitely need to buy unique and artsy souvenirs for Melody, Jules, and Kenji.

Kenji. I miss him so much it aches. Actually aches. This separation is going to be the death of me. But at least I know where he is and we've been in touch. Not like Melody. It's like she fell off the planet. I don't get it. She has my address. She promised she'd write *every* week. I've sent three letters so far, and haven't gotten so much as a birthday card. I try to tell myself she was swamped with the big show and getting ready for that class at the Joffrey Ballet Academy, but *come on.*

Nonna nudges me again, pointing to another building off to the right. "You see there? *Nuovo Mondo*, for the *rifugiati*. The refugee children who get our pastry monies."

The sisters had told me about New World, the refugee school, during our daily task of making breakfast pastries for the students. Nearly a decade ago, they had approached local government officials about opening a school for the children of refugees. It took a year of convincing, and another two before it got off the ground, but the unstoppable Sisters of St. Teresa made it happen. Twice a week Sister Francesca teaches art, and Sister Mary tutors math students. All of the pastry profits, every penny, is given to the school.

"Most of them are from Tunisia," Celeste explains. "But some are from other countries, too."

"Is Tunisia close to here?" I know it's somewhere in Africa, but that's where my geography knowledge ends.

"Very close. Northern Africa. Just over two hundred miles across the sea. A lot of poverty there. No jobs."

"Is much better life here." Ezra chimes in from the driver's seat. "Now I work. My family have food. My boys have school. Place to live. Now we are Italian citizens. The sisters help many people like us. We just want chance to work. To have good life."

The sisters explain that the school is completely dependent on donations, along with the sale of pastries and Celeste's photos.

"We must sell every item to help those children." Nonna gives my arm a gentle squeeze. "Shilo Marie, you are so beautiful, you can flirt with the men and they will buy the pastries. Yes?"

Umm...no. "Why don't we just tell people the money supports a school for refugee kids?"

"Oh, yes, we do that always. So *we* will tell about supporting the school." She gestures to herself and the nuns to ensure I catch the meaning of "we," then cups her hands around mine. "But *you*, Shilo Marie. You do the flirt."

Pretty sure every dead feminist just rolled over in her grave.

Sister Celeste turns to face me. "It was your nonna's idea, you know."

"The flirting? Yes, I know."

She giggles. "No, the school. We heard that dozens of refugees had set up a tent town on the beach near Catania. We brought food and water, but there were so many. We could only help a few. We were heartbroken, especially when we saw the children. Your nonna said we must do something." She gives Nonna's hand a pat. "So we did."

The world could learn a lot from these sisters. "But where are their families?"

"Behind the school are two apartment buildings. The families live there and work on the nearby farms and vineyards."

"You guys are amazing."

She laughs, and the other nuns join in and keep on going, nearly to the point of tears. Clearly I missed something.

"What are you guys laughing at?"

That sets them off all over again, and Ezra joins in with his baritone bellow. Sister Francesca's round cheeks are poppy red as she struggles to breathe through her giggles. She pats my leg. "You, you…" but she can't get the rest out because another peel of laughter steals her words. "You, you…"

"What? What about me?"

She takes a breath. "You guys."

If laughter were energy, our mini-minivan would have exploded. The sisters can hardly catch their breath. Even old Sister Angelina is nearly hysterical. They take turns saying accented versions of "you guys" and convulsing in cackles, chuckles and chortles, but now I've joined in, because there is nothing more hilarious on Earth than a group of nuns cracking up and saying "you guys" with Italian accents. Who knew?

An hour later we pull up to the *piazza*, and it doesn't disappoint. In fact, it far exceeds my high expectations. The seventeenth century Acireale Cathedral is flat-out fairytale material. Eerily beautiful. Mysterious. It's nearly impossible to tear my eyes away from the white marble carvings over the doorway, and the immense gothic towers bathed in early morning sunlight. I grab my camera, but only get off two shots before a groan turns my attention to Sister Angelina, her frail, wrinkled arms reaching into the van for a large box of croissants. Not particularly heavy, but still…

"Sister!" I grab the box, but she hangs on with every shred of strength her gnarled hands can muster. "Please, let me. Why don't you wait in the van and I'll come get you when we're set up?"

"I will rest when I'm dead, young lady. I made these croissants, I will carry these croissants."

The determination in her eyes tells me it's time to relinquish the box into her hands. There are still plenty left in the van, so I grab as many as my arms can hold and head for our designated spot on the *piazza*, walking alongside the aging nun. Just in case.

We arrive to find Ezra setting up a canopy and table for Sister Celeste's photos, each one more mesmerizing than the next. My playful little goat is among them – my favorite shot of him leaping with all four feet in the air, like he's made of springs and happiness. When Ezra sets up another two tables, the nuns cover them with delicate lace tablecloths before setting out the tantalizing array of freshly made pastries. Their aroma draws customers even before we've finished setting up. Next to the pastries sits a box marked "Donations for the Refugee School." Throughout the day, we serve our sweet delights to a steady stream of tourists and locals, many of whom know the sisters by name and generously drop euros into the box. We sell out shortly after noon, and never once do I need to 'do the flirt.'

"Now, Shilo Marie, you must go to the *duomo*." Nonna

stops folding the tablecloths to gesture toward the amazing cathedral that shadows us, providing a welcome reprieve from the heat. "You must see the beautiful frescos, the carvings, the windows. Look down to see floor. Such lovely marble tiles, beautiful designs. You come out and find us there." She points to a vendor selling paninis stuffed with a variety of meats, cheeses, and vegetables. "First a panini, then gelato. It is our treat each week."

Her smile reflects the joy of these simple pleasures. She stands before me, emitting a glow that others may not see amidst the wrinkles and gray hair, and I think of all that led her to this point. The tragic death of her husband, coming to faith, receiving The Gift, and choosing to use it for the wrong reasons, which led to 'The Fall' – her suicide attempt. And there, in the depths of despair, God's grace found her and brought her to the Sisters of St. Teresa. Everything I've discovered about her on this trip has been a testament to the God who takes shattered bits and pieces and creates a beautiful mosaic.

"What is it, Shilo Marie?" Her smile diminishes as concern weaves through her words. "Where did your mind go?"

"I was just thinking about all you've been through. It's been an incredible journey – all the highs and lows. I'm just glad that you found a great home here with the sisters."

Her smile returns, but this time with a slight shake of her head. "We *all* take journey, from the time we are born. Sometime we fall, then we stand again. The convent, this world—" she sweeps one arm across the piazza. "This is no home. Is all just for short while. When time is right, God will take me to my real home. Now that, Shilo Marie, that will be oh-so-much wonderful." The glow is back, far brighter than when she talked about lunch. "Now, you go. Take your time. See *duomo*, shop, explore piazza. Test you friends."

I open my mouth to question it, but the translation pops into my brain. "Text. I'll *text* my friends."

"*Si, si*. That is what I say. See *duomo*. Test friends. Go."

She doesn't have to say it twice. We part ways and in moments I'm strolling toward the *duomo* while calling Melody, but her phone goes to voicemail, again, and I leave a message…again. Next up is Kenji. It's seven hours later in Indiana, so I'm not sure what he'll be doing. Hopefully not hanging around with the mystery girl I heard in the background last time we talked.

"Hey, Blue! I was just thinking about you."

His voice makes my heart leap. I want to reach through my cell, wrap my arms around his neck and never let go. Sounds fill the background, making it a challenge to catch his words. Voices. Music. Children laughing.

"I miss you. What are you doing? Sounds pretty noisy."

"Miss you, too. Every minute." He shouts the words, but I still strain to hear above the racket. "And yeah, it's totally noisy. We're at an ice cream parlor for my little cousin's birthday. It's insane. They break into song about every eight seconds. What are *you* doing?"

"I'm in a *piazza* with a gorgeous *duomo*, which I'm going into—"

"What? Can't hear you. You're in a pizza? With a donut?"

"*Piazza*. It's like the Italian town square. I was helping the nuns sell pastries. And there's this huge *duomo*. It's a cathedral, you know, a huge church, and —"

"What? I'm sorry, Blue. I want to talk to you, but I can't hear and can't go outside. They're coming with my cousin's cake and —"

Whatever else he was going to say gets drowned out with a chorus of "Happy Birthday."

"Shi, you there? I have to hang up. I'll call you in an hour, okay? Promise. Love you."

And with a click, he's gone. The conversation I'd anticipated for days lasted three minutes and twelve seconds. Today was my chance to connect with everyone, and so far I'm pretty much batting zero. My plan to call home, then Misty, takes a back seat to my self-pity. Melody is disappearing from my life, and I never saw it coming. Really thought we were soul sisters and all that. And Kenji...so far our calls have been less than stellar. Maybe that will change when he calls back. All I need to do is keep myself distracted for the next hour.

I continue toward the *duomo*, glancing up at the intricate sculptures of the angel Gabriel, telling the Virgin Mary she would be the mother of Jesus. Who could possibly imagine what that fourteen-year-old girl thought and felt in that epic moment? But she stepped up, without hesitation. I hope I can do the same if The Gift leads me to something even remotely that daunting.

The beauty of the cathedral's exterior pales in comparison to the wonders that await inside. I stop. Stare. Gasp, and forget to release my breath. Sunshine beams through arched windows, reflecting off the fresco covered walls and ceiling, bathing me in golden light. High above, sunlight pours in from a dome window in the arched ceiling. I am dwarfed. Humbled. Enveloped in peace and awed by this masterpiece built and painted to worship the One who gave me The Gift. It is the perfect place to offer thanks. I take a step toward the wooden pews, so stark compared to the ornate beauty of the cathedral, then stop to gaze at the zodiac sundial embedded into the mosaic floor. Everywhere I look, *everywhere*, is lavishly painted, sculpted or architecturally designed in artistic splendor. My eyes fixate on the silver statue of St. Venera, with his ornate crown. They say he protected Acireale from Mt. Etna's eruptions, and I can't help but wonder...

Hairs rise on the back of my neck, obliterating my thoughts of the silver saint. And despite the midday heat, I shudder. Something is wrong. I don't know what, or why I feel this way...or what I'm supposed to do about it. But in the depths of my soul, I know I can't stay in this magnificent place one minute longer, not even to kneel in gratitude. No audible voice is telling me to leave, and there's no reasonable explanation for this feeling, but there is also no denying it. Something is wrong. Horribly wrong. This feeling, calling, premonition - whatever it is - compels me to turn my back on the sunlit statue and head toward the door. Shrouded in an unreasonable fear, my heart races, because it knows what my head is trying desperately to deny.

I am heading into darkness.

Chapter 16

Shilo

Quick steps get me back into the *piazza*, where I break into a run and find the nuns and Ezra enjoying their paninis at a shaded table. They'll think I'm crazy, but it doesn't matter. Why the urgency, the intensity, I don't know. But there's no time to lose.

"We have to go."

Six sets of eyes fix on me. Some with the hint of a glare.

"No, no, Shilo Marie. You get food. Sit here." She pats an open spot on the bench next to her. "Try panini with provolone and ..." Nonna stops, looks at me. "What is it, granddaughter? What has you troubled?"

The group continues to stare at me, except Ezra, who is still munching his panini as he watches an artist paint a Mediterranean sunset.

"Something's wrong. I'm sorry. I know it sounds crazy, but I am asking you to trust me." My heart beats harder. "Begging you. We have to go."

Skepticism shadows each set of eyes. There is no reason, on this blue-sky day in this beautiful place, that they should have to go. This is *their* time, when they sit and relax after all the business of baking and selling. Their little spot in the week when they can just be a group of women having lunch, laughing and chatting. And the outsider is ruining it.

But I have no choice. At least, not one I can live with. And no one's making a move to leave.

"Please. I hate asking, but something is wrong. We have to get back." I look at my great-grandmother, concern adding more wrinkles to her forehead. "Nonna, please."

She turns to the *sorellas*, who are gazing at me like I have three heads. "My sisters, I believe my granddaughter. May I please ask you to trust me on this?"

Celeste is the first to reluctantly wrap her half-eaten panini. Francesca follows suit, but Angelina takes a defiant bite and chews slowly while scowling at me.

"Please, Sister Angelina. I would never ask this if I didn't feel there was something terribly wrong."

"There better be." She wraps the remains of her sandwich and allows Celeste to help her up from the bench.

We make our way back at a pace that would make a snail proud, but there's nothing I can do. We can only proceed as fast as Angelina can walk. With every painstaking step, the urgency of our return intensifies, until I want to scream. My heartbeat pounds at a deafening roar. Ten minutes later, we are at the car. I would have sworn it took an hour. The picturesque hills and valleys, orange groves and pastures, fail to enchant me like they did on the way down. If only teleportation was a thing. Finally, we are passing the olive oil store where Nonna said we should shop for Mom and Dad. Only a few minutes left now before we reach the convent. We pass the grove of trees where the sisters found Riccardo injured and unconscious. His abandoned milk truck will be just around the next bend, followed by the barn, then the convent. We round the curve, and my heart nearly explodes.

The truck is gone.

Whatever drew me here is connected to the missing truck, which is connected to Riccardo. This is the darkness I feared. It's here. Now. And there's no turning back.

"Where is the truck?" Celeste points out the window.

My eyes scan the area around the barn, the convent, the meadow house. There's no sign of them today. No one hanging clothes or gardening. No one playing fetch with Liona and laughing as the giant beast gallops back with the stick. The silence unsettles me. The answer is here. The certainty of it unnerves me.

"You see, there is nothing." Sister Angelina grumbles. "We should have stayed."

Nonna gazes out the window, then turns to me. "Where are the girls?" Fear darkens her eyes. "It's too quiet. Too still."

Sister Angelina is right. There is nothing. But Dad would tell me to trust my instincts. If there's nothing visible, then what can't I see? What's *preventing* it from being visible? I stare at the house, and stare harder, but all I see is the house. Nothing on the sides, nothing in front. So what I can't see has to be…

A flash catches the corner of my eye. Sunlight glints off something protruding from behind the house, and that something becomes the fender of a truck. A truck that isn't moving.

"Ezra!" I half stand as I scream at our driver. "The house! Go! Go to the girls' house! Hurry!" He veers left, off the dirt road and onto the grass, as all the women shove into each other. "Faster!"

The six of us jostle and bounce as the minivan hurdles across the field, closing in on the stone villa. It is pretty enough for a fairytale, but my heart tells me what lies ahead will be the stuff of nightmares. The van stops and I scramble across the women, stepping on feet and nearly toppling out the door. I hit the ground running, with Ezra on my heels, and burst through the front door into the empty living room. Only the sloppy remains of a cooked chicken are there to greet us. Its meat and half-chewed bones are strewn across the carpet. Weird, but there's no time to think about it.

"Search the bedrooms. I'll take the kitchen." We split up and I scan the kitchen for a sign of the girls or Liona. This is crazy. What could he have done with a hundred-pound beast with teeth that can chomp through tree trunks? A thud freezes my next step. It is the distinctive sound of a body hitting the floor.

"Ezra!" The silence that follows tells me whose body went down. I run toward the bedrooms. The first is locked, but shuffling and hushes come from within. The girls. They're safe for the moment, so I move on, hoping I can keep them that way. An open door draws me toward the next bedroom, where Ezra lies unconscious on the floor. A crimson pool forms a gruesome halo around his head. Next to him lies a bloody ceramic angel.

"No! Ezra, please, no."

Movement draws my eyes to the door. "*Ciao signorina.*" A sneer spreads across Riccardo's face, where a drop of Ezra's splattered blood slides down one cheek. "Your timing is perfect. We were just preparing to leave, and now you can join us."

There's no time to stop and think. No time to be afraid. Dad says the element of surprise is often your best defense. I grab the angel, leap and aim for his head, but he ducks and I whack his shoulder. His face contorts in pain, but pain quickly morphs into anger. He glares and curses, grabbing my arm and jerking it so my angelic weapon crashes against the wall. But it is the hand I didn't watch that is my undoing.

White-hot shards of pure agony shoot through my gut, like nothing I've ever felt or imagined. He jerks his hand back, retrieving the bloody knife from my side. Inconceivably, the pain escalates. It steals my breath, my scream, my thoughts. I crumble in slow motion, with darkness closing in before I even hit the floor. Everything in me tries to fight it. He's going to take the girls. He's going to force them into prostitution again. Myriam, Nada, little Farah. There is no one to help them.

Please, God. It is the only prayer I can manage. *Please.*

My body hits the floor, and my hand flops onto something soft and warm. Furry. *Furry.* As Riccardo walks out, triumphantly chuckling, I turn my head to see a huge dark shadow that could only be Liona. I wrap my hand around her massive paw. My vision is fading fast, but my heart…my heart feels hers. There is very little life in her, but a little is all I need.

"*Arrivederci*, young healer." Riccardo's footsteps head down the hall toward the locked bedroom. "It is unfortunate you became collateral damage. You could have been my pot of gold."

Everything in me fights to stay conscious. One hand presses my side in a futile attempt to contain the fountain of blood, while the other holds tight to Liona's paw.

Please.

But there is no miraculous answer from above. Life pours from me, soaking my hand, my clothes. Stealing my strength. Destroying my future. Liona begins to disappear. Darkness closes in as my time on earth draws to a close. Hazy swirls of gray and black become Mom placing my baby sister in my arms at the hospital. Julia's tiny face fades into Dad in his police uniform, picking me up from my fourth grade field trip while the kids gather around him and I beam with pride. But Dad evaporates and the shadowy swirls transform into me running down the soccer field as Melody and Kenji cheer from the stands, then blur into Misty and Tyler. They are walking through our front door to have dinner with us; the first of many. Now I'm roaming through the library book stacks with Julia, kissing Kenji at the carnival, helping Mom set up one of her food shows. The grays and blacks begin to brighten, becoming a golden glow that forms into Aunt Rita. *Oh, Auntie, I've missed you so much.* My heart leaps at the sight of her smiling, radiant, cancer free. Joyful. Are you here to welcome me? To guide me in? She shakes her head and blows a kiss.

And it lands on my heart.

My heart. It fills with the Heavenly warmth, strengthening my pulse, coursing through my veins with a sacred power. My pain dissipates as a wave of summer fills my chest and flows into my shoulders, then streams toward my palms.

Please, God, heal Liona, this magnificent and good-hearted dog You created. You are her only hope, and the only way to protect the girls.

My hand glides over Liona, feeling the feeble heartbeat fading from the poison that's shutting down her organs and rotting her insides. She is nearly gone, but the miracle is here. It fills me with sunlight as I rise above the earth, beyond the atmosphere, to the place where love never fails. Hope bursts in colors that shimmer like diamonds. Grace rains down in radiant hues of gold and silver as the healing warmth pools in my palms, intensifies in my fingertips and releases in rays of miraculous light into Liona.

The miracle ends, plunging me back into darkness, and with it, excruciating pain. The Gift has depleted what tiny bit of strength remained. Muffled sounds reach me. Shuffling feat. Crying. A door.

"Go." I can hardly manage a whisper. "Go, Liona. Save the girls."

A wet tongue licks my face, and the world disappears.

⊱✦⊰

Soft words echo inside my head; the sound of a soul reaching out for its creator, of a precious child petitioning a loving father. But the child is old, nearing the end of her earthly life, and the Father is timeless. Her heart cries out, aching, pleading for an answer. Her sorrow falls in warm droplets on my arm, but I am powerless to comfort her. A frail hand brushes the hair from my face before a gentle kiss graces my forehead, and still her pleas continue.

"Please, Lord, have mercy. Just one more time. One

more miracle." The sweet lullaby of prayers accompanies her request.

"Per favore, Dio." The voices rise together, ascending toward Heaven.

And Heaven responds.

Nonna's gnarled hand gently presses against my wound, and from it, warmth pours in where my life is still pouring out. The gentle warmth stems the crimson flow, then seals the tear. It ebbs and flows through my punctured kidney and severed artery, healing, binding, returning function where none existed. Diminishing the pain. Like a river of love, it courses through my veins, filling them with blood - fresh, life-giving blood that streams into my heart, its final destination. The warmth settles there. I lie on the carpet, awash in love and safe in the power of the Spirit. Earthly sounds return. Murmurs, crying, growling, and in the distance, the wail of sirens. I open my eyes…and gaze into the crystal blue eyes of Nonna Marie.

She smiles, tears streaming down her cheeks, and brings my hand to her lips for a kiss.

"Shilo Marie." Her fragile whisper brings more tears. "God is good. He give me The Gift once more."

The room erupts. Cheering, clapping, sobbing. A cacophony of "Thank-yous" and "Hallelujahs" surge toward Heaven. All of the nuns are there, even Mother Superior, who grabs my hand and presses it to her cheek, wet with tears. The girls are hugging each other, waving to me and calling my name. It is a crazy, beautiful, chaotic scene, bursting with more people and more happiness than one little bedroom can hold.

Through the open door, Liona is embracing her inner demon. Fully healed, she has Riccardo pinned to the floor with ferocious teeth bared in a snarl inches from his face. I wouldn't wish her fury on anyone…except maybe Riccardo. His feet are tied, but I'm not sure that was necessary. Terror freezes him to the floor. He doesn't even blink. Outside, the sirens shriek louder. The police are just minutes away.

I turn back to those topaz eyes, but they are unfocused now as Nonna's skin grows pale and she slumps. The miracle has taken its toll.

"You did it, Nonna. God gave you the power. I'm fine. I love you." I slowly sit, then work up to a standing position. Sister Francesca and I scoop her up and the crowd parts, giving us a path to the bed.

As we lay her down, Mother Superior joins us at her side. "I'm sorry I ever doubted you, Marie."

Nonna pats her hand. "No apologies," she whispers. "You have been good to me."

"Sleep, Nonna." I brush the silver curls from her forehead. "The Gift has exhausted you."

"I love you so very much, Shilo Marie. Tell your mama I love her, too. Now I am going home."

"Just rest here, Nonna. I'll stay with you."

She closes her eyes, but the hint of a smile remains on her pallid face. Peace softens her wrinkles, relaxes her hands.

"Yes. I will rest. And go home."

And then I remember. "Ezra! Where is he? He needs a doctor."

"The ambulance is coming. Ezra is alive. Look." Celeste points toward the living room, where Ezra sits on the couch with Red and a couple of the other nuns. His head is wrapped and he's holding a cup of water. He offers a weak wave with his free hand, and I return the gesture.

One by one, the nuns and girls come up to hug me, repeating the story of what transpired while I lay unconscious. It was only minutes, but it contained enough action and drama for a Hollywood blockbuster.

"Celeste ran across the field to call the police from Mother Superior's phone, while the rest of us ran in." Francesca begins the recap while the others nod to confirm the story. "Just then, Riccardo was shooing the girls out the back door. Then our Liona, oh, you should have seen her! She bounded out of the bedroom like a raging bull and tackled him, knocking that knife right out of his hand."

"We used string from the pastry boxes to tie his feet, while the others tended to Ezra." Red takes over, her Italian hands gesturing this way and that. "By that time, your nonna had found you and kneeled by your side."

"That's when Mother Superior and I came in." Now it's Celeste's turn to share the story. "While she prayed, we told the others that the police and ambulance were on the way. Everyone came into the bedroom to pray for you to be healed. Oh, except for Francesca and some of the girls. They were taking care of Ezra. Don't worry, Shilo, I think he's going to be okay."

It takes awhile before the hugging and storytelling draw to an end. Now I know, from Emily's part of the story, that Riccardo weaseled his way in by wearing one of the nuns' habits over his clothes, so the girls wouldn't recognize him as he walked across the field.

"He fooled us, but not Liona," Emily says. "She ran toward him as he neared the house, but Liona - she sure loves chicken - when he tossed it to her, she couldn't resist."

Francesca continues the story, explaining how Riccardo stole the cooked chicken from the convent refrigerator and soaked it in the rat poison from the closet. Liona wolfed down a fatal quantity before turning her attention back to Riccardo. By that time, the damage was done. The poison flowed through her veins like a river of death, weakening her with each passing minute. I cringe, knowing he would never have known about the poison if I hadn't questioned it in the hallway near his room. In her fragile state, poor Liona wobbled into the bedroom and collapsed just before we arrived.

"We were so scared." Emily is talking more now than she ever did when I visited the little stone house. "We didn't understand what was happening, or who was the person in the nun's clothing. And then..." She looks down. When she glances up again, her eyes shimmer with the memory of unspeakable things. "And then we recognized him. Riccardo. The devil. He grabbed Farah and held the knife to her throat."

My heart quivers. Farah has been through too many horrors already, and has just faced another.

Emily presses her hand to her heart. "We were so scared. He ordered us into the bedroom and took off the nun clothes. That's when we heard the van pull up and he locked us in."

A gentle squeeze to my hand draws my attention back to Nonna Marie. She is pale as pastry dough. Eyes closed. Breaths shallow. She's exhausted, but just needs to sleep for a few hours and she'll be okay.

I ask everyone to leave so Nonna can have peace and quiet while she recovers. When the last person leaves the bedroom, I take her hand in mine so I can hold it while she sleeps. But her hand is limp, and I no longer hear the shallow breaths.

"Nonna." My whisper receives no response. "Nonna, please, please open your eyes." My words grow louder. "Just for a moment, then you can rest. Wake up. Please." The last word chokes on a sob, because Nonna is not sleeping. She did exactly what she said she would do.

She went home.

Chapter 17

Melody

I sit on the edge of the hospital bed, my clunky braced leg dangling over the side, and every single part of me hurting. It took nearly three hours for all my doctors to sign off so I could be released. I'm dressed, packed, and going insane waiting for the stupid wheelchair that I'm required to ride in all the way to the car, where Dad and my flowers await.

"Relax, Mellie, they'll be here soon. I'm sure of it." Mom pats my leg, then stands to look out the window to the little courtyard below.

"Are you? It's been forever. This is ridiculous. Can you go ask them again?"

"They said forty-five minutes when I asked them forty minutes ago, so let's just wait a bit more." She turns to face me. "Do you need anything?"

"A wheelchair. And I don't even want *that*. I just want to go home."

"I know. Me, too. Hey, have you heard back from the adoption agency yet?"

Her attempt to distract me while we wait is obvious, but at least talking about the search for my parents is preferable to staring at the walls, though it's been pretty anticlimactic to this point.

"Just that one response to my email, with the generic 'we'll check into it.' They said it could be a couple weeks."

"At least it's in progress, right? Who knows what you might find out? Are you nervous?"

The question tumbles around my brain, searching for an answer. I've fantasized about meeting my birth parents for years, switching between which one was white or black in various scenarios, considering all the reasons why they might have left me. Sometimes they were international spies who fell madly in love, but knew my life would be in danger if they kept me. Other times they were teens, also madly in love, whose parents forced them to give me up. Getting the answer from the adoption agency will mean trading in the fantasy for reality. And if it actually leads to meeting them, well, "That could go in a million different directions," according to Mom, who wants me to be prepared. But I don't know how to prepare for them not wanting to meet me, or saying they had no interest in having a baby. Or finding out they're dead. The results of this search could be anything from wonderful to painful, or some weird combination of the two. My heart and mind just don't know what to do with that.

"You okay, Mellie?"

"What?"

"You disappeared on me. I asked if you were nervous about what you might discover."

"I am. And excited. And afraid. I guess I don't really know how to feel, but I want to keep going. It'll be good to have answers…whatever they turn out to be."

She stands next to me and takes my hand.

"I won't pretend to know how you feel, but I know how *I* feel, and I'm nervous, too." She opens her mouth to say something more, but closes it again and walks to the door, then returns with a smile. "Your throne is on its way, right down the hall, and your favorite nurse is coming, too. What's her name again? Donna?"

"Adanna." Finally. One minute longer and I would have started screaming...or imploding.

The big wheels enter first, followed by a volunteer I don't know and Adanna in her powder blue uniform. She's all smiles as she congratulates me on leaving, but something's off. Her eyes aren't smiling. Her jaw is stiff. We've talked enough the past eight days for me to know the true Adanna smile that lights her face like a brilliant sunrise. This isn't it. She greets my mom and stands at my side, ready to help me maneuver into the chair.

"Your big day has come, Melody." She grasps my arm like I'm made of crystal as I turn to plop butt-first into the seat. "Tonight, you can sleep in your own bed and have your mama's good cooking. No more hospital food."

"Yeah." Nothing follows, because what am I returning home to, exactly? My new reality. Physical therapy appointments and people visiting with cookies and flowers. Better than the hospital, but not by much. It was supposed to be rehearsals and dance classes. *Don't go there, Melody.* Chen's words echo in my head. *Thoughts like that will only set you back. That's the devil gettin' into your head. Push him out. Fight. Focus on moving forward.*

"Yeah." Let's try this again. "I really want to start moving more and strengthening my muscles. It'll be nice to see my friends, too."

Adanna scoots down so we are face to face, her ebony eyes peering into mine.

"You do that, Melody. Don't let this get you down. You are strong and smart and beautiful. Get better. Live your life and do not look back. Promise me."

Her lips quiver. There's a sheen to her eyes. Does she get this emotional with all her patients? Something in me hopes not, which is ridiculous, but also impossible to deny. I nod, wanting to wrap my arms around this person who was a total stranger just ten days ago.

"I will. Promise."

"And you have my cell phone number, if you'd like to meet with me and Chen."

"Right here." I pat my purse, where my cell holds both their numbers. "Bye, Adanna. Thank you for everything. I'll call. It would be great to have coffee with you guys. I'd love that."

"Bye, now. Take good care of *you*."

She stands, and Wheelchair Guy grabs the handles and unlocks the wheels. In a flash, I'm heading down the hall and toward the big glass door in the lobby. When we reach the car, Dad thanks the volunteer and scoops me up like he's going to carry me over a threshold, then sets me gently into the seat. Not embarrassing at all. Not one bit. The whole scenario is incentive enough for me to jump into PT with all I've got. This simply cannot continue. I want my body back, and I want it *now*.

As we cruise toward home, they offer to stop at every fast food place along the way. Apparently, saying "I'm not hungry" only applies to one food type at a time.

"How about one of those strawberry shakes you love so much?" Dad changes lanes so he can veer into the drive-through.

"Really, I don't want anything."

Mom points to my favorite taco stop. "Let's get you a taco. They're small."

"No, thanks. Really."

"A beef?"

"Still not hungry."

We're nearly home when Dad clears his throat – the cue that he's got something of significance to say.

"You know, lass, that boy wanted to be at the house when you got home."

"It's *Blake*, Dad. Can you call him Blake?"

"Fine. Blake. He wanted to surprise you, but your mom said you didn't want to see him for a while. I told him not today."

I wish Blake would stop trying to postpone the inevitable. We both know he's going to bail when he realizes the old Melody is gone for good. Might as well just get on with it.

"Thanks."

"He left a little somethin' for you, though. Asked if it was okay. We thought you'd like it."

"Seriously? Why did you let him do that? Why didn't you ask me?" I hear the harshness of my tone and regret it, knowing they've practically lived at the hospital the past ten days and spent a small fortune on flowers and stuffed animals.

"Now, Mellie." Mom chimes in from the back seat. "Just wait 'til you see it before you say anything."

"Whatever it is, he's getting it back."

"But it's—"

"I *don't* want it, Mom. Doesn't matter what it is."

We pull up to the house, where a familiar car is parked by the curb – a car I've ridden in countless times since the Giannellis bought it four years ago. Shilo's dad emerges and meets us in the driveway. I love that man, but my instincts tell me I'm not going to love the reason for his presence.

"Why is Mr. Giannelli here?"

"There's six steps, lass. I can carry you, but I was afraid of taking a chance. Don't want anything bad happenin' to my girl. Well...anything *else.*"

Oh, please, no. Getting scooped into the car was humiliating enough. This will be a nightmare of epic proportion.

"No, I can do it. I swear." Desperation saturates my words. "You guys can stand nearby. I'll manage." My right leg rises in an effort to show him I've got this.

Dad shakes his head, determination flashing in his Irish eyes. "No deal. Come on now, let's get this done. No arguments."

Thank God it's Mr. Giannelli, who's practically my second dad, and not one of the neighbors. He teases me mercilessly, of course, but I'd expect nothing less. They each slide one arm under my legs and one around my back and have me in the house before the humiliation can reduce me to rubble. Not pleasant, but not the horror I anticipated.

"Stay for coffee, Nick." Mom carries one of my flower arrangements to the dining room table and sets it next to five others. "I've got a fresh peach pie on the counter, and you can't say no to that."

But Mr. Giannelli does say "no," explaining they're packing for Italy and heading out tonight. I know that wasn't the plan. They visited the Sicily cousins for a week before Shilo went to the convent. They weren't going to return – Shilo was supposed to fly back on her own. And not for a couple more weeks. My heart crunches, eviscerating the remains of my embarrassment over being carried.

"What happened? Is Shilo all right?" Breathing fails me. If anything happened to Shilo…

"She's fine, Mel, but very upset. There was some trouble at the convent. It's all a little sketchy, but whatever happened must have been too much for her great grandma. She passed yesterday."

"What? Nonna Marie is dead?" Oh man, poor Shi. "That's awful. I'm sorry."

My parents join in with their own condolences as I strain to hold in my next question until it's appropriate to ask. The minute it takes for the expressions of sympathy to end feels like hours. Finally, there's a pause.

"What happened at the convent?"

He shakes his head. "Something about girls caught up in human trafficking and a bad guy trying to kidnap them. It's all pretty crazy and scary. Shilo got involved somehow. They say she saved those girls from a terrible fate and got hurt in the process, but she's fine now. All I know is we've got to get out there ASAP. I'm sure she'll tell you the details in a week or so when we get back."

Shilo's coming home. After next week, I won't have to

endure another minute of this torture without her, and she won't have to shoulder her grief without me. What could have happened? We have so much to catch up on, I won't even know where to start. But what must she think about these weeks of silence? First, I was swamped with rehearsals. There was zero time for actual letters, and she was in a no cell zone, so texting was out. Then…the accident. Everything in me wanted her at my side, which is exactly where she would have been if she knew I was lying all broken and battered in that hospital bed. But coming home meant putting her in danger from that stupid gang. I couldn't risk it. And I couldn't risk talking to her, because if I pretended everything was fine, she'd see right through me. Now it's been nearly a month of zero communication.

"Mr. Giannelli, can you tell Shilo something for me?"

"Sure."

"Please tell her I'm sorry. We haven't been in touch since she left. My fault. She texted and left messages, but—"

"She'll understand. When she finds out what happened to you, trust me, she'll understand. And yes, I will tell her."

As we wave goodbye from inside the entryway, something brushes against me. I shriek and jump back on my casted leg, which shoots pain into my other leg and lower back, causing me to shriek again. A gray and white blur screeches, leaps straight into the air, then hits the ground running. It bounds onto the couch, Dad's chair, and the coffee table before I can even take a breath, then stops in the bay window. Jade eyes gaze at me, round as Frisbees. Ears perk like miniature pyramids on its fluffy little head. But it's the tail that grabs my attention. Twice as long as the creature it's attached to, it drapes over the windowsill and down the wall in all its poufy splendor.

I turn to Mom. "What just happened?"

"Meet Cleo." Mom grins, shaking her head at the most adorable kitten I've ever seen. "She's a four-month-old terror, but she's such a sweetheart, we don't mind her craziness."

"But how? When?" Full sentences fail me as the ultimate definition of cuteness continues to peer at me from her spot in the sunlight.

"Oh, that's the surprise from the boy." Dad laughs. "I mean Blake."

I wobble over to the window and hold out my hand for Cleo to sniff. She does, then follows up with a lick. When I stroke the puff of fur extending from her cheek, the resulting purr could probably be heard by the neighbors.

"I love you more than anything in the entire world," I whisper. She answers by nudging my hand with her head, which I kiss. And kiss again. I'd almost forgotten what it feels like. It's been so many years since my cat, Butterscotch, left this world and simultaneously broke my heart. After that, ballet happened. There was never time for pets with all the classes and rehearsals. Never time for so many things. Not that I cared. Ballet was…everything. But this kitten is like cotton candy and fresh snow and summer mornings and all wonderful things wrapped in fluff. I've been a pet owner for all of three minutes, and already this fur ball with the crazy tail is firmly entwined around my heart.

Dad joins me at the window and scratches Cleo behind the ears.

"Of course, since you don't want anything from Blake, we can take her back to the shelter tomorrow."

"Over my dead body."

"That's what I thought." He laughs. "Oh, that Blake."

I scoop Cleo into my arms, and the purr volume increases. "What about him?"

"Gotta give the lad credit. He's not goin' down without a fight. Not that I blame him."

"It's over, Dad. Cleo was a really sweet gesture, but it's over."

As he walks away to grab my suitcase, he mumbles something under his breath that sounds an awful lot like "we'll see." But I've already seen. I've peered into the future with the eyes of a realist, and where Blake's concerned, the vision was nothing short of painful.

But that won't stop me from keeping the cat.

Chapter 18

Shilo

I've never seen so many tears in one place. In addition to the The Sisters of Saint Teresa, the church is packed with nuns from all over, refugee families from the school, the meadow house girls, Ezra's family, and a ton of relatives. Even Liona was allowed to attend. She lays with paws extended and head down next to the casket, grief-stricken as much as any human in the room. Mom, Dad, and Julia sit with me in the first pew, in full view of Nonna's exquisitely carved casket, handmade by Ezra. Celeste's beautifully painted birds adorn the lid, which is propped up next to the alter.

Serenity graces Nonna's face. I gaze upon it with emotions torn over the pain of losing her, gratitude for her sacrifice, and the joy of knowing she is in a place of love so pure, and light so brilliant, that darkness cannot enter. A place I've been blessed to merely glimpse in the midst of healings. She is with the Lord, and there is no place she would rather be. And yet, the tears continue to flow.

Father Antonio walks up to the pulpit and says, "Peace be with you," then talks about Nonna, using words like can-do spirit, a servant's heart, feisty, quick to laugh and always ready to lend a helping hand.

"But when I first met Marie, she was a broken soul, with no interest in engaging with the world. She had lost sight of God's grace and mercy. She could no longer see the sunlight in the world, only the darkness." He steps away from the pulpit and moves closer to the assembly of mourners.

"I believe, with all my heart, that her arrival here was guided by God's own hand. As time went on, she began to grow closer to the Lord. She was washed anew by the Holy Spirit. She came back to life with a vigor not often seen. When someone was feeling down, she was there to encourage. When she saw a problem, she wouldn't give up until she reached a solution *and* made sure that solution became a reality." He turns with a subtle smile to gesture toward the dog flopped on the church floor. "And Marie loved animals. Especially our Liona here."

At the sound of her name, Liona raises her colossal head and acknowledges Father Antonio with a mournful whimper, then lays it down again.

"And she loved children. When she learned about the refugees, she didn't rest until she found a way to help. When she heard about the brothel, she insisted we take action. I'm told it's better for me not to know about some of those actions."

Even through their tears, some of the nuns smile and exchange glances, while the meadow house girls break into full-blown sobs. The priest gives them a moment to settle down before proceeding. He goes on to list other ways in which Nonna touched many hearts that will feel the vacancy she leaves in the world. After prayers and music, he signals the pallbearers – my Dad, Ezra, my cousins, and Domenico - to carry the casket to the hearse.

The sky mourns Nonna's death with a blanket of slate gray clouds, as though the sun could not bear to shine on our dismal gathering. We pray again as the casket is lowered.

And it is done.

∽

I'm sitting between Mom and Jules, three hours outside Chicago, with Dad across the aisle. Jules had offered me the window seat, but I knew she'd be mesmerized by the geography from miles above the earth. Plus, it might keep her distracted enough to stop asking if I'm okay. We enter into a cloud bank and she turns to me.

"You okay?"

"Yeah. I was just thinking about Farah. I hope she likes living with Ezra's family. It was so cool he offered to adopt her. Didn't see that coming."

"I liked him. He'll be an excellent father to her. You can tell." Jules glances back toward the window to make sure she's not missing anything, but we're still stuck in a blanket of white. "His kids seemed pretty nice, too. And now that Farah's healed from that ulcer, she won't be in pain all the time."

If only that were true. Spending the night at the meadow house provided the opportunity to heal her, but didn't erase the horrors she's faced. Or the ache of missing her family. "Yeah, but she's dealing with other kinds of pain, Jules. We should both pray for her, and the other girls, too. I hope the police and sisters can connect at least some of them with their families."

"Me, too."

The flight attendant stops by with pretzels and asks if we want beverages. Jules has been eyeing the cart for the past ten minutes, anxiously anticipating this moment.

"Yes, please!" No doubt she's the most enthusiastic passenger he's encountered. He smiles at her and provides the list of choices, unaware Julia has it memorized.

"Ginger ale, please, with a wedge of lemon and no ice and two napkins." In Julia's world, this is a specialty drink. Her go-to for holidays and birthdays. When she heard they had it on the cart, her joy meter skyrocketed off the charts.

"Coming right up, Miss."

Her eyes catch every move to ensure no ice touches the precious ginger ale, because that will 'dilute the flavor,' and that he doesn't accidentally give her a lime instead of a lemon. It happened once, and I thought the girl was going to need therapy.

She thanks the attendant and squeezes her little wedge into the soda, then cups both hands around the precious drink, sipping slowly. Eyes closed. Savoring. She is ridiculously weird, and I couldn't be more grateful to have her as my little sister. We sit in silence as she relishes the first few sips. I stare into the nothingness of the cloud bank, wondering what I'll find when I get home. Brittany and Lauren will want to get together immediately, and Kenji will be home in a few days, but what about Mel?

"You look sad, Shi. You should have gotten a ginger ale with lemon."

Somehow I don't think that would have resolved anything.

"Not sad, just want to get home and see what's going on with Mel. She's been so weird. Literally zero contact since I left." The little voice in my head whispers *something's wrong* for the hundredth time. It just doesn't make sense. We've been through everything together. Everything. Then, poof, she disappears from my life.

"Well, at least she's finally home from the hospital."

"*What?*"

Our eyes lock for half a heartbeat before hers lower to her hands.

"Oops. Never mind."

"What? What are you talking about?"

"Julia!" Mom's glare crosses the aisle, shoots past me, and smacks into Julia. "We talked about this! I told you I'd tell Shilo when we got home."

"Sorry."

The girl is a walking encyclopedia, but she can't keep a

secret to save her life.

"What is going on? What happened to Mel?" My pulse quickens. My heart fears the answer.

"I'm sorry, honey. Melody made us promise not to tell you because she was afraid you'd come back and didn't want you in danger. We agreed with her."

She goes on to tell me about the fall, the prognosis for her injuries, the end of her professional ballet career. Each syllable weights my heart until I can hardly breathe, and simultaneously fills my head with white-hot anger. They should have told me. I might have been able to heal her. Maybe I still can, but all the pain and heartache she's gone through could have been avoided. My family loves Mel. She's one of us. The fury surges through me, nearly thwarting my ability to speak. Nearly.

"How could you have done this?" My voice rises with each word, but I don't care who hears. "Has everyone gone crazy? What were you thinking?"

Dad leans across the aisle. "Not here. Not now."

"It's *Melody*." The words emerge through gritted teeth. "*Our* Melody."

"I know, and we'll talk about it, but not here." He goes back to tearing open his mini bag of airline pretzels.

Mom places her hand on my arm, which I jerk away.

"She insisted you not come, honey."

"Of course she did. She was protecting me. She doesn't know what I can do. She doesn't know I could have…"

"*Might* have. You don't know for sure. And the risk was too great, though fortunately it's not as much of a risk now. That gang has kind of fallen apart."

"I can't believe you let her go through all that." I don't care about the volume, or the couple staring at me from two rows up and over. "It would have been worth the risk."

Dad shoots me 'the look' and turns fully sideways to face me. "Not to us. Not to Melody. End of discussion until we're back home."

There's no point in going around in circles. Nothing I say now can undo the damage, but that doesn't ease my anger.

"Just drop me off at her house on the way home."

"That won't work, Shilo." Mom lowers her voice to a whisper. "Even if you can...accomplish what you're hoping to, you can't do it in plain view of all of them. And what happens when you, you know...sleep?"

"Don't know. Don't care. I just want to go."

She shakes her head. "It's been a long day. I just hope you're ready for whatever happens next."

By the time we get to Mel's, the sun has set and it's nearly nine. She's not expecting me and doesn't know I know about the fall. I refrain from texting, fearing she'll tell me not to come, though I don't know why. Mom says it's been tough on her. I can't begin to imagine.

Her mother answers the door, surprise giving way to smiles and hugs. It's been awhile since I've been enveloped in a Mrs. O'Hara hug, and the warmth of it envelops my head with memories of countless sleepovers, dinners and annual Halloween parties spanning more than a decade. And it all began on the swings at Veteran's Park.

"I'm so sorry to hear about your great-grandma." Brows knit as compassion floods her face.

"Thank you."

"How did it happen?"

The question takes me by surprise. I hadn't considered people would ask, though it's a normal thing to say.

"Oh...she died in her sleep. It was peaceful. Very sad, but she didn't suffer."

She shakes her head. "Poor thing. I'm glad you got to spend time with her before it happened."

"Well look who's back from the mountains of Sicily." Mr. O'Hara waves me over from his big comfy recliner, where Mel and I used to sit, smashed together, and watch Saturday morning cartoons. He eases out of the chair and I'm wrapped in hug number two. "We haven't seen you in forever."

"I know, it's been too long. How's Mel doing?"

"Why don't you ask Mel?" She grins at me from the top of the stairs. "What are you doing here? When did you get back? Why didn't I know?"

"You don't get to ask questions. Why didn't I know what happened to *you*? Why did I find out *accidentally* from Julia on the plane?"

Melody laughs. "Man, that girl still can't keep a secret." With her leg in a brace, she takes a step toward the stairs.

"No, wait, I'll come up." I tell the O'Haras again how great it is to see them and head upstairs to my best friend, who knows me better than anyone and has shared all of life's joys and sorrows. She'll reach out to hug me, and in that moment, I will know. The warmth will come...or it won't. I fight the fear that threatens to grip me. Nonna Marie said to trust God, because only He knows how each life touches another. "He sees the whole glorious painting," she said that first day when we walked through the olive grove. "We see only a brush stroke." But I need this brush stroke to be beautiful. Perfect. I need this brush stroke to be nothing short of miraculous.

I reach the top, where Melody stands with her pasted-on smile, trying to hide the pain coursing through her body and heart, but I see it in her eyes. She opens her arms, and we hug like there's no tomorrow.

Chapter 19

Melody

Shilo's being weird. So much has happened, and I know she's tired from a fourteen-hour trip and sad about her nonna, but still, there's something more. Something veiled behind the shimmer in her eyes. She denies it, but I see through her words. And even though she came straight here from the airport, she's sure not saying much. She should be bursting with Sicily stories, instead of sitting in my beanbag chair, staring at her hands.

I give her a nudge with my crutch. "Hey, you all right?"

She looks up, those crystal blue eyes contrasting with the pale hue of her face. Maybe she's sick, and doesn't want me to worry.

"I should be asking *you* that question," she says, and smiles the smile of someone who is absolutely not all right.

"You already did. Now I'm asking *you*. What's going on, Shi? I may be a little battered and bruised, but I can still see you."

"It's just…"

I wait, but she can't seem to get the rest out. The struggle boiling inside her is so intense, it's almost visible. Shilo's inability to communicate is a rarity that unsettles me. In a desperate and ridiculous attempt to help her, I grab the toy guitar she gave me in second grade and begin to strum.

"Oh Shilo Marieee, I wish you'd tell meee." I sound like a cat in heat and the scratchy guitar music is the perfect accompaniment.

"Stop. You're killing me." She smiles. For real, this time.

"It got you to talk, didn't it? So again, what's going on?"

Shilo sighs, and those gorgeous eyes shimmer again. Where that girl got eyes like that, I'll never know. She glances at her hands – what's the deal with her hands tonight? – and back to me. "I want to make it all better. It's hard. Much harder than I thought. I want to heal you and I can't."

"Of course you can't, you crazy girl." What did she expect? A miracle? Still, her compassion touches my heart. "I'm going to be fine. I just have to do all the PT stuff, according to my doctor, and stay perky and positive, according to my therapist, and keep the faith, according to Father Ryan. Oh, and be grateful I'm not in a wheelchair or lying in the morgue, according to Adanna."

"Adanna? Sounds familiar. Oh, the hospital. She was Tyler's nurse, right? Really nice. Cool accent. *That* Adanna?"

"Yeah, she was *my* nurse, too. We talked a lot. She's...interesting. Has a backround you wouldn't believe. Anyway, she really helped me get through that first week."

"I should have been the one doing that."

Her guilt is not unexpected. I knew she'd be drowning in it, and prepared my little speech before she got here.

"No, you shouldn't have. From what I heard, you were exactly where you needed to be. And even though I don't have the details, I know there's a bunch of girls who are glad you were on that mountaintop in Sicily. So do not spend another second on stupid, meaningless guilt when you were a hero to those girls." I lean the crutches against my dresser and sit down among the herd of newly acquired stuffed animals.

"Anyway, I was surrounded by people who loved me.

Sometimes so much I could hardly breathe. One more might have killed me."

Shilo grabs the huge koala my dad gave me in the hospital and hugs it as she talks.

"Thanks. I needed to hear that tonight. And I'm glad Adanna was there for you."

"She gave me her number. Said she'd meet with me whenever I feel like talking."

"She wants to meet with you? That's kinda weird."

"No, it didn't feel weird at all. I really liked talking to her. I didn't feel like she was just my nurse. It was more like — don't laugh — like I've known her forever." I don't say the rest, like being with Adanna feels like home. That I've already called her, and it's only been a few days.

"Well, I'm back now, and you've literally known *me* forever, so if you want to talk…"

"For sure."

"How's Blake been through all of this?"

Guilt weights my heart. Poor Blake. He tried so hard to be my shining knight, and I kept knocking him right off that white horse.

"He was great. I was…less than great. Terrible, actually. I figured he's not gonna want the not-a-ballerina Melody, so I decided to spare myself the heartbreak and hate him."

Blue eyes shoot daggers at me. "I'm gone a month and you go and get stupid on me."

"Thanks for your support."

"Seriously, that's the dumbest thing I've ever heard."

I throw my stuffed bunny at her. "Have you considered sensitivity training?"

She grabs the bunny and whips it at me, but misses. "Mel, that boy adores you. What does he care about your career path?"

"I don't know. It's not just that. Look at me. I'm a mess, and I might be a mess for a long time. There's so much going on right now, and —"

"Mellie!" Mom calls from the bottom of the stairs, and I know what's coming next. "Time for your medicine, and you should get to sleep soon."

"Okay," I yell back, then turn to Shilo with an eyeroll. "They're driving me insane."

"No doubt. After all, you *are* their sweet little miracle."

It's the phrase that was quoted in an adoption magazine years ago, and Shilo has never let me live it down.

"Stop. You're horrible."

"Hey, be nice or I won't bring over your Sicily presents."

By the time we say goodbye, I'm exhausted, and I'm guessing she is, too. The strain of walking around with a cast and doing the exercises wears me down, and the meds zap what little remains of my energy. But as I lay staring at my ceiling fan, I can't stop thinking about the transformation that took place in her after we hugged. Heartbreak shadowed her face and glazed her eyes. I replay the moment, searching for clues. She walked up the stairs smiling, we hugged, we released, and she grasped my hands, which she hasn't done since we were ten. When she let go, her face was…different. But not in a way other people would notice. What filled her eyes with anguish? What trepidation drew lines on her forehead? I fall asleep wondering what's going on with my best friend, and why I didn't want to tell her I'm meeting Adanna and Chen for coffee tomorrow.

Mom opens the café door for me, and Adanna waves me over from a booth by the window. I clomp toward her with my braced leg and crutch, fighting the painful image of the grace and poise I possessed just weeks ago. She greets us with a smile, saying Chen just texted about having the flu. A wisp of disappointment is quickly replaced by a small voice saying "Better Chen than Adanna." But why? I like Chen. A lot.

Adanna gestures toward the red vinyl seat. "Please, stay and join us, Bridget."

"Oh, that's so sweet, but no thank you." Mom holds my crutches as I awkwardly maneuver into a sitting position. "Mellie and I have a lot of time together these days. I'm sure she could use a break from her mom." Her emphasis on 'mom' is not lost on me. She laughs and faces me. "You just text me when you're done, honey. I'll come get you."

"If I may, I would be delighted to save you the effort." Adanna graces Mom with her enchanting smile. "I would be happy to take her home."

Mom thanks her and leaves as I look into those hauntingly familiar eyes once again.

"Is something wrong, Melody?"

Apparently, I gazed a bit too long. "Is there any chance we know each other from somewhere? It's just…I keep feeling like we do."

"So, it is not just my crazy head thinking these thoughts. You are just as crazy." She laughs, but when the laughter fades, she looks at me in a way that reaches way down into my heart.

I hear the coffee shop door open and Adanna glances toward it.

"Your mother has returned. It looks like you forgot something." She picks up a packet of sweetener and tears off the corner as Mom draws closer, dangling my purse.

"Melody Yasmeen O'Hara, I swear you'd forget your head if it wasn't screwed on." She laughs as she hands me the purse, but Adanna is not laughing, or smiling. Or breathing. She drops her sweetener packet into her coffee, paper and all. Mom doesn't notice, and turns to leave, but even after she's gone, Adanna remains silent.

"Is something wrong?"

The packet floats like a pink raft in a tiny black sea.

"Adanna, is something wrong?"

Deep ebony cheeks fade to ash. "Your middle name.

How did your parents choose it?"

"When they picked me up from the adoption agency, the woman gave them –"

"A torn strip of yellow paper with blue lines." She cuts me off, her words quiet. Monotone. "Very small. It held the name Yasmeen."

Chills zip up my spine and settle at the base of my neck. My muscles tense, my heart races like a skydiver awaiting her first jump. Part of me wants to push off, leaving the plane behind as I hurtle through the air toward an unknown landing spot. Part of me wants to run back to familiar territory, where I'm safe and risk-free. But most of me is ready to take that leap.

Because in my top dresser drawer, a tiny box holds that piece of yellow paper, given to my mother from the lady at the adoption agency.

"How did you know?" I hold my breath, fearing her response. Craving it. Wanting to hear it in that lovely accent. Aching to hear the answer I already know.

"It was tucked into the side of your diaper," she continues. "I wanted my daughter to have my mother's name."

My lungs forget how to breathe. Fingers clench the edges of the vinyl booth.

"My mom wanted me to have *her* mother's name." I force the words through dry lips. "So she used the name on the paper for my middle name."

We sit frozen, eyes fixed on each other. No words. Neither of us knowing what to say or do. Adanna moves first, reaching into her purse and setting money on the table."Come." She stands and reaches out her hand to help me. I grab her hand - my *mother's* hand – and clumsily slide out of the booth as she gives me the crutch. In moments we are in her car, but she doesn't start the engine. She stares at me, silently crying, while I do the same.

"Your eyes." She shakes her head. "Everything inside me knew I had looked into those beautiful eyes before. My whole self knew there was something special about you."

She takes my hand and places it against her cheek, then kisses my palm. "But my heart was afraid to believe." She wraps her arms around my neck. I hug her back, both of us sobbing. The angle is killing my knee, but I don't care. My mother – my real mother with her beautiful black skin and smile as bright as the summer sun, is holding me for the first time in seventeen years.

Chapter 20

Shilo

I can't understand a word Melody is saying. I keep hearing "my mother," but sobs garble everything else. My mind races. A heart attack? Car accident? If anything happened to Mrs. O'Hara...

"Is your mom all right?"

She draws a breath. "Uh huh."

Silence, followed by sniffing.

"Are you sure? Should I call an ambulance?"

"No!" Deep breaths follow – Mel's way of trying to compose herself during a meltdown. "Come over. Now."

I promise to be right there and hang up, wondering what's in store. If it was an emergency, she would have called 911, so what could have happened to Mrs. O'Hara? In a lucky moment, the car is actually available and I get there in minutes. Mel answers the door and I fight to suppress my shock. On the rare occasions she cries, she lets loose like a hurricane. But today...today she must have reached a whole new level, because her eyes are nearly puffed shut and she's still struggling to catch her breath. I glance at Mrs. O'Hara, who appears physically fine, but weirdly somber.

"*What* is going on?"

Warm, pudgy arms wrap around me. "Don't you worry, Shilo, everything is fine. Let Mellie tell you." She kisses the top of my head and retreats to the kitchen.

Melody leans her crutch against the wall and plops down on the couch. "You won't believe this. You ready?"

"What? Say it already." I join her on the couch, hands clasped, mind grasping at a million possibilities.

"I met my mother." Her faces scrunches up, like she's about to lose it again, but she takes a breath and waits for my response.

Her mom is steps away from us in the kitchen. She would have warned me if Mel was experiencing memory loss. Wouldn't have said "everything is fine." Mrs. O'Hara is the only mother Mel has ever known, so this makes no sense unless...

It hits me like a thunderbolt. "*What*? Seriously? I mean...seriously?"

She laughs, nodding so hard I fear for her healing brain. "Yes! Yes, it's true. And just wait. You won't believe who it is. Someone you know. Well, kinda."

My mind whirls around faces of people I 'kinda' know, trying to figure out who could possibly be Melody's mother. I don't even know if I'm looking for someone black or white, because she never knew which parent was which. The DNA test just showed Nigerian and Russian.

"I don't know, Mel. Honestly, I can't imagine." And then, amidst the faces flashing through my mind, I see brown eyes and a smile as white as the collar on her nurse's uniform. Mel's words from last night echo in my head. *I feel like I've known her forever.* I shake my head. "Oh, man. It's Adanna."

A grin and fresh flow of tears confirms my guess.

"Wow. This is unbelievable."

"I know, right? And if you think *that's* unbelievable, wait 'til you hear her story."

For the next twenty minutes, I'm completely captivated. Mel starts at the beginning, with the young Adanna leaving her family in a poor Nigerian village in hopes of sending them money from her nanny job in the United States. Days later, she's caught in an unimaginable nightmare as her captor, Vlad, forces her friends into prostitution and keeps Adanna for his own sadistic pleasures. She tells me about the birth, *her* birth, and Adanna's gut-wrenching pain as Vlad gave her child away. It is inconceivable that my best friend entered the world amidst so much heartache and drama.

"What did she do?"

"She escaped!"

The next chapter of Adanna's story continues to keep me mesmerized. But as awful as it was, at least she was with people who truly cared about her, and kept her safe. And then there was Owen, who never gave up on her, even through the years of depression and her obsession with finding her baby. It's weird to think the O'Haras were experiencing so much joy over the same child that was causing Adanna so much pain. The drama continues to unfold, with Adanna getting married, graduating from nursing school, and having two more children.

Melody stops talking, and we sit in silence. No words seem sufficient to follow a story like that.

"And then I fell."

I'm not sure how to respond to that, either, so I simply nod and wait.

"I was a thousand percent sure it was the end of the world. Honestly, Shi, once they said I wouldn't be able to dance professionally, I didn't even care if I lived." Her eyes glisten, and my heart aches again from the guilt of not being here to comfort and encourage her. Eleven years of friendship, and I'm a continent away when she needs me most.

"Didn't even want to do the exercises or anything. But Adanna came along, and I started to feel this tiny flicker of hope. Then she introduced me to Chen—"

"Who's Chen?"

"This basketball player who was Olympics-bound until

she had a horrible accident. I'll get to that later. Anyway, after spending time with Chen, I felt that flicker brighten a little more, know what I mean? And then this happened. I mean, I met *my mother*! Can you believe it? And it all started with that fall."

"So…you're glad about the fall?"

"No! Don't be stupid. I hate what happened. Hate it so much. I haven't even wanted to see Jenna or my ballet friends, not that they have much time to see me, anyway. But I get it. Just a few weeks ago, I never had time for anything, either." She shifts, but can't seem to find a comfortable position. "What if I wasn't meant for that life? What if there's a different path for me? What if the different path, and meeting my mother, couldn't have happened if something didn't prevent me from pursuing ballet? But here's the thing, why couldn't I have had ballet *and* Adanna?"

Her words race like a runaway train. Hands gesture. Eyes widen.

"Seriously, why couldn't I have had it all? It's not like I'm asking for someone to hand me anything. I worked so hard to make it in ballet. And other people get to have their real moms without sacrificing a thing."

I cringe, hoping Mrs. O'Hara didn't hear that part. I want to remind Mel that there are also other people who don't get to have *anything*: parents, dreams, education…food. But she's still racing forward at a hundred miles an hour.

"And I have a little brother and sister! Can you believe it? Bayo is twelve. His name is really Adebayo. Ketandu is nine, and they call her Keta. Isn't that cute? Oh, man, I can't wait to meet them. Sorry I'm rambling. It's been so crazy and awful and wonderful all mixed together. My brain is fried. My emotions are on overload."

Overload might be an understatement. The girl is going to tumble right off the tracks if she doesn't slow down.

"Deep breaths, Mel. Deep breaths."

She dramatically draws in her breath and releases it,

which earns her a thumbs-up.

"It reminds me of what Nonna Marie said, that we never know how one life impacts another. We only see a brushstroke, not the whole painting."

"I like that. I wish I could have met your nonna. Oh, man, I've hardly given you a chance to talk about her and everything that happened in Sicily."

Everything that happened in Sicily. I sigh, wondering when or if I'll ever be able to talk about it. Nonna's death is still a raw wound on my heart, while the image of what those girls endured sends silent screams echoing through the canyons of my mind. Worse, it makes me ache for the millions more who haven't been rescued.

"It's fine. You've got life-changing things going on here, so spotlight on Melody." We were eight when Mel's cat, Butterscotch, ran away and I said 'spotlight on you today' to make her stop crying. We did whatever she wanted the whole day.

"You don't have to spotlight me, Shi. We've both got a truckload of stuff going on."

"I stand by my spotlight. You did it for me when Aunt Rita died. Now it's your turn."

She shifts again, stuffing a pillow behind her back.

"Thanks. I guess you don't get much more life-changing than ending your career before it starts, and finding your real mom."

I wince at the 'real mom' again, wondering if Mrs. O'Hara heard.

Mel cocks her head. "What?"

"Your mom might hear you," I whisper.

"So? It's not like she doesn't know what's going on."

"Think about it." I continue to keep my voice low. "She couldn't have kids, then you came along and changed her life. You've been her whole world. She might be hurt if she hears you call Adanna your 'real mom.'"

My concern is dismissed with a wave of her hand. "She's

fine."

Maybe, but there's no off-key Irish ballads emanating from the kitchen today. There is, however, a kitten streaking my way like a gray and white lightning bolt. It leaps onto the couch and into Melody's lap, where it stops to examine me with emerald eyes. A tail made for a much larger feline hangs over Melody's lap and halfway down the couch.

"Who is *this*?"

Melody laughs. "My crazy, adorable, wonderful Cleo." She scratches the white patch between Cleo's ears. "She's four months old. Blake got her for me. She was here the day I came home from the hospital. Whenever I sit on the couch, she jumps up and —"

"Whoa. Go back to the part about Blake. Tell me more about what's been going on with you guys, other than he's been great, and you've been ridiculous."

"I don't know. Let's not talk about him right now. I just want some space from him and from even thinking about him."

If Mel wants space, she can have it. It's her day to get what she wants. But I can't help but wonder what Blake could have done to make her feel that way. I lean down so I'm face to face with the fluffy tornado, and rub under her chin. The resulting purr is nearly deafening.

"You are absolutely the cutest thing I've ever seen, but your tail is preposterous. Mel, what's with this tail?"

"I know, right? I love it. And I love *her*. I never had time for pets after Butterscotch. Now I have a cat *and* my real mom."

A gasp turns our eyes toward the kitchen, where Mrs. O'Hara had silently emerged with a plate of homemade shortbread. She stands frozen, round face paler than usual, green eyes reflecting the open wound created by Melody's words. Her pain saturates the atmosphere of the flowery living room, silencing everyone except the purring Cleo. For no apparent reason, she leaps from Mel's lap to the recliner to the bay window, breaking the tension with her extraordinary cuteness. But the hurt continues to hover.

"Here's some cookies." Mrs. O'Hara sets the plate on the coffee table and walks away. No smile. No commentary on how her grandmother brought the secret recipe from Ireland, or how Mrs. O'Hara left out the sugar the first time she made them, but Mr. O'Hara ate them anyway.

I shake my head. "I told you," I whisper.

Mel fiddles with the latch on her leg brace. "You're overthinking it. She's perfectly okay with all this. She knows Adanna's my real mom."

"She might be, if you didn't say stuff like 'now I have a mother.' How would you feel if she discovered a long-lost biological daughter and just blew you off?"

"Okay, Shi. I get it. Man, I've had enough to deal with, you know? Give me a break."

Her angry tone seems to be aimed more at herself than at me, so I swallow my initial retort and opt for something kinder and gentler.

"Sorry. I'm sure she'll be fine if you just talk to her." I munch on a shortbread and say, a little louder than usual, how delicious it is, but the resulting "thank you" from the kitchen is politely monotone. For the next hour, Mel tells me about Cleo, Chen, and Adanna, and I tell her about the sisters, learning photography, …and Domenico.

"What do you mean he kissed you? Did you kiss him back? Do Italians kiss different? Like…hotter? How could you do that to Kenji? You're crazy in love with him!"

"Geez, girl, you're like a living, breathing National Enquirer. I told you, it was just a moment, and then it passed and I pushed him away. Never happened again. And yeah, just between us, it was hot. The boy knows how to kiss. But so does Kenji, and he's still my one and only."

"What time is he getting back tomorrow?"

"Late afternoon. Can't wait. The next twenty-four hours is going to feel like a lifetime."

"Are you going to tell him about, you know?" She puckers up and makes obnoxious kissing noises.

"We've been apart for almost five weeks. I think there's better Sicily stories to share than that one." My flippant answer satisfies Mel, but doesn't begin to calm the agitation churning in my stomach each time I ask myself that question. Will I tell Kenji? We've been apart for so long, and before that, tons of drama and a break-up. Telling him about one stupid, meaningless kiss would cause more trouble than it's worth. I decide to stray off the Kenji topic by circling back to her relationship issues.

"What about Blake? Are you together? Not? I'm a little lost on whether this is a thing, or an ex-thing. And if it's ex, then I totally blame you."

Mel shifts again, clumsily maneuvering her braced leg to a different position. "I don't know, Shi. But you're right. If we're done, it's all on me. He did everything right. Me? Not so much."

Her gaze lowers to her lap, making it impossible to see her eyes. Even so, I know they're shadowed by sadness. I place my fingertips under her chin, like Dad used to do when I was little.

"Look at me." She complies. "Fix it. You can do this. I did it when I pushed Kenji away a few months ago. You can do anything, Melody Yasmeen O'Hara. You survived smashing to the stage floor, and according to Adanna, you survived getting beaten even before you were born. So a little thing like getting your boyfriend back should be a piece of cake."

Mel smiles, and opens her mouth to respond, but whatever's she's about to say gets stolen by the telephone ringing. She grabs it, listens, then hangs up. "Mom got it in the kitchen."

"So explain why your forehead is all scrunched up. Everything okay?"

"Don't know. It was a lawyer. Sounded super formal. He

asked if she was Bridget O'Hara and said he needed to talk to her about me." Concern darkens those ebony eyes. "You don't think Adanna would try to get custody of me, do you? I love her, but this is my home and I don't want to leave my parents. I'm under eighteen, do I even get a voice in it?"

The irony of her words makes me smile inside. A moment ago she referred to Adanna as her 'real mom,' but even the remote possibility of leaving the O'Haras sends her into high anxiety mode.

"I don't know, but don't worry." Reassuring her comes easy. I know this family all too well. "Your parents aren't going to let you go. The Hulk couldn't pry you from the arms of that red-headed woman in the kitchen."

"Lawyers cost a fortune, Shi. They don't need that, especially with the medical bills coming our way." She glances toward the kitchen, then back to me, with worry lines still intact across her brow. My best friend has bounced through way too many emotions in the past hour. That can't be good for the healing process.

"Stop jumping to conclusions. You don't even know what the call was about. Plus, your broken head has enough problems right now. Don't pile stress on top of it, too. It'll all be fine. You'll see."

Her hands clench the edge of the couch as her brows scrunch together. She doesn't believe me. She's way too quick to see the negative side of everything these days, which is not the way my best friend was wired up. The observation unsettles me, because I've always loved her optimism and fiery spirit, but that accident…it did a whole lot more than damage her body.

Kenji's late. He said he'd be over at four and that passed almost twenty minutes ago. Not a big deal on a normal day, but this is *the* day, the one we've been waiting for since we both got exiled to separate places. Each minute his car doesn't cruise down the street is pure torture. My eyes fixate on the end of our block. Come on, come on, *come on*. The silent urging works. He rounds the corner, and I take a breath I've been holding since this morning. He pulls up, emerges from his car and I run to him like he's been away at war. Oh, those dark, smoky eyes that dissolve me from the inside out. That floppy hair. That smile. My heart leaps out of my chest as he wraps his arms around me and I melt into the warmth of his body.

"Blue." The whispered word lifts me ten feet off the ground. "My Blue. I missed you so much it physically hurt."

He holds me tighter, and the world dissolves. We kiss, and I wonder how I ever let someone else kiss me when he's everything I want forever.

"Let's go in back. We'll have the deck to ourselves."

"Hold on." He reaches into the car and pulls out the largest bouquet of flowers I've ever received, or seen, in my life. Three red roses fill the center, surrounded by brightly colored mums, daisies, and things I can't even identify. No way can he afford something so extravagant.

"You're crazy." We head toward the backyard. "This is too much. Seriously."

"Nothing's too much for my girl."

"They're amazing, but they must have cost your whole college savings." I lift the bouquet to my nose and breathe in the sweet, flowery scent of Kenji's love for me.

He laughs. "Close, but not quite. You're worth it. I don't want to be with anyone but you."

Anyone but you. There's something about the way he said it. Something that sends my giddiness crashing to the sidewalk, where it lies in scattered shards. My heart winces, as if glimpsing something dark on the horizon. I tell myself not to ask the question on my lips, but myself doesn't listen.

"What do you mean?"

He laughs again, but the tone falls flat by half a note. Not in a way anyone else would notice. But *I* notice.

"I'm just saying you're the only one I want to be with. Isn't that a good thing?"

It is. It's a good thing. Of course it is. And yet, there's something in those words that unsettles me. *Listen to your instincts.* Dad's voice in my head again. So far, his advice has been painfully spot on.

"Yeah, of course. I mean, I'm glad you don't want to be with someone else. Someone like, say, that girl that was calling you 'Chicago' when we were on the phone."

His smile disappears as fast as my giddiness. "Why would you bring her up?"

"I don't know. Maybe I've been worried that you were having too much fun over there in Indiana where you said you'd be sitting on fences, staring at cows."

"Is that what you wanted for me?"

"Of course not. But something's off, Kenji. I feel it. Tell me I'm wrong."

I lay the flowers on the deck bench and look up at him. "Please."

He shakes his head. "Those eyes. You're killin' me with those eyes. You're my one and only. You know that, right?"

"Tell me I'm wrong."

His eyes lock on mine, and with every passing heartbeat, my suspicion solidifies.

"Say it."

His gaze shifts to my hands, which he takes in both of his. "Shi…"

All the oxygen evaporates from the atmosphere. Images of Kenji with some nameless, faceless, gorgeous Indiana girl bombard my brain. Kenji whispering her name, kissing her lips. Laughing at a private joke. His ebony eyes fixed on her and nothing else. Oh, God, I have never wanted to be wrong so badly in my life.

But I am not.

Chapter 21

Melody

Two suited lawyers enter our living room, a man and woman, each with a leather briefcase and well-polished smile. We all shake hands amidst introductions and sit on couches that were meticulously vacuumed this morning as part of Mom's cleaning blitz. The scent of lemon disinfectant blends with the lilac potpourri on the dining room table, which gleams under a fresh coat of furniture polish. After declining Mom's offer of coffee or soda, the woman clicks open her briefcase.

Here we go.

"Thank you for allowing us to come on such short notice. I know you're curious about the reason for this meeting, but we wanted to say everything in person."

My parents nod. I worry for them. None of us knows what's about to happen next, and they have no frame of reference for this sort of thing.

She turns to me. "First things first, though. Melody, how are you? I would imagine this has all been quite traumatic for you."

The accident? Or finding out Adanna is my mother? She catches me off guard and I'm not sure which "this" we're talking about.

"Yes. Thank you. I'm doing okay."

"Good. The president of the university sends his regards and says he's deeply sorry for the pain and injuries you've sustained from the accident. He regrets he could not join us today."

The accident. Not Adanna.

Mom lets out a small sigh as her fingers unclasp the edge of the couch cushion. "Oh, that's just fine. I'm sure he's a very busy man."

Dad nods his agreement, sitting stiffly in his shirt and tie.

The woman smiles and pulls two sets of papers from her case, handing one set to my parents and keeping the other in her hand.

"Well, let's get started, so we don't take up too much of your time. We're here because the university feels badly about Melody's injury and is prepared to offer free tuition, along with room and board for four years."

Mom's eyes widen beyond the rims of her glasses. Dad's mouth opens, but no words come out. And I flat-out stop breathing. That school costs a fortune. Even with scholarships, Blake and his parents had to take out some pretty heavy loans. Numbers fly through my head. Numbers so big I sit frozen to the couch, speechless like my parents, waiting for her to laugh and say it's all a joke.

"Additionally," she continues, "the university is offering this check to compensate for Melody's pain and suffering." She pulls out a check and we lean forward in unison to get a closer look. My jaw drops as Mom sucks in a breath. But Dad's eyes narrow like they do when he suspects something's fishy.

"Of course, this is all just a summary. The official language in the papers you're holding spells out everything in detail."

Our small living room now holds two lawyers, three shocked O'Haras, and one awkward silence so huge it's threatening to push out the walls.

Dad glances at the papers in his hand, takes off his glasses and rubs his eyes. "I don't understand. Are you serious?"

"I'm so sorry. I forgot to say that all of the medical bills will, of course, be covered as well. You'll find that on page…" She flips through her set of papers. "Three. Second paragraph. It's an extremely generous offer."

The man clicks open his briefcase and reaches in. "All you need to do is sign at the bottom of page six, and we can hand over this check today." He nods toward the check in Lady Suit's hands. We stare like it's pirate treasure, then simultaneously glance back to the legal document.

Mom and Dad turn to page six and I lean in to read with them. In legal mumbo jumbo, it says we agree not to sue the university. But why would we sue? I fell. That's not their fault. But if it wasn't their fault, this whole scenario wouldn't be taking place. As my parents flip through the pages, I search my memories for the moment I try every day to forget. Bathed in a golden spotlight, I had reached the edge of the platform and pushed off, hoping the Joffrey Ballet School guy would be blown away by my grace and talent. My legs extended perfectly. My arms rose, my back arched, and my shimmering wings billowed. But something felt wrong. What was it? I hadn't thought about it until this moment. Didn't want to. There was something wrong about the push off. I knew it the moment I was airborne. I pushed off with my right foot and the platform moved, then…

The platform moved.

"The platform!" Three sets of eyes lock on me, while mine zero in on the lawyers. "This is about the set, isn't it? It wasn't locked in place. I lost velocity because someone didn't set the brake on the platform's wheels."

Confusion narrows Dad's eyes. "What are you talking about?"

"The set has wheels so you can move it around on stage. The wheels are locked in place for the performance, but the right side gave way." My head is spinning. All this time, that memory was tucked away beneath my pain and grief. Even watching the video didn't bring it to the forefront. All it did was pile shame and grief on top of my misery. "That's why I didn't get enough thrust to reach the opposite side." I turn from my parents to the lawyers and summon my most accusatory tone. *"That's* why I fell."

Miss Poise and Confidence glances down, then sideways, before answering. "We don't know that anything about the set *actually* contributed—"

And there it is.

"Wait." I slip my cell out of my pocket and pull up the video in a heartbeat. "Look. It's here." My parents lean in and watch the video I saw that day in the hospital. And so many times since then. "Watch the cliff on the push-off." The lawyers don't bother to look. They already know.

"Is this true? Were the wheels unlocked?" Dad's volume increases with each word. "Did that school cause my daughter to crash? To go through all that pain and *two* surgeries? To lose her dream of becoming a ballerina? And don't lie to me. It's all on video."

"Mr. O'Hara." The man smooths out the check on his lap. "The university feels great compassion for Melody and all she's been through. That's why we've come to offer this very generous package in exchange for your signature. Just imagine, four years completely free at a well-respected university, plus an extra twenty thousand—"

"I heard your offer the first time." Dad's tone flares with anger. "Now I'd like *you* to imagine seeing your precious child crumpled in a hospital bed, groggy from painkillers, struggling to sit up, unable to walk without assistance. She is only *seventeen years old* and just lost her greatest dream because somebody forgot to press a lock into place!" He leans forward, fury reddening his face. "So don't pretend this offer begins to compensate for that. I may not be college educated, but I'm smart enough to know when I'm being bamboozled."

Normally, I'd laugh at "bamboozled," but the tension permeating the air leaves no room for humor.

"We understand this is an emotional time." The woman's lips form a thin line. "We'd be happy to return with the check tomorrow, if you'd like to think about it overnight."

My parents glance at each other and have one of their silent conversations. I swear they can read each other's minds. Mom fixes her eyes back on the suits.

"By tomorrow we'll have called a lawyer," she says. "So unless you have an offer that actually compensates for the nightmare our daughter has been through, and the future that was stolen from her, there'll be no need for you to return."

The lawyers gather their papers and briefcases, offer a stiff "Thank you for your time," and head out. The three of us stand in silence at the bay window, watching them go.

"What just happened?" It's like I just finished watching a play.

"I don't know." Mom looks as dazed as I feel. "But I think we turned down a truckload of money and four years of free college. It felt like the right thing to do, but it might just be the craziest thing I've ever done in my life."

"No, it was right." Dad shakes his head and plops into his recliner. "We're not being unreasonable. Their offer doesn't make up for what happened to our Mellie. I'm not looking to go to court or sue them for millions, but I want our girl to get what she deserves."

"This is crazy." I can't think of anything else to say, which is a phenomenon in itself. Four years of college at a great university we never could have afforded, plus all that cash. And they turned it down. "Why didn't you take it?"

"Relax, Mellie. They'll be back. I didn't know that set was the reason you fell. Somebody didn't do their job right and you paid the price. A very, very high price. And they know it. We're not going to be greedy about it, that's not who we are. But you need to be treated fairly, and that offer wasn't fair." Dad rubs his temple, which is probably throbbing after this movie-worthy scene. "We'll see what they come back with, then the three of us will discuss it and decide, okay?"

I don't share his confidence. "What if they don't come back with anything? What if we never hear from them again?" Four years of college. Medical bills paid. Twenty thousand dollars. Did we just tear up a winning lottery ticket?

"We'll hear from them within forty-eight hours. Trust me. Now let's get you to your therapy session."

The little girl with the walker always arrives just after I start my set of warm-up stretches. She is possibly the cutest thing I've ever seen with her big brown Bambi eyes and auburn curls. The staff sang to her last week for her sixth birthday and gave her a fluffy stuffed unicorn that made her shriek with delight. She hugged it so tight, I thought its pink sparkly horn might pop right off. Six years old and using a walker. Six years old and coming to physical therapy three times a week. How does that happen?

"Car accident." My therapist stretches my leg in a way it doesn't want to go. I wince, but let him do his thing, knowing the pain is a necessary part of getting better. "Happened about a year and a half ago. That's how long it took her to get this mobile. Can't tell you anything else though. Probably shouldn't have said that much. You know, patient confidentiality."

Her name is Daisy, which is super cute, but more than that, it's so who she is – a bright, beautiful flower reaching for the sun, bending with the wind, setting the room aglow with her smile. She doesn't always smile, though. Sometimes she cries. Sometimes the therapy hurts, or she gets frustrated, or simply doesn't want to do it anymore. I think being a six-year-old with damaged limbs probably just sucks. I want to help her so badly it hurts. Seems like her therapists feel the same way. The difference is…*they* can actually do something about it. I envy that every time I watch them working with her. They're so good. So patient. I want to be that person making a difference in her life, helping those little legs walk again.

"How does it feel, you know, to do what you do?" My therapist had to answer a phone call, so I'm with Daisy's PT for a few minutes.

"Oh, that's a tough one." He massages her legs. "I love my job. No regrets. But sometimes, when the kids are little like Daisy, it kinda hurts your heart, you know? And I just want it to all go faster so she can get rid of that walker, but these things take time. Right, Daisy?"

"Yeah. But I'm doing good, right Dr. Harry?"

"Super good today. I'm very proud of you." His words elicit a brilliant grin from his miniature patient. He turns back toward me. "She's made a lot of progress."

He tells Daisy and me to walk to the window and back, each of us in a specific motion designed to benefit our damaged muscles. It's at the far side of the therapy room. Weeks ago, I could have leapt there in a blink. Now…the distance looks daunting. *You can do this.* The words are my PT mantra three days a week. *Whatever it takes.* Daisy's expression reflects the same conviction. We take the first few steps and my heart hurts to see the combination of struggle and determination in her cherub face, but it sparks an idea.

"Hey, Daisy, do you like ballet?"

"Oh, yes! Mama took me to see a ballet. It was sooo fun, 'til a really bad thing happened. *Really* bad."

I freeze as a memory punches me in the gut. Could it be the same "really bad thing?" My mind zips back to the terror. The pain. And then…an image of a little girl coming down the aisle with a walker, right before the performance. Daisy.

My miniature therapy buddy witnessed my demise.

"There was a beautiful butterfly ballerina and she crashed!" Daisy's hand floats in the air, then smacks her thigh. "Boom! Just like that. Right on the floor. Then people took her away." We take a few more slow steps, stretching the muscles badly damaged by our accidents. "Maybe someday I can be a ballerina, when my legs get all better. I just know I'd be great at bein' a ballerina."

Her words bring me back to the present. Daisy is a few steps ahead of me, but has stopped to look back. Focus, Melody. Focus. The plan was to help Daisy. I can't let the painful memory derail it.

"Well, guess what? I'm a ballerina. And I bet we could be ballerinas together all the way to the window and back."

"Really? A real one?"

I nod. "Really real."

"Show me!"

"Okay, but the tricky part is, we have to do our ballet movements while still doing our therapy movements." I lean close to her ear to whisper. "We don't want to get in trouble with Dr. Harry, right?"

She nods and giggles at our secret, her face lit with anticipation, completely unaware that I have no idea what movements we can do that combine with therapy. She doesn't have her walker, so something with arms might work.

"In ballet, there's five positions, and they're numbered, like first, second, third, and so on. First position for arms is this." I hold both my arms out low in front of my body, slightly bending my elbows so each arm forms a semicircle with my fingers almost touching.

Daisy copies my position, each of us working our way toward the window at a snail's pace. "Like this?"

"Arms a tiny bit higher. Hands in front of your rib cage."

She complies.

"Perfect! Ready for second position?"

Her energetic head bob leaves no room for question.

"Now raise your arms to your sides, keeping your elbows

just below your shoulders." Her arms fly up like airplane wings. "Elbows down a bit, like you're holding a big beach ball. Wrists down just a little. Relax those arms so they're not so stiff." She follows each direction. "Perfecto! Look at you! Okay, missy, back to first position." My heart soars as she lowers her arms and does it perfectly. "Now second position." She completes the movement as we reach the window and turn around. "Now we'll move to the music, starting with first position, then second position. Follow my lead." I hum a waltz from "Swan Lake" as we repeat first and second position until we're back in front of Harry.

"Bravo, bravo!" He claps, much to Daisy's delight. But she is not the only one riding a wave of joy. Helping her get through her exercises by adding ballet to the mix made me happier than I've felt in…I can't remember when. It was just a simple thing, some basic arm moves, a little humming, and yet it made a world of difference.

When she goes to the water fountain, Harry leans toward me. "Nice! That was a great idea."

"Thanks. Will she ever be okay?"

"She should be fine eventually," he whispers. "But the road from here to fine is all uphill. On the bright side, we can get her there. Years ago, that wouldn't have happened."

His words intrigue me. "What does it take to be a PT? Schoolwise, I mean."

He explained that first you have to get your bachelor's, usually in biology, then go three more years to become a Doctor of Physical Therapy.

"Sounds like endless years of school."

He laughs. "Felt that way, too, but so worth it. How many people can honestly say they love their job? I can. And the last three years, you're working on people, so it's not all classes. That's way more interesting."

I almost had a job I loved. There were times I hated the commitment, got tired of the pain, or wished I could spend time with Blake or Shi, but mostly I loved it. Dancing made me feel complete, like I was doing what I was born to do. But it's gone. That's what I need to wrap my head around. It's gone, and I can either make a new future that has meaning for me, or stagnate as I wallow in self-pity.

Daisy heads back toward us, moving her arms in first and second position as she walks. I offer a smile and thumbs up. She smiles as bright as the sunbeams pouring in through the windows, then glances toward the door as someone walks in.

"Mama!" She waves at her mom, who stops to blow a kiss.

"How's my Daisy Doll?"

"Dr. Harry said I did super good today!"

Her mom walks over to us and glances toward me. "Looks like you've made a friend."

"She's a real ballerina!"

I extend my hand. "I'm Melody."

"Nice to meet you. I'm Kate."

"Your daughter is a sweetheart. She inspires me to work harder and stop feeling sorry for myself."

"Aw, that's sweet. Thanks. She's been through a lot." Kate lifts up Daisy, who wraps loving arms around her mama. "She gets a free ride to the car after working so hard." She gives Harry a half hug while holding Daisy. "Harry, how can I ever thank you enough? You've been amazing. We'll miss you."

"Bye Dr. Harry." Daisy's mouth quivers. The joy from a moment ago has disappeared. "Thank you."

Kate turns back to me. "Well, we better get going. Nice meeting you."

"See you Tuesday, Daisy." We wave to each other, but Kate surprises me by turning around.

"She won't be here after today. That's why we were saying goodbye to Harry."

"But…I thought she needed more therapy."

"She does. Lots. We'll have to do it at home until we can

figure something out." Kate glances down. When our eyes meet again, hers are glassy. "My husband lost his job a few weeks ago. This was the last session the insurance company would cover, and it's way too expensive for us to afford."

My jaw drops. How is that possible? Daisy needs therapy, plain and simple. "I don't understand. She can't just stop coming. There's got to be something somebody can do."

She shrugs. "Not really, but we're going to do our best to work with her at home. Harry printed out papers with diagrams of all her excercises, and promised to stop by once in a while. We'll be okay."

They walk out, with Daisy waving to Harry and me until they're out of sight. My therapist returns and I finish my session with my mind on Daisy and the injustices that seem to permeate this world.

Chapter 22

Shilo

"You *what?*" Anger, hurt, indignation. I try to cram all three into those two small words, as if I don't have my own little secret locked away in a place I never intend to unlock. But that moment with Domenico meant nothing. I ended it. It doesn't count. *This*, however, is another story.

"It was just a kiss, Shi. It was a mistake. I was lonely. She was friendly. Like, *really* friendly, know what I mean?"

Yes, I'm painfully aware of what 'really friendly' means. I grace him with my best eye roll. "Spare me."

"I would have told you eventually, even if you didn't bring it up. I just didn't think we needed to start on that note. Not after all these weeks of missing each other."

"Missing each other? When did you have time to miss me, Kenji? In between make-out sessions with farm girl?" Hypocrisy has never been so blatant. My head says I should forgive him and offer up a confession of my own. But my fractured heart keeps spewing angry words.

"I cannot believe this. How could you do this to me?"

"It just happened. No matter how much I want to undo it, I can't. But I stopped it right away. Told her I have a girl-friend."

"Like she would care. Like that changes anything. Man, Kenji. I trusted you…with everything." My eyes well up as my heart continues to splinter into shreds. "You betrayed me. You cheated. You…you…you did *this*."

"I told her—" He gazes at me with eyes that turn my heart to Jello, but I'm determined not to cave. "I told her—"

"What? You told her what?"

He takes my hand. "I love you. I told her I love you, and that you had my whole heart."

And just like that, the fracture begins to mend. The next set of angry words die on my tongue. Kenji loves me. We'd told each other before I left for Sicily, but in this moment his words soothe me like aloe on a burn. Kenji loves me. And love…what's that verse? Love covers a multitude of sins. "You told her that?"

"Yeah. I swear. It was done after that. I just wish it never happened. You're the only one for me. You're my Blue."

"One kiss?"

"Well, two. Technically."

I pull my hand back.

"What? I'm being honest. We were watching the new foals run around in the pasture. It was hot and she was standing close, so close I could feel the heat from her body, then she leaned over and —"

"Okay, okay! Enough honesty. I don't need a play-by-play."

"Oh. Sorry." Kenji takes my hand back and gives a gentle squeeze. "Are we okay? Say yes, Shi. I've missed you like crazy."

He steps closer, our bodies nearly touching, eyes imploring, loving, looking into me like no one else can. Knowing me like few others ever will. He knows about The Gift. He brings me flowers and M&Ms and elicits feelings that I've never felt and can't begin to describe. Warm lips touch mine. The only lips I ever want to kiss.

"Let's start fresh, okay?" he whispers. "Just you and me."

Another warm sweet kiss that weights my heart with the guilt of what I'm not confessing. And with every heartbeat, the weight grows heavier until it's nearly crushing me. I pull away, desperately needing air.

"Come on, Blue. Please. On my life, I swear it will never happen again."

He misinterprets my reluctance. I stare at the grass around my shoes, unable to lock eyes. My throat tightens, threatening to cut off the words that desperately need to be spoken. But how can I tell him now, after everything I just said? I take a breath, knowing I can't savor one more kiss until the truth comes out. "It's not you. It's me."

Dark eyes narrow at my pathetic cliché. "Oh, come *on*, you're not going to hand me that old break-up line, are you? Seriously?"

"No." I force myself to look up, afraid he'll see the deception in my eyes. "No, I mean, it's *actually* me. I did something, too."

"Like?"

A soft breeze ruffles his hair, making him look cuter, if that's even possible. It gently bends the daisies along the fence line and whispers "say it, say it, say it" into my ear, but my voice does not comply. Kenji waits, but there is no patience in his gaze. "*Like?*" The word emerges louder this time.

I take a breath. "Same as you."

Kenji's arms fall to his side as he steps back. Sweet chocolate eyes that brimmed with love one slim second ago now darken and smolder, making me wish I'd just kept kissing.

"*What?*"

And here we go.

"Are you serious right now? I stood here confessing and apologizing while you glared and played the victim? And all the while you'd done the same thing. Man, Shi, what was *that?* And with *who?* I mean, you were with *nuns.*" Eyebrows raise as he cocks his head. "Was it one of the nuns?"

"No! What is wrong with you? They're nuns. No, it was a guy. My cousin's friend. One kiss. We were swimming in this cool place with towering rocks and suddenly we were alone. The whole thing was surreal and it just happened."

"Surreal? That's the best you've got? You kissed another guy because it was *surreal*?"

I sigh, knowing that what I've really got is nothing. "No. It's just...I don't know. For a moment, it felt like we were in a different world, but I told him, Kenji. I pushed him away and told him right away. Okay, well, after a few seconds, but pretty quickly."

"Told him what?"

"That I have a boyfriend."

"Not that you love me?"

"No, but—"

"But?"

"But I do. With all my heart. And I'm sorry for the kiss, for not telling you, for being a hypocrite. Everything. It just hurt so bad when I pictured you with someone else, and I wanted to be mad about it, which I couldn't if I admitted doing the same thing." Now it's my turn. I take his hand, and he doesn't pull away. I step closer, and he doesn't step back. We lock eyes. "I love you."

My cell goes off, but I ignore it, unwilling to let anything interrupt this moment. I slip my hands from his and wrap my arms around his neck. He responds, kissing me the way I dreamt about since the day I headed for Sicily. Sweet, deep kisses that make the world disappear. My cell goes off again, and still I ignore it. There is nothing more important right now than kissing Kenji in my backyard until we make up for all the kisses we missed during the past five weeks, four days and eight hours. Moments after the second call, my cell tells me I've got a new text.

"Somebody's really trying to get you." Kenji steps back. "Maybe you should check."

Whoever it is better have a life or death problem to be

cutting into my long-awaited Kenji kisses. I grab my cell from my pocket. Mel. Two calls and a text that reads "911." We've used that code for years, but only when it was something huge, and very, very bad. Butterscotch dying. Aunt Rita getting diagnosed with cancer.

I call back.

"Shi?"

"What's going on?"

"It's Mom. She had a stroke." Mel's words are slurred beneath a veil of tears. "We're at Northwest Community."

"Leaving now." I never imagined having to ask the next question, but need to know. Especially with the way she's been so chummy with Adanna lately. "Umm, which mom?"

"My *mom*, Shilo!" She screams the words. "My mom, my mom! The one you've known your whole life. My *mom!*" Hysteria rips through every word. It is not a pitch I've ever heard in my best friend, and it scares me.

"It's going to be all right, Mel." My words are velvet, spoken to calm her, even if they are meaningless. "I'm coming right now."

"Okay." She sniffs. "Thanks."

⸎

I reach Mrs. O'Hara's curtained-off section of the ER to find her lying with eyes closed, her face whiter than its normal shade of pale. Kenji remains outside the curtain, waiting. We talked about what may or may not happen here, and I trust him to play his part if the circumstances are right. Oh, please, let that happen.

A priest sits with Melody and her dad, cupping one of Mel's hands as he speaks somber words that elicit a nod. She has stopped crying, but the terror shadowing her eyes is visible even from several feet away. Mr. O'Hara fares no better. He focuses on his motionless wife while the priest continues the hushed conversation. My heart crumples in the midst of this private moment as I watch pain tear through people I love, and hear words I do not want to hear.

"Last rites." The phrase is practically a death sentence. The priest's next words elude me, but my heart knows he is recommending this Catholic end-of-life prayer ceremony be performed as soon as possible. He would not suggest it if he expected Mrs. O'Hara to live.

Mel shakes her head. "No, not yet. Please." She turns to her dad. "Can we just wait? Give her some time?"

"Absolutely. Let's just pray for healing and guidance. Nobody's saying goodbye yet. Okay with you, Father?"

The priest nods. "Of course."

It is a painfully private moment, one that crumples my heart as I search for a way to slip out unnoticed, but Mel glances up before I make the move. We freeze in place, like a million years ago when we used to play "Statue," and lock eyes. My knees nearly collapse under the weight of Mel's pain, but there is no time to lose. In three steps I'm at her side, where my hand can easily reach the nearly lifeless Mrs. O'Hara. Fear reminds me that The Gift was not available to Nonna or Melody. Or Aunt Rita. It threatens to stop me from trying, with unbearable images of failure and another heartbreaking funeral. But faith steps in, pushing out the fear and reminding me that, whichever way it goes, God's got this.

My left hand rests on Mel's shoulder and I lean down to hug her as my right casually presses against the soft pudginess of Mrs. O'Hara's upper arm. But the priest extends his hand, so I have to break contact.

"Father Ryan." He shakes my hand, his smile warm. Sincere.

"Shilo. Mel's friend. Nice to meet you."

Mel rests her hand on her mom's arm, where mine was just a moment ago. "We were just about to pray for Mom."

Normally, I would join them, but I need to know if today, right now, a miracle is about to change the course of three precious lives.

"You guys go ahead. I'd just like to sit here and hold her hand for a minute." I wrap my fingers around Mrs. O'Hara's palm.

Mel and her dad turn their backs toward me in order to face the priest, who closes his eyes as he folds his hands. Quiet prayers of comfort, strength, and healing fill the small ER cubicle. Mel sniffs. The heart monitor quietly beeps. And I hold my breath.

Please.

It is all I can say in the tormented silence of my mind. This woman cannot die. My best friend is broken in body and spirit. She just can't take another hit. And Mrs. O'Hara…she's like my second mom. I can't take another hit, either. But my heart beats its normal beat, feeling nothing extraordinary.

Until it does.

The miracle is undeniable, flooding my heart with a torrent of warmth that quickly intensifies as it spreads through my chest. My plan was to steal a moment alone with Mrs. O'Hara, but clearly, God has a different idea. With each wave of warmth, He tells me this will happen here. Now. Who sees me and what they think is no longer my concern. My veins infuse with heat that permeates my shoulders and upper arms. It radiates toward my hands with the life-giving healing power as it simultaneously diminishes my strength. My knees hit carpet, though I don't recall summoning them to kneel. My hand glides toward her head, settling on her wavy red hair.

But it is not the hair I feel, it is the clot. Thick. Menacing. Blocking her artery so blood cannot flow into her brain. It has excelled in its vile assignment, for without blood, there is no oxygen. And without oxygen, her brain dies. Under attack by clot-dissolving drugs, the killer is slowly breaking up and will soon allow blood to flow again. But it has taken too long. Death has captured sections of her brain, devouring many of her cherished memories, her ability to speak, the use of her left arm and leg. Even if she lives, it is too late for the medicine to return Mrs. O'Hara to the woman I've known and loved since I was six.

Father in Heaven, have mercy on this woman You created and love immeasurably. Please hear my prayer for healing. Mend her brain, wrap Your arms around her. Restore her. Please, Lord. Only You know what she needs. Only You can provide it.

Only You.

The hospital room fades into a hazy mist. No more beeps or priestly prayers. I am weightless, floating amidst hues of blue and lavender that brighten into swirls of colors never seen. The Spirit fills me, fills the atmosphere around me, and whispers of love so pure, so powerful, that nothing can stand in its way.

Not even death.

The heat concentrates in my palms, then my fingers, intensifying before it radiates into Mrs. O'Hara. The miraculous power disintegrates the blood clot and permeates her brain, restoring precious life to millions of cells that had shriveled and died. They resurrect, stronger and healthier than before their death, returning her memories and her ability to move and speak. To sing beautifully off key while she makes shortbread for the people she loves. It flows through her body, destroying a small, undetected breast tumor with horrific intentions.

The Gift has prevailed, but it has consumed every last shred of my energy. Sounds return. Beeps, shuffles. A priest's "Amen," echoed by Mel and her dad.

"Shi, are you okay?"

The words drift toward me from somewhere far away.

"Praying," I mumble. "For your mom." There's no energy for anything more. I'm fading fast.

"Oh. Thanks. That's really nice. You could have just prayed with *us*, though."

I grasp the edge of the mattress to avoid keeling over. My

eyes catch movement. Kenji. Thank God.

"Hi. Sorry to interrupt. Sorry to hear about your mom, Melody."

"Thanks. This is my dad, and this is Father Ryan."

Darkness edges my vision as my grip on the mattress weakens. My mind screams, *Get me out of here!*, but Kenji seems oblivious.

"Pleased to meet you." He takes a step and shakes hands with the men as my body slumps closer to the floor.

"Hey, I'm really sorry, but I drove Shilo here and now I have to leave." His effort to sound nonchalant is admirable, but his words are edged with stress. "Family emergency. Sorry, Shi. We gotta go."

"It's fine. She can stay and we'll take her home." Mel wants me here with her, but I can't. There's nothing left. "Okay with you, Shi?"

So tired. What was her question? The room darkens. My body wants to collapse on the Emergency Room floor and remain there for hours.

"Shi?"

Please, Lord. Get me out of here.

A trickle of energy returns. Just enough.

"Honestly, I don't feel very good." Slurred words tumble from my lips. "Think I'll go with Kenji. Text me, okay?"

"Sure. You don't sound so good. Hope you're okay."

"Thanks."

We are two steps away when the beautiful music of Mel's next words reaches us.

"Dad, look! Mom's eyes are open. We're here, Mom. We're here."

I force my legs to take a step, then another. If I can just get outside. Just to the car.

"Come on, Blue. Keep going. Keep going. You got this."

A soft glow of sunlight tells me the door is not far ahead. Step. Step. Head for the light. One more. But I don't have one more. Kenji was wrong. I don't "got this." The light fades and my knees collapse. Strong arms catch and lift me.

"It's okay, Blue. It's okay. *I* got this."

I breathe him in, engulfed in his strength and warmth. Enveloped in his love. The world disappears…and I am gone.

Chapter 23

Melody

She stands at the counter where flour, salt, baking soda, and buttermilk wait to become the Irish Soda Bread I've grown up on. I watch, undetected, from the kitchen doorway, as she blends it all together with her wooden spoon, singing "You Are My Sunshine" in a way that would make most people want to rip out their ears. But to me, it is the sound of love. The sound of my living, breathing mother, who rescued me when I was brand new to this world, and held my hand and heart through every victory and defeat. Who never cared if people gave us looks because she was plump and pasty and I was skinny and mocha. And yeah, I wasn't formed in her body, but there has never been a doubt that I live in her heart.

The doctor called it "nothing short of a miracle" and said there's no way the medicine burst that clot in time for her functions and memory to be so absolutely, perfectly fine. No way for her to recover so fast. No way for their to be zero signs of damage. *No way.*

And yet…

"Mellie!" She smiles, knowing that moments like this almost disappeared from our lives. "I didn't see you standin' there. Are you spying on me, young lady?"

"Yep. And getting a free concert from the world-famous soloist."

She laughs, a sound more beautiful than her crazy singing. *Nothing short of a miracle.* The words echo in my head. I've heard about miracles. Read about them. Listened to Father Ryan sermonize about them. I've even looked at nature as a miracle. Sunsets that paint the sky in gold and red, delicate orchids too gorgeous for words. Babies. All of them and every species. But my half-dead mom walking out of that hospital, healthier than she's been in years? I just can't wrap my head around it.

"In another hour or so, this will be nice and hot and ready to eat. Why don't you call Shilo over? That girl loves my soda bread."

"Okay." Every word she utters makes me want to cry. It's been that way for three days – ever since she came home. Shi says it's because there's just been way more going on these past few weeks than one person can handle. Physical, mental and emotional pain. Stress. Shattered dreams. And wonderful as it was, the complete and utter shock of meeting my biological mother. It's a reasonable explanation. I really do deserve to be an emotional basket case with all that going on. But those aren't what put my emotions in overdrive. It's the one that Shilo left out.

Guilt. It weights my heart every time I look at Mom. Every time my callous words echo in my head.

She's not my real mom.

Adanna's my real mom.

I can't believe I finally met my real mom.

Meeting my real mom is the best thing that's ever happened to me.

Words that slapped my mom in the face, time after time, and she just took it. And I know why. Because to my mom, seeing me happy mattered most. It was why we went to Disney World instead of seeing the Cliffs of Moher in Ireland, and why she went back to working full-time when I started ballet classes. The list goes on, playing in my head like a funeral dirge, because I stuck all those memories in a coffin and nailed the lid the minute Adanna entered my life.

"Melody Yasmeen O'Hara, what on earth?"

Her soft words snap me back to the present, where I realize tears are dripping off my cheeks. Mom wipes her floury hands on a damp cloth and steps toward me. Open arms envelop me. She smells of dough and buttermilk, with a hint of lavender from the lotion that's meticulously rubbed into her arms and neck every night. In these arms I am safe, content, at peace. It is a good place to be. The best.

"Shhh. We will get through this together, Mellie Bear. It might be hard, but there's good things ahead, I know it. God's got great plans for you. I know that, too. He said so Himself, right there in the Bible. Shhh. It's all right."

She thinks I'm crying about the accident, but I'm so past that. Hopefully. I gently pull away so we are face to face. "You're my mom."

"I know, honey. Of course I am."

"You're my real mom. I know you didn't birth me and all that, but you're the one I run to. You're the one that knows me and all my flaws and broken parts."

"Oh, Melody. I—"

"Wait. There's more and I need to say it. I've been a jerk, and you didn't deserve that. First, I felt so sorry for myself that no one else mattered. Then I got so excited about Adanna, it blinded me to you. Until…until you almost left me. Left this world. It shouldn't have taken something so huge and awful for me to realize what you mean to me. I'm sorry. Really sorry. I hope you'll forgive me."

She brushes a strand of hair from my face. Probably the same one that kept distracting me the night I fell. "You don't need one single splattering of forgiveness, you crazy girl. I know you love me. And I know that Adanna deserves to be in your life, too. Poor woman. All that horror she went through. But I have a confession, too. I was jealous of her, and jealousy is a bitter pill, you know what I'm sayin'?"

She takes a step back, so she can look me full in the face. "She seems so perfect, with her pretty face and lovely accent, and having a job where she's saving lives. And you even look like her – there's no denying. I didn't want to share you with her, but then I realized she was the one who shared *you* with *me*. Not intentionally, of course, but the point is...you weren't mine, but I got to be your mom, anyway. Now I want her to be part of your life, too. So let's both shoo away all the guilt and jealousy and what-have-you and just be happy."

"Okay." Her words make me smile. I love the way she looks at a situation and breaks it down to its simplest form. We'll just get rid of the bad feelings and focus on the good ones. Job done.

"But don't love her *more*, okay?" She laughs. "I'm not that good at shakin' off the jealousy. Don't love her *more* than me. Promise?"

I grin, knowing that will be an easy promise to keep. "Yes, ma'am."

She squeezes my hand, green eyes peering into mine. Eyes that laugh even before her smile emerges. "We're a mess, we two." And now her laugh is audible. "Go on, missy. Wipe your face and invite Shilo over for soda bread. Tell her I'm never adding M&Ms to the soda bread, no matter how many times she asks. And tell her I've got that orange tea she likes so much."

It's a good idea, and one that I'd normally act on immediately. But not today, when my mind keeps wandering back to Blake. There are things that have been left unsaid. Frayed heartstrings in danger of snapping. It's time to step outside my comfort zone which, in truth, hasn't been all that comfortable anyway.

"I'd like to invite Blake, instead. Not sure he can come, but...are you okay with that?"

Emerald eyes sparkle. "Oh, goodness. Yes, yes, yes!

We've been wondering when you'd come to your senses about that boy." She pats and shapes the dough that's now resting on a baking sheet. "This will be lovely."

We haven't seen each other since the stroke, even though he offered to come to the hospital when I texted him. I wanted him out. At least, that's what I thought. Out of my life, out of my heart, out of my world before he realized I wasn't ballerina Melody anymore. Before he saw the me inside. A little nerdy. Kind of awkward. Not really sure how to act around boys. Dance gave me confidence on and off the stage, but maybe, like Chen and Adanna, I could find it inside myself. And maybe a prayer or two wouldn't hurt, either. It sure helped Mom.

"On my way." His response takes less than a second. Now I've only got twenty minutes to look Blake-worthy, and these days it takes nearly that long just to get up the stairs.

"He's coming," I call out to Mom as I head up for a quick outfit change and a little eyeliner and mascara.

Dad's face emerges from behind his newspaper in the family room. "Who's coming? We're havin' company? Mom didn't say anything about company."

"Blake."

He grunts, rolls his eyes and returns to reading.

Blake loves the soda bread, or seems to, at least, and even asks for seconds. That alone is enough to hook my mom. Talking to Dad about the pre-season Bear's games scores points on that side, too. He converses like he's known them forever, with a casual confidence that leaves me envious and enormously proud to call him my boyfriend. If, after everything, he still wants that title. Any normal person would not.

We head down to the basement – our game room – where a ping-pong table and pinball machine take up most of the space. A couple of blue bean bags are nestled in one corner, but we opt for the couch along the opposite wall. We sit, angled to face each other, and make small talk about the room and pinball machine for a minute before that thing happens where nobody knows what to say. Silence permeates the room. Gone is the casualness that seemed so easy upstairs. He takes my hand – just the fingertips, actually – and I think maybe he's going to kiss me for the first time since I told him to leave at the hospital. But he doesn't lean in, so I sit frozen, still unable to muster the confidence of before-accident Melody.

He gives my fingers a squeeze. "Why am I here, Mel?"

Gray eyes lock on mine and melt me, making me forget all the words I'd rehearsed in my head.

Blake shifts, positioning himself a few inches closer. "I mean, I'm glad I'm here. It was great to get your call. But…there's been a lot of mixed signals, you know? Some not so mixed, actually. You seemed pretty intent on calling this quits in the hospital. So I need to know. Where are we at? Why am I here?"

Because being with you feels better than anything else I've ever done, I want to say. *Because you make me feel alive and beautiful and smart. Because even when we're not together, you're in my thoughts and I know you're mine and I love that. And I love you.* But none of that makes it from my head to my mouth, and only the humming of the air conditioner fills the empty space.

"Do you even know why you invited me?"

This is ridiculous. *Melody Yasmeen O'Hara, you are a strong and confident woman. You are so much more than a ballerina. You might even be helping children heal someday. So get your act together and say what needs to be said before you lose this amazing guy who wants to be your boyfriend.*

"The accident."

His eyes narrow in confusion.

"It…unravelled me. I mean, it was hard on my body, and there's been so much pain, but it was even harder on my heart. My thoughts and emotions got all screwed up."

His thumb rubs the top of my hand. "That stupid lock. I told those guys…"

"Blake, wait. Let me finish. This isn't easy for me."

He nods.

"When they said I couldn't dance professionally, it was like something in me died. I was angry and frustrated. They wanted me to talk to people, go to counseling, but all I wanted was my body back. And my future. I felt like nothing without dance, and to be honest, sometimes I still do. It's been my sole focus for so long. I figured you were just being nice to come around while I was in the hospital, but eventually you'd figure out there wasn't much to me without dance."

"It was never the reason I wanted to be with you. Don't you get it? You weren't Ballerina Melody to me. You've always been Melody. Amazing, beautiful, smart, funny Melody. I couldn't believe you were my girlfriend. I only loved watching you dance because *you* loved it."

His words dissolve me.

He lets go of my hand and shakes his head. "Did you really think I was so shallow?" His tone is edged with a hint of anger.

"What? What do you mean?"

"Did you think I wanted you because you were a dancer?"

"No. I don't know." Confusion swirls through my brain, blocking the right answer. Is that what I thought? And why would I, when he never once gave me the impression that dancing mattered. At least, not in our relationship.

"You don't know? Seriously? Man, Mel. Give me some credit. Don't turn my feelings for you into something so meaningless. And whatever you do, stay away from guys who want you for your talent."

He stands. "I think I should go. Let me know if you figure this out."

Oh, no, he's not leaving. Not when I got this far. Fear of

losing Blake, coupled with my own insecurities, sends confidence racing through my veins. I grab his arm and tug him back to the couch.

"Sit down."

"What's the point?" He remains standing.

"I asked you to let me finish. I admitted this wasn't easy for me. You don't get to interrupt and then walk out."

He sighs and sits. "Fair enough."

At least he's willing to listen. Now I just have to say something to make him glad he did. I search my thoughts, my heart, way down deep to the place where my self-pity convinced me I was not worthy of this incredible guy.

"So I was this huge mess. Pain all the time. Dreams up in smoke. Hating the world. Hating everybody who oozed encouragement and smiles. I knew they were trying to help, but all that positivity just made me madder. And more depressed. And lonely. Don't you get it? Before the accident, I never thought you wanted me because of ballet. Never crossed my mind. But after, I sank into this really dark place."

Cleo streaks down the stairs and bounces onto my lap. Without warning she smacks my cheek with her paw. Claws in, thank goodness. We both smile and Blake scooches her onto his lap.

"Father Ryan said that's when the devil gets his claws in people. Whispering lies in their ears. So I convinced myself to hurt you before you could hurt me." He rolls his eyes and opens his mouth to speak, but I want to finish my thought while it's still flowing. "And yeah, that was stupid. I'm still working through a lot of things, but I've got my parents and Shi and Adanna and Chen to get me through it. And you, Blake. If you'll still have me. I'm asking you to give me another chance, even though I'm still kind of a mess."

He leans in, his face inches from mine. Close enough for me to feel his breath. Close enough that I fear he'll hear my heart pounding. Intensity shades his eyes, deepening them from gray to pewter. If he doesn't say something soon I'm going to combust.

"I'd give you a thousand chances."

My heart leaps from my chest, and suddenly, there is no space between us, only lips pressed against lips. Warm and delicious and hungry. Cleo jumps to the floor as he wraps his arms around me and mine slide around his neck, caressing the wavy brown hair that feels like heaven in my hands. How could I have been so willing to let him go? He breaks away, tracing my cheek with his finger, his gaze lowering from my eyes to my lips. I tilt my head and lean in again, wanting these kisses to last forever.

"Melody!" Mom calls from the top of the stairs. "Don't forget we've got those lawyers coming back today. They'll be here in fifteen minutes. I'm sorry, but Blake will have to go soon."

The lawyers. Leave it to them to ruin the moment. I roll my eyes and Blake laughs. "Sorry."

"It's fine. I couldn't stay much longer anyway. We've got a birthday thing tonight for my six-year-old cousins. Triplets. Wouldn't want to hang out here, kissing you, when I could be playing superhero with six-year-olds."

I laugh. "No, I definitely can't compete with that."

We walk hand in hand toward the front door, passing Dad, who glances up long enough to scrunch his eyes into the 'mean face' that has made me laugh since childhood. Blake doesn't see, and I press my lips together to hold in a giggle. One last luscious kiss on the front porch, then he walks away. At least this time, it's not forever.

I'm closing the front door when the gray sedan pulls up, instantly altering my happy mood. Out step the same two suits, looking exactly like they did last week. A breeze rustles through the trees, but I swear that lady lawyer's hair doesn't move an inch. It probably isn't allowed to.

I wish we had our own lawyer, but it's just us against them. At least, that's how it feels. They might be perfectly nice people, but their job is to make this whole thing go away for the least amount of money, and without any bad publicity for the university. I've seen enough lawyer shows to know the basics. Dad says we're not looking to get greedy, but they need to pay up to make up for all the pain, and for my body being permanently damaged. And the whole ballet thing, of course. I wonder what the going price is these days for broken dreams.

I hold the door open and they enter; all of us pasting on polite smiles for each other. Dad sets down the paper and there's more plastic smiles and handshakes before we settle in the same spots as last time. It's a big, awkward déjà vu, with one significant difference. This time we're ready. This time we know what's going on, and they know we know. After last week's visit, they called the next day to set up this meeting, just like Dad predicted.

"We appreciate your willingness to meet with us again." Lady Suit opens her briefcase and pulls out papers. "We discussed your concerns with the university and have revised our offer. I think you'll find it quite generous."

"With all due respect, ma'am, that's for us to decide." Dad's words are polite, but firm. He didn't like being caught off guard last time, and he's letting them know he won't be "bamboozled."

She clears her throat, then hands us each a duplicate copy of the new offer. "Yes, of course. You'll find the new amount at the bottom of page six."

We flip to page six, my eyes land on the number, and my stomach flips. Blood drains from my face and my head feels light. Faint. Oh. My. Gosh. Ohmygoshohmygosh ohmygosh. They quadrupled the first offer. More money than I ever could have imagined, plus free tuition and payment of medical bills. It doesn't fix me, or bring back my ability to dance professionally, but oh, man, what that money can do. Can change. A tornado of thoughts and ideas swirl through my mind. I want to leap from the couch, do a double pirouette and hug both suits, but Dad's words at breakfast echo in my head. *No matter what, play it cool. This is very important, Melody. No show of emotion. We'll do the talking.*

Dad clears his throat. "Hmm." He flips to the first page, reads a little, and does the same with the next five. Tension permeates the room like rumbling thunderheads. "Hmm. This is a better offer, which we appreciate. Of course, you're aware that if we choose to take this to court, the offer would far exceed this one."

"Far exceed" is not a normal term for Dad, who clearly practiced what to say for this meeting.

Man Suit nods. "Yes, sir. However, we felt it was quite gen…I mean, a high enough offer that you might like to receive it immediately, rather than deal with the stress and expense of hiring a lawyer. It could take years for this to get settled if you take it to court."

"I'm aware of what's involved with going to court." Dad's eyes lack their usual sparkle as he locks eyes with the lawyer. "We'll have to look this over and consider our options. The pros and cons and all that. We'll have someone examine it."

The woman taps a pen against her thigh. "You know, we'd be happy to present you with a check right now, immediately, for the full amount. This whole business could be over and Melody would have a nice chunk of money in the bank."

Mom sits up, back straight as a pole, her chin tilted slightly upward.

"I believe my husband said we'll need to think about it." No Irish drama, just cool and resolute. "We will do that and get back to you."

"I see." She nods and sighs, glances at her partner, then back to my parents. "Mr. and Mrs. O'Hara. Melody. The university would very much like to settle this matter, and left us one last option to encourage you to do the same. If you sign this agreement today, we'll add another twenty-five thousand to the offer in your hand. But only if you sign it today." She holds out a pen to my parents. "I hope you will consider doing so."

Mom and Dad look at each other and engage in another one of those silent discussions. Mom's nod is barely visible, but it's all the affirmation my father needs.

"Let's go over this document together." Dad turns from the lawyers and looks at me. "All of us."

A torturous half hour is spent reading through the legal document line by line, with the suits taking turns explaining any unfamiliar terms. I try to pay attention, but my mind keeps zeroing in on that crazy big amount of money. When we finish the final page, Dad says we need a moment to talk privately, and the suits retreat to the kitchen.

"Now listen, lass, because this is very important." His whispered words are meant only for me and Mom to hear. "This is your decision, because this happened to you. They're offerin' a lot of money, plus college and all the rest, but if we take this to court, they'll be payin' a whole lot more."

My head can hardly wrap around the current amount. I can't imagine what 'a whole lot more' would entail. "Seriously?"

"Yes, but they were right when they said it would be tied up in court for years. And we'd have to pay a lawyer a hefty chunk to represent us. It's your decision."

The thought of repeating my story over and over, Dad having to take off work for court appointments, the stress it would cause all of us, tightens my gut. I don't want that. I want this to be done, so we can all move on with our lives.

"Let's take their offer." I hear the confidence in my own words, and know it represents my heart.

"You're absolutely sure, Mellie Bear?" Mom loops an arm around me. "You know we're on board a hundred percent no matter which way you go."

Fighting for more would come at a price for all of us. I

look at my parents, worry and weariness adding lines to their faces from all they've gone through since the night my butterfly wings crumbled on that stage floor. We just don't need more.

"Absolutely."

"All right, then." Dad picks up the pen from the coffee table and places it in my palm. "Let's tell those lawyers you've come to a decision." He walks into the kitchen, and returns with two relieved looking suits.

We all sign or initial the highlighted places, then Lady Suit writes out a check and places it in my trembling hands. That's when I realize it can't be real. It can't. Any minute now I'll wake up to my usual morning pain and no big, fat check to lovingly call my own. But we say our goodbyes with more fake smiles and they drive off as we watch from the living room, staring at the empty street, until my mom hugs both of us hard enough to wake someone in a coma. And still, that crazy check sizzles my hands, thanks in large part to that horrid, humiliating video.

Chapter 24

Shilo

There's a golden-hued room in a corner of my mind. Small and private, it shimmers with the memories of my best moments. All the healings are in there. Meeting Kenji…and Misty. Racing Mel to the sky on swings when we were six. Playing guitar at a bonfire, surrounded by my best friends, and again just weeks ago, surrounded by the meadow house girls. My first kiss and, even better, my first Kenji kiss. Holding newborn Lambie in Sicily. And now…healing Mrs. O'Hara. Seeing the joyous light in Melody's eyes when she talked about the miracle that took place after she and her dad prayed with Father Ryan. No need for her to know about The Gift – either way, it's all God.

It's been nearly a week since the stroke. Mrs. O'Hara is walking, talking, baking, and singing. Melody got some sort of settlement from the university – didn't see that coming – and has 'big news' that requires meeting for coffee. But that can wait. Right now, I'm right where I want to be, with the person I most want to be with. And maybe this moment will be added to that golden-hued corner of my mind.

"Look." Kenji tugs my hand and points to a tree just off the prairie path, where a masked cardinal rests on a low branch. "See him?"

I nod, taking two slow steps toward the bird without making a sound. *You must be stealthy and patient with wildlife.* Sister Celeste's words fill my head as I set the aperture on two for a shallow depth of field, then zoom in as best I can without an actual zoom lens. Sunlight illuminates his fiery red feathers, with no branches blocking my view. Three shots go off before the crimson beauty takes to the sky. Thanks to Celeste's lessons, the shots are perfect. The cardinal fills the frame, clearly focused against a blurred background. Julia will love it...and tell me how many species of cardinals there are, what they eat, how long they live, and on and on. Still...I look forward to showing it to her.

"Good eye." I pat Kenji on the back. "Now find me a blue jay. Better yet, a deer."

He grins. "Not if all I get is a 'good boy' pat."

I tilt my face up and we kiss. A soft breeze rustles the tall prairie grass as his hand caresses my hair, then slides tenderly down my back.

"Much better." He laughs. "For that, I'll find you a unicorn."

To think, we almost blew it...again. We each faltered this summer. We each regretted it. But in the face of a life-giving miracle, we realized our ugliest moments don't have to destroy something beautiful.

"Come on." He grabs my hand and we head toward the woods. "Let's go find more things for you to shoot." He shakes his head, grinning. "Definitely not something I ever imagined saying."

As we walk, he reaches for my camera and presses the playback button.

"Let's see that bird. Wow." He keeps scrolling, looking through my last dozen or so shots. "You should sell these or something. Seriously, these are great."

"Really? Thanks. But there's still a lot to learn. I can't believe how much I love this, though. It's like a whole new world. I've actually decided to major in it."

"Photography? I thought you were pretty set on journalism. What would you do, shoot weddings and stuff? That doesn't seem like a Shilo thing."

"Because it's not. I'd want my photos to make a difference. I mean, wedding photography is great because it's happy memories and all that, but I want to show people what's really going on in the world. It's one thing to tell people about a situation, but when you actually *see* starving kids, or a town hit by a tornado or people living in poverty, like the families we saw on our mission trip, it's more powerful, you know? And wars. You can read about war, but what about the impact on the people living in those countries? Photos show you that."

A squirrel shimmies up a nearby oak, its mouth stretched around an acorn. I grab the camera, switch to a fast shutter speed and get a few shots before he disappears into the branches.

"And animals, Kenji. Imagine taking photos of animals in Antarctica or the Galapagos Islands; showing people what global warming and pollution is doing to wildlife. Photos can inspire people to take action. So…I'm thinking about photojournalism. Imagine if I could work for a big international magazine. How cool would that be?"

No response. Silence fills the space between us. Even the birds stop chirping. We leave the sunlit prairie and enter the shadowy woods, where I'd hoped to find some deer, but my mind is not on deer photos now. It is whirling in a futile attempt to figure out why no words are coming from Kenji's mouth. Nothing.

He stops and faces me.

"You'd have to travel for that. Everywhere. All over the country. All over the *world*. Sometimes in dangerous situations. And then there's…you know what. You might heal somebody and pass out in the middle of a war zone or a hurricane. Then what?"

Disapproval saturates his words, but I wasn't looking for approval.

"You'd be gone all the time, Shi. What about *us*? Haven't we been through enough? Separated enough? Am I the only one who pictures a future with us together?"

A soft rustle to our right turns our heads simultaneously. A doe and her fawn step gingerly over a fallen tree, then freeze to stare at us. I let my camera hang off my shoulder and contemplate his words. *A future with us.* When I imagine my future…he's in it. But the thing about futures is, they're up for grabs. Fragile. Time twists and turns everything like a kaleidoscope of shapes and colors moving in what appears to be a random design. But it's not random at all. I know that now more than ever. God knows exactly when and how those shapes and colors will emerge into masterpieces we could never imagine. My gaze switches from the deer to my boyfriend's knitted brow.

"Not *all* the time. It would depend on the job. I don't even know how this whole thing works yet, Kenji. That's a long time away."

Mother and fawn bound away, disappearing into the trees. The shot is lost forever. "We've still got senior year and college. Let's not worry about five years down the road, okay?" I step closer, sliding my arms around his waist. "*Okay*? We just got back to being 'us' again. Let's just immerse ourselves in the 'now' and deal with the rest when it comes." He stands motionless, but I remain in place, pressing my cheek against his chest, where his heart beats a sweet melody into my ear. "Let's just love each other right now. Can't that be enough?"

It feels like forever before his arms wrap around me. "Okay," he says, and kisses the top of my head. "Okay."

Jules stares at my cardinal images, swiping back and forth

through the three I took before the bird headed skyward.

"Excellent. The middle one is the best. His eye is in the sunlight, not shaded, like the other two."

"Thanks. I like that one, too." Hopefully, she'll relinquish the camera now and we can avoid an Audubon Society-worthy lecture on the Northern Cardinal.

"Did you know cardinals often attack their reflections in windows and mirrors?"

And here we go. I shake my head, hoping my lack of commentary encourages her to conclude with that one simple fact.

"They're very territorial. Males *and* females. They get obsessed with defending their territory from intruders. It could even be a car bumper. As long as they see their reflection, they'll continue to attack. As a human, I find it difficult to relate to that form and degree of aggression."

But are *you human, Julia?* I ask it silently, knowing she's easily hurt. Not that I haven't said such things in the past, but I'm trying to do better. To *be* better. To remember what Nonna Marie said about how difficult it is to be different, like Julia.

"I didn't know any of that, Jules. I agree, it's hard to imagine they'd keep attacking a mirror or something for hours. Pretty crazy."

Her smile beams at me and illuminates the room. All because I listened and responded. The warmth that floods my heart is nothing like what I feel during a healing, but it's a good kind of wonderful, all the same. *Note to self. Do more of that.*

"Did you know I'm going to visit my friend, Deepthi?" She turns off the camera and hands it to me.

"Who?" My ears perk up. Julia has just attached a name with the word friend, and that's a rare and precious phenomenon.

"Deepthi Kapadia. We met at Mensa camp. She shares my interest in geology *and* astronomy. What are the statistical probabilities of that? She's been researching black holes in space. Isn't that fascinating? And she only lives half an hour away, so Mom's taking me there tomorrow and I'm staying for two nights. Maybe she'll let me help with her research!"

I have no words. My sleepover memories involve playing video games, walking to Frosty Freeze for shakes, and taking magazine surveys.

"And here's the best part. Her parents are taking us to the Adler Planetarium! They are currently featuring a Venus exhibit. Did you know Venus—"

"Shilo!" Mom calls from the living room. "Your phone's ringing upstairs."

"Sorry, Jules." I sprint upstairs, thankful for the interruption, and see Misty's face on my cell. We haven't talked since my first day back. Man, it's great to be connecting with people again.

"Hey, Beach Girl." She hates when I call her that…so I do. "How's life in North Carolina?"

"Livin' the dream, Shi. Killin' it at college, but only because Mrs. Howell, I mean *Mom*, watches Ty when I'm at school and studyin' and stuff. Just two classes this summer, but I'm already signed up for more in fall. Oh, and volunteering when I can with that anti-trafficking group I told you about. Met some pretty cool people there, too."

"Good. A lot of changes for you in the past two months. I'm glad you moved in with the Howells."

"Me, too. It's been kind of a whirlwind, though. A little exhausting sometimes, but all good. I'm starting to figure out some stuff, you know? Like maybe I'll major in somethin' I can use to help the anti-trafficking efforts. Or help girls like me. Or both. What about you? What's goin' on?"

"I'm starting to figure out a few things, too." I tell her about my photojournalism idea, and Kenji's response. She tells me about her new roles as sister, daughter, and aunt, and how sometimes it's overwhelming to be around so much family after not having anybody but Tyler for so long.

But mostly it's been "killer amazing." We talk a little about the things that happened in Sicily, but most of that was covered in our last conversation.

"How you doin'? I know your nonna's death was pretty tough."

"I think I'm okay. Sometimes I hear something, or smell fresh-baked pastry, and I fall apart a little. But I know she's in a place too wonderful for words, and that helps a lot."

Thinking about Nonna Marie weights my heart, and if it gets any heavier, I'll have to end this call. "How's the munchkin? Getting spoiled rotten by his Grandma and Grandpa?" I still miss Tyler's goodnight hugs, followed by "Happy sleeps, Sheebo." I pretended to be mad that he never said my name right, but…it was adorable.

"Totally. They're completely wrapped around his little finger…and he knows it."

Misty's laughter vaporizes my sadness. There was so little of that when we first met. It was all she could do to survive and keep Tyler safe and healthy. Now, her life's full of love and her future's full of possibilities.

"He's doin' good, though. Friends, cousins, playdates like crazy. Learnin' tons of stuff at preschool. Oh, hey, speakin' of school, we're comin' for your graduation! All of us. Mom and Dad insisted. They want to come anyway to visit relatives, and we're gonna stay with you guys for a week. I know it's not 'til May, but I'm super excited."

"*What?* Seriously?" My smile feels like it's going to tear my face in two. I already can't wait until May. We talk a few minutes longer, until the digital clock on my nightstand reminds me I'm late for coffee with Mel. We say our goodbyes, happy knowing we'll see each other in spring.

ॐ

Melody rests her salted caramel macchiato on the table, having barely said a word since I picked her up. Adding to the weirdness is the ashy hue of her face, like when she had the flu last winter. Most of my conversation attempts have fallen flat, so it's up to her now. I sip my mocha latté and wait.

"Sooo?" Waiting is not among my strengths. "What's going on?"

She sighs and sips her coffee. "Something happened. Something so crazy I keep waiting to wake up, but I think it's real. But it's crazy. Just crazy, Shi."

I narrow my eyes at her. "We've established that it's crazy. Perhaps we can move on with a detail or two?"

She pulls an envelope out of her purse and hands it to me. "It's this. You know how I said the university gave me money for the accident? Well, look at this. Don't say anything. I wasn't supposed to bring it, but I had to show you."

I slide a check out of the envelope. Her name appears, followed by a number big enough to buy a small country. "OH MY—"

She smacks her hand over my mouth. "Shhh! I told you not to say anything."

I remove her hand from my face. "That's…that's *yours*?"
She nods.

"No. No way. If that's real, you're paying for me to go to college…in Paris." I laugh. She doesn't. Oh my gosh. That thing is real. I grab it back for a second look. "This is crazy."

"Right?"

"Now you can just *buy* the Joffrey Ballet."

She laughs. "Not quite. And there's no point if I can't be a prima ballerina. But…I was thinking about a twist on that."

For the next half hour she tells me about a plan that spans eight years, starting with getting a biology degree, then a Doctor of Physical Therapy degree, *then* opening a dance studio for kids with injuries and disabilities. She finally stops, probably because she hasn't breathed for far too long, and sips her coffee.

"Where did all this come from?" I'm blown away by these

new goals. "One minute your life is over—*your* words, not mine—and now this grandiose plan. And it's good, Mel. Awesome, actually. But, wow. I mean…there's a lot to this, you know? You're talking about starting a business and you haven't even graduated from high school yet."

"I know, but there's plenty of time to learn, and people I trust to help. I saw God work a miracle with my mom, Shi. If this idea's good, if it can help kids, maybe He'll make it work, too."

Her faith unravels me, like being in Florida and watching a fuchsia sun rise over the sea. She divulges the source of her inspiration - watching Daisy struggle, then seeing her smile when they pretended the exercises were ballet moves – and relates her conversations with the PTs and Daisy's mom. That's when she launches into the part about secretly paying for a few more months of Daisy's physical therapy.

"But that's not all."

"How can there possibly be more?"

"Just wait." She grins, her eyes sparkling with an excitement I haven't seen since returning from Sicily. As she reveals Part Two of her plan, envy stirs inside me. Man, this girl's mind must have started spinning like a tilt-a-whirl the moment she saw that check, and hasn't stopped. If only I could be a fly on the wall when she unveils her plan to her moms.

Chapter 25

Melody

Talking to Shi, revealing my ideas out loud for the first time, felt like Christmas and fireworks and birthday cake all rolled into one. Still, my head is nearly exploding. I open my laptop and get it all in writing, figuring out a timeline and some details as I go. But Shilo's right, there is *so* much I don't know how to do, so many parts I need to leave blank...temporarily. There's just something official to having it on paper, like it's less dream, more reality. Now it's time to get things in motion, starting with Adanna.

She's cooking when I call, and invites me to come later for a dinner of pounded yam and suya, which she says is like a spicy kabob. It's been fun tasting Nigerian foods. So far I've loved them all, except for Egusi soup, which I pretended to like anyway. She saw right through me, though, and laughed at my pretense of liking it. When I tell Mom I'm going to Adanna's for dinner, there's a pause before she smiles and says, "Oh, that's nice." But I see through Mom just like Adanna did with me. I walk into her room and plop down on the bed while she hangs freshly washed shirts in the closet.

"Are you going to be home tonight?"

She makes a space for her favorite green blouse. "No, Dad and I are going clubbing til midnight, then hitting a couple of wild parties til about 3 a.m., more or less. Maybe from there we'll catch a flight to Vegas."

I roll my eyes, but can't supress a laugh.

"Then you won't be available to sit and look through photo albums when I get back from Adanna's?" It's one of her favorite things, and something I'm always too busy to do.

She shakes her head and smiles, but her eyes do not. "You don't have to appease me because you're going to Adanna's. I'm not that thin-skinned. It's fine. I told you, I'm fine with all of this."

Sincerity permeates her words, but I'm not buying it.

"The truth is…I want to talk. Just me and you. About the money, about a lot of things. But I want to talk to Adanna, too, so the dinner invitation was the perfect chance. Can we do that?"

"Absolutely. We can *always* do that." She picks up another shirt from the laundry basket, but stops to kiss my head before hanging it. "You don't have to make an appointment, Mellie. I'm always here for you."

And so she is. Through rebellions and emotions and all my drama, she has always, always, always, been here. Always done things for me. Lived her life around me. Now…it's my turn to do something.

⸙

I clean up the kitchen with my new brother and sister, still trying to wrap my head around the fact that I actually have siblings. Keta is adorable, with her big brown eyes and dimples so cute I can hardly stand it.

"Do you like cake, Melody? Me and Mama made cake just for you."

"Really? I love cake!"

Her smile lights the room, just like Daisy's. "Do you like yellow cake with chocolate frosting and pink and purple sprinkles?"

"That's my absolute favorite kind."

"Well, guess what. That's the very kind we made!" She bounces with springs for legs. I went seventeen years without a sister, and now I have the best one in the world.

"What? No way!"

She nods and grins and nods some more, like the world's most precious bobblehead doll. I hope all our conversations are this much fun.

"Really! I'm not kidding at all. That's really what we made."

Bayo rolls his eyes, but does it out of Keta's line of sight. He seems to be struggling to decide whether my existence is a good thing, or not so much. It's got to be weird to suddenly have a big sister. I'll have to find ways to get to know him better. So far my attempts at asking questions have resulted in painfully short responses, but we have time.

We finish up and I slip on my shoes for a walk with Adanna.

"In a house full of nosy posies, it's the only way to talk privately," she'd said when I told her I had something important to discuss. We head into her neighborhood, taking a route that leads to a pretty park with wildflowers and a little playground. It's only two blocks away, but progress is slow. My knee still has a lot of healing to do. I lumber and limp, hating my new reality, forcing myself to focus on better things. Like this conversation.

"I've been thinking about what to do with the settlement money, especially since I don't have to pay for college."

"Ah, yes. Quite a sum. But there is no need to think about that now, Melody. You are young, and you have plenty of time to consider how best to spend it. Perhaps even help some people in need, yes?"

"That's the thing. I already have ideas. Really good ones,

I think. And there will still be plenty left to save."

"I am listening."

I tell her about paying for Daisy's physical therapy, and donating to that human trafficking group that Misty volunteers for. Her eyes glisten, and my heart contracts at the thought of what she must be remembering. No one should ever have to go through that.

"These are admirable plans. I am very proud of you. Please promise me you will involve your parents in this. You were raised by good people. God blessed *both* of us with them. They will provide wise guidance."

I know she's right, and promise to get their input.

"Are you ready for Part Two?"

"You have mischief in your eyes, daughter. I like the way they sparkle. Now tell me about this Part Two."

Excitement sends my heart racing. I hope she loves the idea as much as I do. "It's a trip. For me and my moms. We'll fly to Sokoto, Nigeria, look for your family, spend a week or so, then fly to Madrid, hang around and do whatever cool things there are to do in Madrid." We come to a bench under a shady maple and she motions for me to sit down, for which I'm grateful. She sits next to me, silently waiting for me to continue. "It's a good halfway point to our next destination, the Cliffs of Moher in Ireland. My mom's always wanted to go, and it looks pretty amazing. We might have to visit some relatives there, too. Next…stop in Nova Scotia, just because it's really beautiful there and I want to see it. Plus it's on the way back."

A family with three little kids, two dogs, and a tiny human in a stroller passes by in a flurry of noise. Adanna smiles and waves to the children, and they all wave back. After they pass, she squeezes my hand.

"My crazy, beautiful daughter. I could not afford such a trip. But it is a wonderful fantasy."

"We'd use the settlement money! That's the whole point. I've got this covered." Maybe I should have made that more clear.

"Oh, my goodness, no. I am not touching your money. Oh, no, my sweet Melody Yasmeen. That is for you and your future. You go to Ireland with your mama. She has been through so much. It will be good for her."

What? She can't be serious. I've researched this whole thing and thought about nothing else the past few days. She has to come. She just *has* to.

"You know who else has been through so much? Me. And you. All three of us. Please don't take this away from me, and don't do this to my grandparents."

Her eyes widen, then narrow. "Your grandparents? I do not understand."

"My Nigerian grandparents, your mom and dad. They don't even know if you're alive or dead. Imagine how that feels. They don't know about me or Bayo and Keta. And I want to know *them*, and my other relatives in Nigeria. I've gone my whole life not knowing anything about my past. Please don't take that away from me…or them. Wouldn't that be a great use of my money? To reunite with your parents *and* introduce your long-lost daughter to her relatives? Please Adanna. Don't say no. This is huge, and it can't happen without you."

She sighs, gazing out over the pond where gulls dive for carp and bluegills. "Melody, this would be a very long trip."

"I figured on three weeks."

"What about Bayo and Keta?"

"They have Owen and three aunts, plus grandparents right down the block. This will work, Adanna."

"And your Irish mother? How does she feel about such a trip?"

"Can't answer that 'til tonight, but she's going to *love* it."

"You are very persuasive, but this does not feel right. I do not like the idea of you spending money on me."

"I'm not. This is something I want to do for myself, and for my grandparents. It's not for you."

She shakes her finger to admonish me, but smiles through the gesture.

"Ah, you are a clever one, but you cannot fool me. You know how much I miss my family. If we do this, and that is a big *if*, we may not even find them. It has been many years."

"So you're considering it? Please say yes."

She sighs. "Yes to considering, but no promising. It is very generous of you, and it touches my heart deeply that you want to do this thing. We shall see."

Three photo albums are piled next to the couch's armrest when I walk into the living room. Mom's locked and loaded for a journey into the past. We'll probably start with my first day of kindergarten, our Disney trip, and six years of Halloween and birthday parties. *Every classmate gets invited, Mellie. No one gets left out.* Then we'll move on to ballet photos, with me in a variety of warm-ups, leotards and tutus over the years. At some point she'll make an awkward comment about how you can "really tell when the curves started to emerge." Adanna never got to see all of that, though. I make a mental note to bring them over one day soon. Maybe Keta would like seeing the pictures, too.

"Hi, honey." Dad lumbers in with a cup of coffee and a book, plopping down in his easy chair. "Nice visit?"

"Yeah, real nice. I want you to meet my brother and sister real soon. Maybe we could have a dinner or something. All of us together. Would you be cool with that?"

"Sure, sure. You set that up." He turns toward the kitchen. "Bridget!" He yells loud enough to reach the west wing of the White House, which is just a tad bigger than ours. "Mellie's home."

"Okay. Be right there."

He turns back to me. "She's been waitin' for ya. Guess I'll go read in the bedroom so you gals can talk."

I tell him to stay for the first part, and when Mom comes in, I share my plans about Daisy, and how I want to pay for her sessions anonymously. Hopefully, it won't be long before her dad gets a job and they have insurance again. They ask a bunch of questions, and in the end, agree it's a great idea.

"Time for photos?" Mom leans over and grabs the top album.

"Not so fast, Bridget. Mellie says there's somethin' else she wants to talk about." He stands up, grabbing his novel. "I'll be upstairs, seein' if I can figure out if the murderer was the math professor or the astronaut. My bet's on the professor. He seems a little snaky to me."

Dad is every author's dream. When he gets into a book, he becomes one with the pages.

"Okay, missy. Let's hear it. A big shopping spree? A spa day? I know you want to do something besides that wonderful donation. And that's absolutely fine, long as you put away the rest into savings. You'll be glad it's there when you're done with school."

I take a breath and slowly release the buildup of excitement and nervousness jumbled up inside me.

"I want to take a trip. A big, fat, amazing trip across oceans, over mountains...all that stuff."

"Ah, well you're a bit young for that. It may have to wait a couple of years."

Now comes the good part. I force myself to act casual. "I'd really like to see Ireland after all these years of hearing about it. What if my mom was with me?"

"Oh." Her gaze drops to her lap. "You want to go to...to Ireland? With Adanna?" When she raises her eyes, they are laden with the anguish of an Irish ballad. It would break my heart...if I didn't know what was coming next.

"No. I want to see the homelands of both my moms...with *both* my moms. That is, if you're up for it."

She sits back against the pillows and tilts her head. "What

are you talking about?"

I tell her the plan, just like I did an hour earlier with Adanna.

"Oh, no, no, no. I don't want you using a penny of that money for me. No siree."

My crazy moms. Different backgrounds, different ethnicities, same mentality. I repeat the speech I gave Adanna, then tack on a part about seeing the Irish relatives I've never met, whom she hasn't seen in two decades.

"And won't it be a great educational experience? Geography, culture, all that stuff. And those Cliffs of Moher!"

I flip open my laptop and we look at gorgeous photos of her beloved, but never seen, Cliffs of Moher. They rise over the Atlantic in photo after photo, sometimes washed in the golden streaks of sunset, other times standing out like green emeralds against a blue ocean and even bluer sky.

"Oh, my," she says over and over again. "Look at that one. And that one." And each time she points, a click of the mouse makes it fill the screen. Nothing could veil the longing in her eyes.

"But Mellie, you're in no shape for all that walking."

"We could go after graduation. First week of June. I'll be way better by then. The doctor even said so. Please, Mom." I rub my knee. "This has all been such a nightmare. I just want something huge and wonderful to look forward to."

I can't believe I have to work this hard to get my moms to let me do something for them. It's exhausting.

"Just say you'll consider it. Adanna felt the same way, but she's considering it." I switch my image search to 'scenic Ireland' and pull up green meadows with flocks of sheep, mountains bursting with wildflowers, and ocean waves crashing at the base of her precious cliffs.

She sighs. "You're killin' me, missy. All right, all right, I'll consider it. No promises, though. It's an awful big trip. And Nigeria, too. Wouldn't that be somethin'? But I'll have to think about it."

I can't suppress a grin, because in my heart, I know they'll go, and this is going to be an absolutely insane adventure.

⌘

Shilo sits on the floor, strumming her guitar and wearing a nightshirt splashed with the colors of the Northern Lights. She says she wants to shoot them someday, and wonders out loud what the shutter speed and aperture should be.

"I'd probably need a tripod," she mumbles, more to herself than to me. The technical stuff doesn't interest me, but I love seeing her photos and hearing the passion in her voice when she talks about photography. It's a good distraction, with all that's happened this summer, and a really cool career path if it all works out.

"What about soccer?" She hasn't mentioned it once since she's been home. "Tryouts are next week."

She plays the chords to a song I've never heard; maybe something she learned in Sicily, then rests her hand on her guitar. "I'm done." Soft words, tinged with a hint of sadness, exude a certainty that surprises me.

"With soccer? No way. You live and breathe it."

"Weird right? I had this whole plan. Soccer camp this summer at Perdue, tryouts, playing varsity this fall, club soccer in spring. Even getting a soccer scholarship."

I know this plan backward and forward. It was all she talked about last spring. "And when that plan got derailed by the Sicily trip, you flipped out. So what happened?"

The pause that follows happens a lot lately, like she's struggling to say something, while leaving something out. Something big. Significant. More and more, I sense a secret within her, but I've been her confidant forever. She wouldn't keep something from me. And yet...the feeling is undeniable.

She shrugs. "It just doesn't feel important to me anymore. I'll still play for fun, but I want to use my time for things that matter, like those nuns. They're up there on a mountain in Sicily and most of the world doesn't even know they exist. But they're making a difference. Rescuing people, giving families a future, giving refugee kids an education."

"So what are you going to do?"

Cleo leaps onto my dresser, startling both of us, and immediately knocks my mascara onto the floor. Without a second's pause, she smacks a pen, launching it at Shilo's head.

"Heyyy, Miss Thing!" She rubs her head, then shakes a finger at Cleo. "Knock it off." Firm words lose their intention as she reaches for my mischievous kitten and cuddles her.

"What am I gonna do? For starters, I'll see if the school newspaper could use a photographer. And I was all signed up to volunteer at Chicago Suburban Hospital before I got whisked off to Sicily, so hopefully, they'll still take me."

"It's just so different than everything you've wanted for the past decade. Good, but different. Hard to wrap my head around."

She laughs that bubbling brook laugh I've loved since first grade. "Ditto. Look at *you*, with your whole new plan. You could potentially change the course of children's lives. I want to change lives, too. I feel like I could do that as a photojournalist, you know?"

She goes on about how photos are a great way to get people to care about issues like child abuse, modern day slavery, animal poaching, and on and on. "But I've got so much to learn. And I'm anxious to start, Mel. Just like you."

Bittersweet emotions surge through me.

"You have a choice, Shi. I didn't. I was forced to come up with something new when everything I'd worked for fell apart." I hate the part of me that resents her freedom to make her own choice.

"But look how excited you were when you told me about combining physical therapy with ballet. That would have never crossed your mind before the fall. Now it's this huge, exciting goal. And you *do* still have a choice. You could coach ballet or do all kinds of other things. But would they mean what this plan means to you?"

She's got a point. I have a world of other options, except the one I wanted most. And probably a ton of career possibilities I don't even know about yet. But this PT-dance idea feels beyond right, like a spark, tiny and bright, that's intent on igniting everything in its path until it blazes into a roaring fire. And I want to be the one to fan those flames. "No, but you never know, I might have thought of it, anyway. I'm just saying, I wish it didn't come about the way it did. It's not the same as you waking up one day and deciding to trade in soccer for photography."

She rolls her eyes. "Photojournalism. And it didn't just happen like that. I mean, I didn't have an injury that stole my soccer future, but there were a lot of painful circumstances that led me to take a different path."

Suddenly we're in a pointless competition to determine who went through the worst experience before changing their career plans. That was never my intention. I absolutely acknowledge the amazing things that resulted from my crash, but I wish Shilo understood what I was forced to sacrifice, unlike what she *chose* to let go. Still, this needs to end.

I nudge her knee with my foot. "Crazy summer, right? We'll still be talking about this one when we're sixty."

"Definitely."

I pick up the remote. "TV?"

"Another definitely."

It's nearly two when we decide to call it a night. I click off the TV and Shilo stands to flip the light switch, but says "mosquito" and smacks my arm instead.

"Sorry," she says, "I know how you puff up from bites. Hopefully I got it before…before…umm…"

Her eyes become crystal blue saucers, fixated on my arm. I glance down, but see nothing except her hand. She doesn't move it from my arm, and doesn't speak.

"Shi?"

Her mouth parts, but still no words.

"Hey, you okay?"

"I'm warm." She whispers the words. "My heart. It's warm."

I reach over and gently pry her fingers off my arm. The dead mosquito hits the carpet, but Shilo's eyes remain fixed on my arm.

"Why don't you lay down? You look a little pale. Maybe you have a fever." I say it just to break the silence, knowing full well nobody goes from fine to fever in twenty seconds. But something about her looks different, unless my over-tired brain is playing tricks on me.

"What? Oh." She smiles, with shimmery eyes like when she's watching a sappy chick flick and everything finally works out in the end.

"What's going on? It was like you left the planet for a minute there."

"Nothing. I'm fine. Everything's fine now, Mel. Let's go to sleep. Tomorrow's going to be a good day. I can feel it."

Could it have been a seizure? Whatever that moment of weirdness was, it seems to have passed. I'll think about it more tomorrow, when my brain and body aren't beyond exhausted. I haven't stayed up this late since the accident, and my energy is zapped from the combination of pain, therapy, and lugging around a leg brace. My body melts into the mattress and drifts toward the edge of sleep, ready to be done with this long day. But as my consciousness ebbs away, I feel the warmth of Shi's hand on my injured knee, which doesn't make sense. No matter. It's just a dream.

"*Sei guarito*, Melody. Which path will you choose?" Shilo's question floats on a whisper while I walk through verdant woods, breathing in the delicious, earthy scents of leaves and rain and bark. My legs and back are strong, with a dancer's toned muscles and power. No pain. No limp. Ahead of me, a fallen tree blocks the path, but I perform a perfect *grand jeté* and sail over it—legs outstretched, arms spread like wings, back arched—and land at a fork in the road. One trail erupts with the beauty of autumn trees ablaze in vibrant hues of crimson and gold, while the other blossoms with spring flowers bursting from pink and violet buds. Both paths are so breathtaking, they nearly hurt my eyes. Both beckon with the beauty of hope, given by the only One who has the power to provide it. My heart reaches toward one path, then the other, unsure of which to choose.

Until a soft whisper speaks to my soul.

I pirouette and blow a kiss to the sky, then take the first step and keep walking, without looking back.

About the Author

Faith, family, and a passion for nature, writing, and photography nurture Susan's soul. She loves to visit the world's amazing places and has a travel bucket list that includes the Northern Lights, sunsets anywhere, Jamaica's Luminous Lagoon, and basically anything that glows.

Susan began her career as a Chicago-area newspaper reporter before moving to Albuquerque to work as a television reporter. Back in her home state, she works in public relations for a library and presents writing workshops and travel programs throughout the Chicago suburbs. Susan is president of the American Christian Fiction Writers Chicago chapter and a member of the Society of Children's Book Writers and Illustrators.

Website: www.susanmiura.com

Acknowledgements

Writing a book is a weird dichotomy of flying solo and working as a team. The latter, however, is what truly transforms words on paper to the status of novel. And for each member of my *Shards of Light* team, I am truly grateful.

Once again, my heart and gratitude go to my daughter, Kasie Miura, who provided valuable content critique as well as excellent line editing; and my son, Nico Miura, who wrote "Blue," an amazing theme song for my Healer series.

Melody would not have survived her accident without the expertise of occupational therapist Christine Rojas and the OT/PT team at the Early Learning Center in School District 54, Schaumburg, IL, who made sure my physical therapy references were relevant and accurate.

Another huge help with the Melody chapters was Michele Holzman, director of Schaumburg's Northwest Ballet Academy. She took time from a busy schedule to correct my ballet blunders and help make Melody the ballerina she was meant to be.

With zero knowledge of what it's like to be Nigerian-American, I turned to my good friend Yasmeen Bankole, from whom Melody Yasmeen O'Hara derives her name. Huge thanks to Yasmeen for her insight and excellent suggestions.

To the American Christian Fiction Writers Chicago Chapter, my own personal writing community, thank you for sharing your experiences and offering support and encouragement.

Where would I be without family? From my husband and kids to my brothers, sister, in-laws, nieces and nephews, I'm blessed with the love and inspiration that sustains me through the challenges and victories of being an author.

Last on this list, but first in my heart, is God, to whom I'm grateful for everything.